EXPECTING
AN ARGUMENT

First Edition: February 2026

Names: Jay, Perci, author
Title: Expecting an Argument by Perci Jay
Audience: Ages 18 and up
Summary: Lawyer Olivia and billionaire Beau must overcome their old rivalry when an unexpected twin pregnancy forces them together.

Printed in the United States of America.

For all the twin parents.

Author's Note

This story contains explicit sexual scenes and is not recommended for readers under age 18.

Content Warnings

Off-page: Death of a mother, death of a grandparent, abandonment by a father, alcohol use, illegal substance use, childhood poverty, childhood bullying.

On-page: Alcohol use, high-risk pregnancy, grieving a lost parent, body image discomfort, emergency c-section.

Nothing bad ever happens to the dog. He is a good boy.

Check out Perci Jay's Spotify account for the official "Expecting an Argument" playlist along with themed ambient music to enhance your reading experience.

1

Olivia

"Why can't this bitch GROW UP???"

My phone lit up in my hand as the text came in. I quickly dropped my buzzing phone into my tiny purse and sucked in a breath.

Damnit, Ashley. Did she have to text me *now?*

I looked over my shoulder as I was halfway out of the window of the grungiest apartment I had ever seen. Thankfully, my hookup from last night was still snoring on his stained pillowcase.

The angry texts kept rolling in, so I quickly made my exit with my stilettos in one hand and my vibrating purse in the other.

Only after I hopped off the final step of the fire escape did the message alerts finally stop. With my bare feet safely on the pavement, I scrolled through Ashley's rapid-fire texts.

"Remember how I couldn't book the Silver Hall for our class reunion?" Ashley had texted. *"Remember how I said it was bullshit*

that the Hall had EVERY weekend next year booked? I just found out that CAITLIN COLE is the Hall's new manager!"

The memory of Caitlin yelling "Trailer Trash Ash and Off-brand Olivia!" from her Mercedes still lived on in the back of my mind. I was about to ask Ashley if the Silver Hall was still the only event venue in the county when my screen lit up with another text.

"She's trying to force me to have our ten-year reunion under the rodeo pavilion. I would DIE of embarrassment! Caitlin is pushing thirty and hasn't changed since she tore my dress at prom!"

As happy as I was to have left all that small-town shit behind, I wasn't about to let my best friend suffer. If Caitlin Cole and all those other rich assholes back in Elren wanted to be petty, I could be worse.

I started my walk of shame and quickly typed a response. *"Sounds like Elren needs a new event venue, then."*

Our old bullies rearing their ugly heads had been the kick Ashley needed to take on the renovation of the abandoned department store in downtown Elren. Ashley and her husband were already social media famous for documenting the renovation of their house, but turning the dusty department store into a ritzy event venue was a feat even her most devoted fans doubted.

But Ashley and I never backed down from a challenge.

We grew up as the trash without fathers, the girls the church ladies would pray for but wouldn't let their kids play with. If we wanted respect, we had to work for it.

Though Ashley had charmed her way to become class president and I had taken up a second residence in the library to be valedictorian, throwing the best class reunion in our hometown's history would prove to all the gossipy diner dwellers and social media stalkers that our success wasn't a fluke.

And after a year of planning and hard work, we were finally put to the test.

When our class trickled into the reunion after the Friday football game, Ashley and I beamed as we showed off the "Copeland Corner" event venue. Fairy lights strung high on the exposed brick walls glittered off the restored copper tile ceiling. Silver mylar balloons spelling "10" surrounded the room.

Boots danced scuffs onto the new varnish of the stained pine floors as throwback hits from high school played through the speakers. The old cliques reunited around the cocktail tables, but an unexpected few blurred the previously un-crossable lines between groups. The jean-skirt wearing church girl was now sporting a full tattoo sleeve and was sharing cigarettes with the old potheads. The lanky star of the boys' basketball team married the quiet farm boy. The kid who got suspended for drawing dicks on the door of every bathroom stall stood with the honor society members and bragged about his Ph.D.

Though one might think a passing decade was powerful enough to metamorphose a burnout into a better person, I doubted that anyone truly changed.

People don't get better, they just get braver.

Even Ashley, who had cowered in the gym bathroom after Caitlin Cole stepped on her train and split the seams of her prom dress wide open, stood in the center of the party with the confidence of a newly-crowned homecoming queen. She wore a silver cocktail dress that hugged her slim figure and complemented her strawberry blonde hair. Her husband, Tyson Copeland, proudly held his arm around her waist as the crowd gathered around him.

The crowd of Elren locals congratulated Ashley on the renovation, but those who had moved out of town were falling over themselves to snap a selfie with Tyson—the college football star turned hometown hero. After enough insistence, Tyson bashfully rubbed his tightly-coiled black hair and raised his hand to show off his national championship ring for photos.

As soon as the crowd broke, I took out my phone and snapped my own photo. I had the perfect vantage point from my barstool, but I still smiled at my luck of capturing the candid shot of Ashley's sparkling eyes as she mooned over her husband.

Oh, how Caitlin and all the other overgrown mean girls would *seethe* when I posted that tomorrow.

I leaned against the bar and my cheeks strained from how hard I was smiling. Ashley and Tyson were the twin stars of the show, but we had wanted the other entrepreneurs in the class to shine too. Ashley had posted a video of Marisol Martinez giving me a blowout for the reunion to promote her salon. Two months earlier, Ashley had staged a photoshoot inside Nicole Liu's boutique where I modeled my navy dress that Nicole had ordered in a size 16 just for me. Each post was strategic, crafted to highlight the local businesses, expand the reach of the reunion, and persuade more of our classmates to buy tickets to fund the renovation.

Nearly every one of our graduating class of 170 showed up. Trailer Trash Ash and Off-brand Olivia had won again.

Even better, all the pampering I had received on camera made me look *hot*. My dark brown hair was glossy and full and my navy dress sparkled like the night sky. Everyone wanted to look good for their first high school reunion, but I was determined to erase the image of the valedictorian hiding beneath a hoodie from everyone's minds.

I swiveled on my barstool and gently leaned on my toes, showing off the bright red soles of my stilettos—my reward to myself after securing a *big* money verdict on the case I had worked on for the past two years.

Was it a slimy lawyer move to flash the red-bottom heels at a small-town class reunion? Sure, but I wanted to make it loud and clear that my "off-brand" days were over.

My career was taking off like a rocket to Mars and I was leaving the small minds of my small town behind for good. The success of the reunion was the first step to healing my inner child, but I was beginning to suspect the wounds from poverty never truly closed.

Being away from the office for so long was making my nerves twitch. I needed a distraction before I started mentally calculating how much money I was losing by partying instead of working.

As I waited for the bartender to return, the tips of my acrylic nails traced the small tiles on the bartop—made from the remains of a century-old floor mosaic that was once at the store's entrance. Ashley and Tyson had recovered most of the original department store while completely modernizing the antiquated building. Instead of changing rooms, they added bathrooms. Instead of clothing racks, they had purchased circular tables. The bar used to be a soda fountain, so instead of a soda jerk in front of me…

…there was just a regular jerk beside me.

I held back a scowl as a familiar face sat on the bar stool directly to my right. Even after ten years, I couldn't forget that oh-so-perfectly combed head of blonde hair. His cheekbones cut deeper across his face and his eyes had hints of crow's feet like most of us, but otherwise Beau Fontaine looked exactly the same.

Back in high school, Caitlin Cole and the other rich assholes followed him around like designer-bred puppies because he was too much of a snob to associate with anyone else. Beau groaned any time we got paired for a group project, threw hard candy at my head from the homecoming float, and even tried to run me over in the school parking lot once.

And he couldn't have picked anywhere else to sit?

"Adams," he said in greeting, not bothering to even glance in my direction.

I cringed at the sound of his voice. He was still too good to say my first name, huh? Was Olivia really that hard? Even Liv would have been easier.

"Well, look who strolled out of his manor to pay the peasants a visit," I said with a laugh that anyone else would interpret as friendly.

That made him slide those blue eyes my way. In true Fontaine fashion, he wore a midnight blue suit rather than the typical sportcoat-and-jeans combo that most of our classmates showed up in. He didn't have on the white lapel rose that all the other former members of the football team wore, either.

He was probably too afraid to sully his thousand-dollar suit with a grocery store flower.

"Drinks?" asked the baby-faced bartender.

"Old fashioned," Beau ordered.

I took a quick glance at the chalkboard drink menu and gave the bartender a smile. "I'll have the 'Top of the Class,' please."

The bartender turned to make my drink and Beau scoffed. "Rub it in, why don't you?"

This time, I turned to face him. The moment he mooed at me as I crossed the graduation stage still haunted me in the brightly-lit hell of dressing room mirrors—so, yes, I was going to rub it in.

"Don't be such a sore loser," I teased. "Some men are happy coming second."

His eyes locked with mine. A heartbeat passed and the corner of his mouth flicked up as we both caught my unintended innuendo. Just as my cheeks started to grow hot, the bartender set my drink down in front of me.

"One 'Top of the Class' for the lovely lady," the bartender said. He placed Beau's drink on the bartop. "And an Old Fashioned for Mr. Fontaine."

I popped my straw into my mouth to stifle a laugh. Beau's cut crystal glass contained whiskey with a bright, waxy cherry and an orange slice perched on top of a pyramid of cubed ice.

Beau stared at the drink like he had just been served a dead mouse in a cup. He was probably going to throw a fit and have the poor kid tossed out of the reunion.

"Oh, don't you be mean to him!" I whispered to Beau as soon as the bartender walked off to serve another guest. "He can't be older than twenty-two. Hell, I think I might have babysat him at some point!"

He cut me a look. "You really do think the worst of me— assuming I would be cruel to the help."

I rolled my eyes and took a sip of my own drink, a fizzy cocktail that was the same bright coral color that my graduation dress had been. The bubbles tickled my tongue as I drank, but Beau looked at his own drink like he was trying to solve a puzzle.

"So, what brings you to my barstool?" I asked. "I would think you would be sitting with Bethany Whitecloud. Didn't you take her to prom?"

Beau picked up the orange slice and then gave me a half smile. "You mean, didn't I take *him* to prom?"

Heat crept across my cheeks as Beau sank his teeth into the orange.

"Oh, I'm sorry," I said as my eyes dropped to the mosaic bartop. "I guess I hadn't kept up with our class as well as I thought."

Beau pulled the orange from his lips, having stripped all the flesh from the rind in one mouthful. "Well, isn't that the point of tonight?" He turned his head and met my eyes. "To finally catch up?"

The glow from the fairy lights scattered across his blue eyes like a sunset sparkles across a pool. Damn, I had forgotten how pretty his eyes were.

Warmth bloomed in my lower belly and I pressed my thighs together. Nope! I might have had the worst taste in men, but I wouldn't consider him—not the shit head who had sneered at my torn jeans and had worn shoes that cost as much as my mom's rent.

I gulped my drink to cool down as Beau lazily rubbed the orange rind around the rim of his glass.

"So, um," I said with a cough, "what have you been up to?"

The ice clinked as Beau picked up his glass with his slender fingers. "You know exactly what I'm doing, Adams."

He took a sip of the caramel-colored whiskey as I bit the inside of my cheek. I could have assumed he was living on his sprawling ranch and working for his family's oil company—or "working" as much as the only son of the owner would actually do—but he didn't have to be a dick about it.

"And what about you," he said, glancing down to my left hand, *"Miss* Top of the Class?"

I made a fist on the bartop to hide my lack of an engagement ring. "Commercial litigation. I work for Parker & Hill in the city."

He let out a low laugh that echoed around his glass. "Of course you do. Do you have a list of all the men whose balls you've stepped on, or have you lost count at this point?"

"You know me—perpetually organized." I bit the end of my plastic straw. "And *always* ready to add more to the list."

He smirked. "I bet you are." He caught the stem of the cherry between two fingers and lifted it from his glass. "Do you like cherries?"

I swallowed, but my mouth was suddenly dry. "N-not particularly."

His eyebrows raised briefly in consideration and he hummed. "Shame."

The entire cherry disappeared behind his perfect white teeth and I had to quickly find my straw and chug for dear life.

What the hell was wrong with me? I had come to the reunion to look hot, not get hot-and-bothered for *Beau Fontaine III,* of all people! I needed to pay the bartender and make a quick exit before I left a wet spot on the new barstool.

Beau's cheeks pitted as he swallowed the cherry.

"You haven't changed a bit, Adams." He plucked the cherry stem out of his mouth and held it up in the ambient coppery glow of the room. He smirked. "If only we could all get as lucky as you."

He placed the cherry stem on the bartop between us—he had tied it into a knot with his tongue.

The warmth in my lower belly ignited again and I sucked on my straw, only to discover with a loud slurp that I had drained the glass.

"Need another drink?" Beau said cooly before taking another sip of whiskey.

The sharp edge of the straw pressed into my lower lip as the air around us thickened. My eyes fell to his big hand wrapped around that glass, his fingertips pressing into the rigid facets of the crystal. I was approaching that all-too-familiar point of no return where I was just seconds away from crawling out of a bar and into a bed.

I shouldn't—I *really* shouldn't—but it wasn't like I lived in Elren anymore. I would never have to speak to him again. It could be a one-and-done. Yeah, just to see what that snarky little mouth of his could really do.

What a fine *distraction* Beau Fontaine could be.

I pushed my empty cup away and leaned on the bartop. "Did you know this place has an attic?"

He sipped his whiskey. "A three-story building has an attic? Color me surprised."

I pursed my lips. God, he was such a fucking dick. "Did you know the attic is haunted?"

His lips hovered over the rim of his glass as he gave me a half smile. "Are you saying you want to ditch the reunion to go on a little adventure?"

I leaned forward, letting the neckline of my dress slip down *just* enough. "Up for a challenge, Mr. Fontaine?"

Those pretty blue eyes dropped to my cleavage. The tip of his tongue pressed against his canine tooth as he smiled.

"You're on, Adams." He drained the last of his whiskey and pulled out a money clip from his jacket pocket.

I hopped down from my stool as he carelessly set a stack of bills on the bartop. I headed for the stairs in the back, giving him enough space to discreetly follow me out.

The din of the party and the thumping of the bass from the speakers faded as I crept up the creaking staircase. Four inch stilettos and steep rickety stairs didn't mix, so I clung to the worn handrail that was bolted to the wall. My ankle wobbled and I gasped, but then large hands gripped my waist from behind and held me steady.

I held my breath as heat rushed to my core. My legs trembled, but I carefully climbed the rest of the two flights of stairs as Beau silently rested his hands on the curves of my hips.

When we reached the top landing, I turned the porcelain knob and pushed open the creaking attic door. The scent of antique lace filled my nose and I blinked as my eyes adjusted to the low light. The amber glow from the street lights outside barely illuminated the dark room. Old mannequins and stacked cardboard boxes lined the brick walls.

The heat of my arousal ignited into the harsh the burn of embarrassment—had I really just taken the wealthiest man in town to a dusty attic for a hookup?

Beau closed the door behind him and I turned around.

"Look," I said, "I really should have just booked a hotel—"

With a single step forward, Beau backed me into the wall and I lost my breath. He rested his forearm above my head and my cheeks flared—how had I forgotten how tall he was?

I took in a shallow breath and suddenly all I could smell was the cologne on his neck. The light, yet masculine scent hooked me in and made me want to move closer, but my knees went weak. I pressed my palms into the rough brick wall to brace myself while he leaned down until I could feel his soft breath against my skin.

"Birth control?" he asked.

"IUD," I answered in a whisper.

"Perfect."

He grabbed my jaw and his lips crashed into mine. My eyes widened with a gasp that softened into a moan as he kissed me. The sweetness of the cherry flavor on his tongue mixed with the naughty burn of whiskey on his breath. My hands reached up to grip the lapel of his jacket as his hands slid beneath my skirt.

He broke the kiss and smiled against my swollen lips.

"Never imagined you would wear these." He slipped two fingers beneath the thin band of my thong and popped the elastic against my hip. "Not so angelic anymore, are you?"

Just before I made good on my earlier threat to drive my stiletto into his balls, his hand disappeared into my panties.

"And you shaved," he said with an amused lilt into my open mouth. "Almost like you were expecting me."

"Don't flatter yourself," I huffed as I melted into his touch. "You egotistical—*oh.*"

He slipped a finger inside me and the lower half of my body went slack.

He let out a low laugh. "That shut you up." He wrapped his arm around my waist, bracing me against him. "How about another one?"

A second finger joined the first and he curled them as he stroked me in a delicious rhythm.

"*Fuck,*" I whimpered against his mouth as he brought me closer and closer to an orgasm.

"I don't remember you ever using that word," he said. "I must be really getting to you."

Just as I was at the edge of my climax, Beau stopped. I opened my eyes to find him staring across the attic.

"The hell are you doing?" I asked as I pushed through the needy ache between my legs. "I was close to—"

He quickly took his hand out of me and wrapped both his arms around my thighs. I gasped as he picked me up and carried me across the room. I locked my legs around his waist and gripped his jacket to stay upright, but he plopped me ass-first onto a cushion. A cloud of dust floated up around me.

"The–*fuck*, Beau—" I coughed.

He dropped to his knees in front of me. "I got you a couch and you still complain? I like you better when you're moaning."

Before I could get my bearings, he dove beneath my skirt. He ripped off my thong before flattening his tongue against me. My head fell back in ecstasy against the carved wooden frame of the couch. My palm covered my mouth to quiet my moans as he showed me exactly what he had done to that cherry stem. My thighs shook against the sides of his head, but just as I got close, he pulled away with an evil smirk across his face.

I let out a frustrated breath. "Come on, Beau, stop this—"

He rose to his feet and took off his jacket. "Say please, Adams."

I balled my hands into fists against the couch cushions. "You asshole."

He folded his jacket into a loose rectangle and shot me a look. "God, I'm getting sick of your mouth."

Just as I was about to finish myself off in front of him out of spite, Beau tossed his folded jacket onto the edge of the couch and pushed me onto my back across the cushions. His jacket protected the back of my head from dust as he joined me on the couch and positioned himself between my legs.

I glared at him as he unfastened his belt. "You know, I wondered how a man as wealthy as you wasn't married yet. Apparently, even a net worth of half a billion can't compensate for how *rude* you are!"

"Oh that's what I'm worth to you?" He unzipped his pants. "I think you'll find that I don't have to compensate for anything."

He thrust inside me and my head fell back onto his jacket as I gasped. Oh fuck—he was big.

He flashed me an evil smile. *"That's* what I wanted to hear."

I took a breath to tell him to shut up, but he thrust into me again before I could speak. The smell of his cologne enveloped me as he fucked me with a punishing rhythm. The couch shook beneath us. My nails clawed at the back of his starched shirt and my eyes rolled back into my head as I tried to contain my happy noises within my throat.

Beau picked up pace and the frame of the couch creaked, then cracked beneath us.

The couch tilted down and I gasped in panic. His chest pressed into mine to keep me from sliding, but two of the legs of the couch had snapped off.

"Shit," I breathed. "This thing is an antique—"

"Shut up." His lips captured mine as he grabbed my right leg and hooked it across his hip. "I'm not done with you yet."

He locked eyes with me as he went in slowly, agonizingly slowly. I twisted and wiggled beneath him, my body aching for release. My moans turned into needy whines as I nearly pleaded for him to go faster.

He was teasing me on purpose. He had to be.

I looked up at him through half lidded eyes. "God, I hate you."

"I'll make you beg one way or another," he said darkly as he slowly pushed into me. "Nothing would delight me more than finishing and leaving you angry and frustrated, so you'd better surrender. Be a good girl and say please."

I clenched my jaw. Never.

I locked my legs behind his waist and squeezed, making him dive deeper. His eyes rolled back into his head and he bit his lip as he fully sank into me.

"You little *bitch*," he moaned.

He gripped the armrest above my head for leverage as he picked up pace, giving into that irresistible need. I smirked and tilted my hips up, taking full advantage of the increased friction. I weaved my fingers through his soft hair and pulled at the roots on the back of his head, completely fucking up the perfectly-combed style. I yanked harder and he let out a pathetic, irritated noise, but he couldn't stop fucking me.

Who was the little bitch now?

Then, with his breath huffing across the shell of my ear with every thrust, I came *hard*. My back arched and a strangled cry left my throat. My vision blew out. I dug my nails into his shoulder muscles and claimed my glorious victory.

With a shuddering gasp against my skin, he finished inside me. His thrusts slowed and his chest sank down onto mine as his grip on the armrest loosened.

My breasts squished against him as I panted. I fluttered my eyes open to find beads of sweat on his forehead that glistened in the low ambient light.

"I came first...again," I teased. "I won."

His eyes met mine as he hovered above me, our noses a mere inch apart. He smirked. "Tell yourself that when my cum drips down your thighs in a few minutes."

The attic stairs creaked and both of us whipped our heads toward the attic door.

"Come on, y'all, I heard something!" said a voice from the stairwell. "It's got to be the ghost!"

"The spirit of Miss Kaye wants to party with us!" said another. "Maybe we can finally get footage of her for our channel!"

Beau jumped off me and I quickly scrambled up from the couch. I snatched up his jacket and hurried to hide behind a tall stack of cardboard boxes. My heart pounded as I held Beau's jacket against my chest—as if that could hide the evidence of what I had just done.

Suddenly, a cool September breeze blew against my legs and I turned to my left. Beau was straddling the frame of an open window that led out into the alley. Dust stained the knees of his pants and the collar of his shirt was soaked with sweat. His hair was a tousled mess and his mouth was stained pink from my lip gloss.

He raked his hair out of his eyes and shot me a look. "Thanks for the ride, Adams."

My eyes dropped to his jacket in my hands. "Don't you want this?"

He shrugged. "Keep it. It's going to get chilly tonight."

With a wink, he ducked out the window and disappeared down the fire escape.

I held my breath as the attic door swung open and two pairs of footsteps stumbled in.

"Damnit, John, there ain't shit up here!" said a voice.

"I didn't make up what I heard," came the reply. "There was moaning, dude!"

"Maybe the ghost was here, trying to warn us that a Fontaine was in our midst and up to some sketchy shit."

I pressed the jacket closer to my body as one of the men sighed. "Aw, hell. Let's not waste the one good party this town has seen in a decade."

I only released my breath once the footsteps had disappeared down the stairwell. My knees shook as my inner thighs grew sticky.

Ugh. The sooner I could get to a shower, the sooner I could erase every trace of that little tryst.

I didn't know where my underwear went, nor did I know how I was going to inconspicuously sneak back down to my car.

But at least I knew I would never have to see Beau Fontaine again.

Olivia

It couldn't be. It was impossible.

And yet…

I stared at the white plastic strip perched on the edge of my bathroom counter, hoping that if I stared hard enough, the result would change.

"*Fuck,* Liv!" Ashley groaned through the phone. "Are you sure? I thought you had an IUD?"

I walked over to the bathroom counter and peered down. I stifled a groan as the word "PREGNANT" burned into my eyes.

The test might as well have read, "PREGNANT…you dumb bitch."

I rested the back of my head against the wall as I held my phone up. "I do, but…I got so focused on the Herringbone case last year that I forgot to track the expiration date."

"How do you just forget that your IUD expired?" Ashley exclaimed. "I thought you had your shit together!"

"I *did* have my shit together!" I pushed myself off the wall. "How else do you think I earned that $98 million verdict?"

She sighed. "The verdict was badass, Liv, but you can't forget to take care of yourself. You are more important than your job."

"I'm only important *because of* my job." My slippered feet paced across the black hexagonal tile of my bathroom. "Fine, I neglected my self-care to take on the largest oil company on the planet. Hell, I even neglected my other cases to make sure I secured that verdict when it went up on appeal! I was busy playing catch-up all month but then I got sick and made everything worse."

Just before Halloween, I started the most violent spells of vomiting I had ever experienced. I couldn't keep anything down, not even water. I could barely walk. I couldn't think. When I wasn't at the office, I alternated between hiding in bed and clinging to the toilet.

When I collapsed while crawling toward my front door to go to work, I finally forced myself to call in sick for a week and a half. I had thought the illness was just the worst stomach flu known to man, but then Ashley told me to take a damn pregnancy test.

"And...you're sure the baby is his?" Ashley quietly asked.

I sighed. "Couldn't be anybody else. I didn't hook up with anyone while the Herringbone case went up on appeal and that started months ago. And after the reunion..." I shrugged, letting the neck of my sweatshirt slide down my shoulder. "...I don't know, I just haven't wanted anybody since."

Though I usually told Ashley all the sordid details of my hookups, I was too embarrassed to admit that I was still pining after my old high school rival. I hadn't even opened my dating apps because I was too busy thinking about that night in the attic. Why go on another mediocre date when I had a vibrating arsenal in my nightstand drawer and a good memory?

I bit my lip at the thought of that egotistical rich boy buckling as I made him finish. Damn, what a sight to behold.

"So, Beau Fontaine is your baby daddy," Ashley said a little too loudly.

"*WHAT?*" Tyson exclaimed in the background.

I retched, holding my fist to my mouth to stop the vomit.

"Hey, I'm still in denial," I croaked. "Let me enjoy it a little while longer. Also—hey, Tyson."

"Heyyy, Liv," Tyson responded sheepishly. "So...I guess congratulations are in order?"

"That depends," Ashley said. "Are you keeping the pregnancy?"

I pursed my lips and stepped out of the bathroom. Being "Aunt Livvy" to Ashley's kids made me want my own baby eventually. My plan had been to go to a sperm bank once my career was settled and established...but I wasn't there just yet.

My shoulder rested against the wall as I stared out my big windows that framed a perfect view of the cityscape. I had made it into an apartment on the twentieth floor, clawed and scraped for an office at Parker & Hill, and had just scored the highest-value verdict the firm had seen all year. My career was finally kicking off and a child would kneecap me before I could start a full sprint toward true stability.

I bit my lip as I looked across my apartment. My spindly-legged chairs weren't exactly child friendly. My granite counters had sharp corners that I could just imagine a toddler running head-first into.

I didn't even have a bathtub...was my kitchen sink big enough to clean a baby in?

Though I'd need to do some major child-proofing, I did have a spare bedroom and enough floorspace for a playpen and a high chair and all the other baby stuff Ashley and Tyson had for their kids. My mom didn't have any of that when I was born.

My eyes drifted up to the shelf with my mom's photo—she was bright-eyed and smiling at my college graduation, right after her cancer diagnosis. Then my eyes fell to the small pewter canister containing her ashes. The "Dead Mom" club was the shittiest club in all of human existence. I had never needed to talk to her more than I did now.

I pictured a teenage Mom crying in my grandma's pink bathroom as she held a positive test in her own hands. She raised me on a small-business owner's meager earnings, then on government assistance as she hunted for jobs, and we still made it through. It was a childhood full of hand-me-downs, shared beds, and afternoons spent window-shopping downtown with our hands stuffed into our empty pockets—but it made me into the woman who held the world's largest oil company accountable at only twenty-seven years old.

Staring at her ashes triggered the memory of me sobbing in her living room because I was ready to quit law school. She was bald as an egg and had deep purple bags beneath her eyes, but she gripped me by the shoulders and told me to look at her as we recited, *"I can do hard things."*

I rested my hand on my lower belly as my mother's brave words repeated in my head.

"Yeah," I said into the phone. "I'm keeping my baby."

I pushed off the wall and walked over to Mom's shelf. I picked up a framed photo of her beaming with pride next to me at my third grade history fair. I wore a creative interpretation of a flapper dress fashioned out of old rags and gave a partially-toothless smile as I held my "First Place" certificate in my little hands.

"And this changes nothing about our plans," I said as I stared down at the photo. "I'm still all-in."

"No, Liv," Ashley argued, "I am not asking you to fund the renovation of Miss Kaye's house while you're *pregnant!*"

I frowned. "I get my bonus from the Herringbone case at the end of the year. According to my contract with the firm, my cut out of the attorney's fees is going to be $2.9 *million*. I'm going to be fine. My baby is going to be fine. And you know Miss Kaye's house is personal for me."

I set the photo back on the shelf. Miss Kaye had been Elren's original business woman. She owned the downtown department store, invented a patent for sewing machine parts that's still in use more than a century later, and never married. After she died, all her money went into an endowment for the betterment of Elren's up-and-coming young women. The endowment paid for my entire education at Plains State University for my bachelor's degree *and* law school.

Miss Kaye reminded me of what Mom could have been…had she never let my dad into her life.

After she got pregnant with me, Mom and my dad opened a successful restaurant downtown. She did the cooking and the serving while he handled the business. "Handling the business," I later learned, really meant committing tax fraud, swindling other vendors in town, and then cleaning out the registers and disappearing without a word.

I had just started preschool. Mom went bankrupt and her reputation in town never recovered.

Even though the faded memories of my dad haunted me, I stared lovingly at my mom in the portrait—still in her twenties and holding us together. The eight-year-old dressed as Miss Katherine Kaye smiled back at me through the glass frame. I had once promised myself that if I ever made it big, I would give back to the people, just like Miss Kaye did.

I'd do it for Mom.

"Call the city and sign the contract for the house," I told Ashley. "It's time we showed Elren the power of an independent woman again."

"OK," Ashley replied lightly, but with commitment. "But don't change the subject. When are you going to tell Beau about the baby? I'll come with you for support!"

I turned from my mom's shelf and scoffed. "Why would I tell him? I'm about to be a multi-millionaire, I don't need him."

"You have to tell him," Tyson said. Their infant son quietly babbled in the brief silence. "He needs to know."

"Beau is not a family man like you," I replied. "He doesn't want to see me, and frankly, I never want to see him again either."

Baby Tarik clapped his chubby hands and giggled as if Tyson had bounced him.

"Come on, Liv," Tyson scolded. "You can't do that to a man and you know it."

In the background, I swore I heard Tarik babble "Dada." I held my breath as my stomach tightened into a knot.

"He's right," Ashley said. "You have to tell him."

If the pregnancy wasn't making me queasy, their guilt trip definitely was. What was the point of having friends if they didn't let you run away from your problems?

I bit my lip. "I don't have his contact information."

"We do, from his reunion registration," Ashley replied. "I'll send it right now so you don't have an excuse."

My hand trembled as it gripped my phone. Telling Beau about the pregnancy didn't mean involving him. I could still raise my baby myself, on my own terms. I wasn't beholden to him.

I didn't need him. I didn't need *anyone*. I just…needed to enter this new phase of my life with a clear conscience.

I blew out my breath and suddenly my knees felt weak. "OK, just…send it now and I'll do it before I fall back into denial again."

"Give me two minutes," Ashley said. "And good luck—tell me what happens."

"Nothing *has* to happen!" I stressed. "I can tell him, he blocks me, and then we live happily ever after!"

"Oh…you *are* in denial," Ashley said with a smile in her voice. "See you at Thanksgiving! Love you!"

My stomach filled with dread. "Love you too."

"You're doing the right thin–!" Tyson called as Ashley hung up.

With a groan, I fell backward onto my bed. I rested my sleeve over my glasses to block out the light, but my head still spun. My trashcan was beside the edge of the bed, but somehow I was too sick to even vomit.

I was pregnant. A baby was growing inside me. Beau fucking Fontaine was the father. How was I supposed to tell him? What was I going to say?

My phone vibrated and a shock raced down my spine. I slowly lowered my sleeve from my eyes and peeked at my phone screen—there was the fateful text from Ashley with the number of my child's father.

I swiped to open the message. Sure enough, there was the contact information for…Beau Louis Fontaine III. Of course that douchebag had registered with his full fucking name!

And those douchebag genes were inside me, building a whole person.

The thought of packing everything and moving to the woods crossed my mind, but I shook the thought away and started a message to Beau's number. I held my breath, forcing myself to type out the message before I let myself breathe again.

The time crunch made me decide what I was going to say, and fast. My fingers quickly typed out the message and then I gave myself a cleansing gulp of air.

As I read the message over again, my thumb hovered over the "delete" button—my way out of the mess I was about to throw myself into. As I almost gave into the temptation, my mom's voice crept through my mind again.

"I can do hard things," I whispered.

And I hit send.

Beau

Every time I started a run, I couldn't wait for it to end.

But I still ran every damn morning.

The sun had just risen as I came to the end of my five-mile run. The crisp chill in the air was melting with the buttery sunlight. Tiny rocks and dry grass crunched under my feet as I followed the country road to the manor.

My heart was pounding, but my thoughts were quiet.

My podcast still had another five minutes left, so I jogged down our long driveway and headed to the back of the manor. According to the Bored Bros, my Lindsay University Crimson Knights had a good chance of winning the upcoming Thanksgiving game.

"I don't know, Bobby," Bret Bogeman groaned into the mic. "We can't count out Plains State's new running back. Lindsay's defense might not be able to stop him."

"He's fast," quipped Bobby Ballinger, "but he's no Tyson Copeland. No one at PSU has gotten close to breaking his record—"

I pulled out my earbuds and tossed them into my hoodie pocket. Bobby had never played a down of football in his life, don't know why he thought he was such a fucking expert.

I made a turn around the manor's southern wing and finished off my run at the back patio. I picked up a new tennis ball out of the wire basket at the end of the patio sectional and rolled it in my palm as I passed the firepit and outdoor bar.

As soon as I reached the covered pool, I found my favorite pile of white fluff lying on the glazed tile deck between two lounge chairs.

"It's November, boy," I said to my big silly dog. "You're not going for a swim until May."

Titus lifted his head and let out a low whine.

Poor boy, I missed the pool too. The patio was much too quiet when the waterfall wasn't turned on.

I tossed the tennis ball up in the air and caught it. "Come on, nothing makes you forget the silence like a run!"

I turned and launched the tennis ball. The ball soared about eighty yards before rolling down the grassy hill to the pasture where the cows were having their morning graze.

Though I expected to see Titus's giant body fly down the hill after that ball, I turned back to find him still between those deck chairs, looking up at me like I was some dumb asshole.

I sighed. Get a working breed, the managers at headquarters had said, they'll keep you busy. None of the breeders I spoke with ever mentioned that a Great Pyrenees was the biggest baby money could buy.

My phone buzzed. Odd, I wasn't expecting any messages.

I took out my phone to see that my finance guy was calling.

"I swear to God," I answered, "if you're about to tell me about another charity gala invitation…"

"How about *five*," Chuck answered with a groan. "But I do hear Mistletoe Masquerade in the city is actually pretty good—"

"You go, then." I sneered. "Wear some goofy mask and pretend to be me. See just how fun it is when all those opportunistic women corner you and 'inconspicuously' whine about how single they are."

"You make it sound like a bad thing…"

"Chuck, I will gnaw my arm off before I'm caught dead at another gala," I snapped. "Just give them money."

"Which galas? And how much? You've already maxed out your tax-deductible charitable contributions for this year, so there's no financial reason to—"

"All of them," I said. "Find the highest pledge tiers and add an extra zero to the checks. Send a message that my absence is much better for charity than the sight of me in a tux."

Chuck sighed. "You're a real Kris Kringle, Beau."

"And if I don't hear a peep from another gala until next year," I said with a tight smile, "you'll get another zero added to your Christmas bonus too. *Ho ho ho.*"

And I hung up.

I whistled for Titus to follow me as I headed back inside. He padded across the patio after me as I pushed open the French doors into the manor. My footsteps and the little clicks of Titus's paws echoed in the foyer. Just as I nearly turned into the media room, my phone buzzed again—a text this time.

Furrowing my brows, I pulled out my phone to read the message.

"About to fly over international waters. Aunt Liz is already two martinis deep. Won't activate phone service until we land on the island. Only call me if the Crimson Knights win."

Damnit, Mom.

I held back a sigh. I knew I shouldn't have filled the fridge with all the old family favorites for Thanksgiving, but I got my hopes up anyway.

I glanced at the family portrait hanging in the foyer, where little six-year-old me sat in my mom's lap. My hair was plastered against my head with gel and I wore a baby blue outfit with puffy sleeves and a girly collar. Growing up, I had hated that Mom chose to immortalize that goofy look with an oil painting. Now, I was just happy to have a portrait of Mom's smile where her eyes wrinkled in the corners—a smile that was now extinct.

The cigarette burn over my dad's face was a less pleasant sight, but I kept the painting up anyway.

"I'm going to cook you the best Thanksgiving dinner of your life," I said to Titus as I pulled up my bank app. "Half of the turkey in the fridge has your name on it, boy."

With a few swipes, I sent my mom a thousand dollars and texted her, *"Drinks are on me!"* As soon as I hit send, I shoved my phone into the pocket of my sweatpants and headed to the bar in the media room.

I slammed my steel tumbler on the marble bartop and mixed a post-run cocktail of coconut water and lime juice. The cold prick of the first sip through the metal straw hit my tongue as I crashed onto the leather sectional and turned on the TV for some noise to fill the silence.

A five-person sports panel started playing and I groaned. Monday morning football broadcasts were for sports gamblers. I had already learned the hard way that I wasn't lucky enough to gamble and it was already too late to save my fantasy football season, anyway.

I pulled out my phone and checked my fantasy stats—I was dead last. Chuck adding me to his fantasy league let me indulge in the illusion of having friends, but getting my ass kicked week after week wasn't doing much to lift my spirits.

I couldn't even beat Aunt Liz's team, the *"Pretty Ponies,"* and I was damn sure she picked her players at random!

A sigh left my lips as my eyes settled on the TV. I had three days until the next football game, so what else did I have to do other than watch the panel?

I tossed the remote aside and took another sip of my drink. Titus settled on the floor near my feet.

"I'm telling you, Lindsay has no chance!" Lamont Odell emphasized to the other panelists. "Their win against Rocky Mountain College was solid, but their defense is too spotty for Plains State."

Come on, Lamont. You haven't been in the game for two decades. What do you know?

"And we all know the most explosive running backs come from Plains State," said Perry Switzer.

The screen flipped to an old clip of a familiar player in an orange jersey sprinting toward the endzone.

"AND HE'S GONE!" the announcer cried. "He's gone! Like lightning from the heavens, it's TYSOOOOON COPELAND!"

I cursed under my breath. My metal cup clinked on the granite-top end table as I slammed it down.

"Before carrying the Stallions on his back in the national championship game," Perry said, "Plains State University recruited Copeland from small-town Elren—where he made *every single touchdown* in the state title game his senior year."

My hands scrambled across the leather cushions as I searched for the remote.

Don't need to fucking remind me about the state title game, Perry. I was there.

The front page of the Sunday paper after the fateful game flashed through my mind. Some jackass had taken a picture of me as I was slumped over in defeat, the harsh lights from Fontaine Stadium highlighting my sweat-soaked hair. The headline read: *"FONTAINE III DROPS THE BALL, OILERS LOSE STATE!"*

A fucking lie. I never dropped the ball...I threw interceptions, the final one costing us the game. The same reporter that said I had a golden arm when we won the semi-finals had turned on me— said it was clear my head wasn't in the game.

Of course, the reporter could only speculate. Despite how much he had pressed me for an interview afterward, I never let anyone in Elren know where my head actually was that night.

"It really does come down to recruiting, huh, Perry?" Lamont agreed.

Yeah, and the recruiters were at the game for *me,* but someone else got lucky instead.

I found the remote between two cushions. Just as I turned back to the screen to change the damn channel, more footage from the Plains State national championship win flashed across the screen.

Ashley Kouba, now Ashley Copeland, was in the stands bug-eyed and screaming after Tyson scored the final touchdown. She shook the girl next to her like a bobblehead, nearly strangling her in the frenzy of her excitement.

"Win aside," said Ryan McElroy, *"that* was the moment that went viral."

Lamont chuckled. "I even used that clip in the group chat last week."

The show played the clip over and over and I couldn't help but smile. The girl with her glasses falling off the end of her nose as Ashley gave her neck trauma was no random PSU student—it was Olivia Adams. The Crimson Knights had barely scraped by with a bowl win that year, but that clip had been the saving grace of an otherwise garbage season. Olivia had been such a smug little shit in high school that I had wanted to shake her like that myself.

She had annoyed everyone when her hand would be the first to shoot up after the teacher asked a question or when she started every sentence with "Did you know…?," but her true colors came out senior year. After we took our semester finals before Christmas break, she had passed me in class rank after chasing it like a dog for the past three and a half years. She could have just taken the valedictorian title and just fucked off like a normal person, but Olivia was not a normal person. As soon as she was announced as valedictorian, she finally took off the good-girl mask and became a complete sadist.

I had kept up appearances after the…*family event* happened senior year, so no one could have known why my grades had suddenly slipped after years of being on top, but Olivia had sensed my pain and relished in it. I couldn't even receive my silver salutatorian medal in peace without her cutting me a smug glance and whispering, "You're *nothing*, Beau Fontaine."

I wanted so badly to call her a bitch in front of the entire class, but I kept my mouth shut. The family had kept everything too quiet for me to blow up at some girl from the bad side of town.

If I hadn't lost my cool over losing the state championship game, I sure as hell wasn't going to lose control over Olivia Adams.

Though just because I kept quiet didn't mean I forgave her cruelty. A few months ago, I had been doom-scrolling through my socials when I found a video of Olivia doing a silly little twirl in a blue dress. The insufferably uptight valedictorian was all tits and hips in that dress, so I formed a plan for my revenge as I watched the video on repeat.

I was going to get under that little blue skirt at the class reunion and humble her once and for all. Either I was going to leave her so sexually frustrated that she combusted or fuck her so thoroughly that she would beg on her hands and knees for more. And since I had chosen the latter plan…

I took out my phone and checked the direct messages of all my socials—dry as a bone.

I furrowed my brows. Nearly two months had passed and *nothing?* Sure, my profile picture was a photo of Titus and all I ever posted were landscapes of the ranch and a few pics of fun drinks that I had made, but Olivia could have found me if she tried.

Damn. My plan may not have gone the way I wanted, but Olivia's black lacy thong in my dresser drawer was a fine trophy regardless.

Titus lifted his head and gave me a look.

"Absolutely not," I replied. "I don't care how good it would feel to humble her, *that* is not worth chasing."

Though I couldn't help but wonder how her luscious thighs would look dotted with bruises from my fingerprints…and I did miss the way her lip gloss stung the tip of my tongue.

No. I hadn't lost control over Olivia Adams when I was young and I sure as hell wasn't going to now.

I tossed my phone onto a nearby cushion, leaving Olivia in that dusty attic—a fitting place to store old memories and forget about them.

The cold of the steel tumbler bit my fingertips as I picked up my drink. That was all a man needed—a good drink, a good dog, and some good football. Thanksgiving week couldn't get any better.

My phone buzzed against the leather cushion and I paused mid-sip. After I had already heard from Chuck and my mom, I couldn't think of who else would be texting me. Everyone at Fontaine Energy headquarters was off for Thanksgiving break. Aunt Liz was probably passed out drunk next to Mom on their flight. Dad didn't even have a cell phone anymore…

The ice clinked in my tumbler as I gently set it down. I held my breath as I picked up my phone and read the notification—a text from an unknown number with a local area code.

With a flick of my thumb across the screen, I opened the message to read:

"Hey…it's Olivia Adams. I'm pregnant."

Olivia

Ashley and I sat on her back porch listening to Tyson work in his shed while Tarik napped in the living room. Ashley chattered about all the happenings in town, but I focused on the whine of Tyson's buzzsaw to keep the vomit at bay. We usually had our elbows pressed against her quartz kitchen island and buried ourselves knee-deep in gossip before family events, but even *standing* in her kitchen made me gag.

"Did you hear about Jessica Stalls?" Ashley said from her end of the porch swing. "Apparently, Clark found out their son wasn't his and he filed for divorce last week. My mom heard from her friend that the actual father might be Dwayne Gibson."

I turned to her, lifting my forehead from the cool chain of the porch swing. "Mr. Gibson? Our old gym teacher?"

"Yes!" Ashley shrieked.

I made a gagging noise, trying to not trigger myself to actually gag. "I thought I couldn't have a worse baby daddy than Beau… but at least it's not the man who wore knee-high socks and made me run laps until I cried."

"Speaking of which, did Beau ever specify where he was meeting you for brunch?" Ashley asked.

I took a saltine cracker out of the sleeve that rested in my lap and nibbled on the corner. "No."

Ashley pushed the toe of her black leather boot against the porch, letting our swing have a bit more momentum. "I'm surprised he waited so long after you told him."

I swallowed my bit of cracker. "Well, he wanted to meet me sooner, but I told him I had Thanksgiving plans. Then I told him we were shopping the next day. I didn't have enough energy to make up an excuse for Saturday, so…"

"So the procrastination train had to come to a stop," Ashley finished before taking a sip of her hard cranberry seltzer.

I buried my hands in my hoodie pocket. Though I always had a tummy, my palms rested against an undeniable baby bump. Ashley never showed this early, not even with her second baby.

I cut a glance at Ashley's pretty orange smock dress. She looked like a cover model for an autumnal magazine whereas I resembled a pumpkin that would sit in the background.

"I hope you sent Mrs. Copeland an apology text on my behalf already," I said softly. "My PSU hoodie is all that fits me right now."

Ashley shook her head. "She wouldn't care if you showed up to Thanksgiving wearing a potato sack, especially once she finds out about the baby."

The back door slid open and Ashley's daughter stomped onto the porch in her pajamas with her pink silk bonnet over her curls.

"What baby?" Kierra shouted.

I winced.

"None of your business!" Ashley scolded. "And why aren't you dressed, young lady? We go to Granny's in an hour!"

"No, you said there's a baby!" Kierra crossed her arms. "I wanna know!"

Ashley had no one to blame but herself. Kierra had to inherit the gossip gene from somebody, after all.

Ashley shot me a questioning look and I nodded, giving her permission to tell. What was the harm in letting Kierra know?

"OK," Ashley said in a quiet voice. "Aunt Livvy is having a baby."

Kierra gasped in excitement. "She's sick like you were with baby Tarik!"

My stomach roiled and I clamped my teeth down.

Ashley sighed and held her finger up. "Yes, *but* it's a secret. We can't be telling people."

Kierra furrowed her brows. "But you told me kids don't keep secrets from adults."

Ashley bit her lip and her eyes glanced up, as if the answer were written on the blue porch ceiling. "It...it's not a secret. It's a surprise!"

She pointed to the shed. "Like how we aren't telling Aunt Destinee that Daddy is making her a bookshelf for Christmas. She'll find out when the time is right."

Kierra nodded. "So, everyone should know about Aunt Livvy's baby when the time is right?"

"Yes, exactly," Ashley said. She kissed her daughter on the forehead. "Now go put on the outfit Aunt Destinee made for you."

Once Kierra ran back into the house, Ashley let out a long sigh. "That's the life you're in for as a mother, just making shit up on the fly."

I shrugged. "I'm good at that. I was a trial lawyer, after all."

Tyson shut off his saw and the crisp November air suddenly became too quiet. My stomach turned, but not with sickness for once.

"Ash, I'm sorry," I said quietly. "I'm sorry I told you to buy Miss Kaye's house. I'm sorry I had you sign that contract with the city and then—"

"Don't," Ashley said, short and clipped. "You couldn't have known they were going to fire you."

I closed my eyes and held my tongue against the roof of my mouth so I wouldn't be sick. Although, I would have rather vomited my crackers all over Ashley's porch than remember the morning when one of the partners walked into my office, said the two fateful words, and I was escorted out by armed security like a fucking criminal. The bankers boxes with all the shit from my office were still stacked in my backseat, but I was finally coming out of denial that my career, my insurance, and my $2.9 million were gone.

"Your law license is still good, right?" Ashley said with an optimistic lilt. "Why work for some assholes in thousand-dollar suits when you can open up your own firm?"

I shrugged. "Opening my own firm would mean a lot of upfront costs—money I don't have. Right now, my best option is working from my apartment and taking on contract work from other firms—you know, like reviewing documents and writing briefs. Might not be enough to pay all my bills and it wouldn't come with insurance, but I'll just have to try."

Ashley glanced at my belly. "You could tell the other lawyers you're pregnant. They'd feel bad for you and want to help you out!"

I snorted a laugh. "City lawyers don't feel bad for anyone. If they can't use you, they want to destroy you."

Ashley pulled her seltzer from her lips. "Jesus, Liv. How you survived three years in that hellscape is beyond me."

Late-night happy hours every week and meaningless sex with strangers—that's how I survived it.

I patted my belly from within my hoodie pocket. All my favorite coping mechanisms were out the window now. If I hadn't been fired, I don't know how I would have survived the stress and long hours while being pregnant. Sacrificing my own health while pushing toward the finish line was fine, but I couldn't do that to my baby.

I would just have to be like Mom and…make it work somehow.

"Regardless, don't worry about us—we'll figure out how to fund the renovation," Ashley promised. "We have over a million followers across all our platforms, I'm sure we can get some of them to chip in. Maybe we'll give donors exclusive renovation content or something."

I glanced at Ashley as she took another sip of her seltzer. Going viral our senior year of college with that clip of her strangling me had been like catching lightning in a bottle. What would have been a week of internet fame for most people, Ashley and Tyson had turned into a career. That one viral moment snowballed into recognition when they started filming their house renovation, then became credibility when they documented turning the abandoned department store into Copeland's Corner.

If anyone could get the eyes and support needed to turn Miss Kaye's house into the most-booked event venue in the state, it was Ashley and Tyson. They had better fortune than anyone I had ever known.

I ran my hand across the swell of my belly. If only I could be so lucky.

Ashley spared me the embarrassment of squeezing between Tarik's and Kierra's car seats by letting me ride shotgun as Tyson drove us to his mother's house for Thanksgiving dinner. I balanced the pies Ashley had baked on my lap while Tyson led the entire car in the Plains State school chant.

"Ride on, Stallions!" Tyson chanted as he pumped his arm.

"Ride, ride, ride!" cried Ashley and Kierra from the back seat.

I wanted to chant along with them, but I was too afraid I would vomit if I opened my mouth. Besides, I couldn't stop thinking about my upcoming meeting with Beau.

Beau had sent me the address of where he wanted to meet to discuss the pregnancy, but I couldn't find any information on the place. My phone's map showed that it was near a small lake—maybe the brunch spot didn't exist and he was going to fill my shoes with concrete and throw me in the water to cover up a scandalous pregnancy.

I tapped my nails against one of the pie dishes. As much as we hated each other, Beau was too cowardly to kill me. No, he was probably sending me to an exclusive lakeside country club—so exclusive that the *poors* weren't able to even look at it online. We'd probably sit at a table with crisp white linens and drink grapefruit juice from crystal goblets as I explained that I was carrying his child.

My cheeks grew hot as my slightly puke-stained hoodie felt even grungier. Beau wasn't going to hurt me, he was going to humiliate me. The thought of walking into this meeting when I was about to be a multi-millionaire was tolerable, but now that I again had nothing...

No, I didn't have nothing. I had savings. Ashley and I were going shopping before our meeting. I could get a new outfit so I could charge into the battle of the brunch with some confidence.

But could I still afford my favorite stores? Maybe with their Black Friday sales, I could get a few pieces...practical pieces...*maternity-friendly* pieces...

Memories of cabinets full of plastic restaurant cups and packs of ramen weighed on my mind. I wiggled my toes in my sneakers if only to prove I wasn't just pretending they weren't too tight. I mentally ran through my morning routine—I had showered and put on deodorant so I was sure I didn't smell, I had brushed my teeth in the sink of Ashley's guest bath and not with a bottle of water I had filled from the school drinking fountain, and the only reason I hadn't eaten breakfast was because of my nausea and not because it was the easiest meal to skip.

I grounded myself in the pressure from the glass pie dishes against my thighs. I was an adult now. I had control over my life and my finances. My bills were paid. My car wasn't about to get repossessed. My Thanksgiving dinner was coming from Tyson's mother and not out of a cardboard box from the Beau L. Fontaine Family Center.

The back of my head fell against the headrest as I stifled a groan. When I was in school, not a year had gone by where my mother's name wasn't on a list for holiday meals at the F.F.C. I had always told myself that it was Beau's *grandfather's* name on the building to spare myself the mortification that I was only eating thanks to his charity.

But even if Beau had never set foot in the F.F.C. and never seen that highlighter-yellow clipboard with undeniable proof that my mother relied on his family, he knew what I was. He never had to say it, but I saw it in the way he looked at me and how he talked to me—I was poor, dirty, and worthless.

It didn't matter that I had beaten him in the valedictorian race, or that I had cleaned up enough for him to want to fuck me on a couch, or even that I was bearing his child, Beau Louis Fontaine III was never going to let me forget that I was beneath him.

I set my jaw. No, I hadn't let him win when I was a kid and I wasn't about to let him win now that I was about to be a mother.

I would fulfill my moral obligation to let him know he had a child on the way and leave. I wouldn't ask for his money or his involvement. My dad wasn't around and I had turned out fine, and my child was going to be just fine too.

My child would grow up knowing we were strong, independent, and worthy. I had a long road ahead, so I needed to set that example *now*. I would walk into our brunch meeting, dressed my absolute best, and hold my head high.

I still had my dignity, damnit.

Tyson parked in front of his mother's house and we all got out of the car. Everyone except me was dressed to the nines. Kierra wore the sparkly dress her Aunt Destinee had sewed for her and her hair was pulled into two curly puffs accented with adorable orange bows. Baby Tarik even wore an orange button-up shirt and tiny black leather shoes.

Ashley had complained about how tough it was finding "Sunday best" clothes in PSU orange and black, but Tyson said we needed school spirit to win the Thanksgiving game and no one was going to argue with the man who had secured our first national championship.

Tyson opened the front door and the cacophony of smells of the Thanksgiving meal hit my nose. My mouth watered. My stomach knotted. Ashley had only just taken the pies from my hands before I turned on my heel and sprinted off the porch.

I threw myself on my hands and knees on the lawn as the first wave of vomiting tore through my throat like liquid fire. My stomach jerked painfully as it purged all my crackers and water from earlier.

I coughed and spat into the brown grass once the sickness finally stopped. If I vomited in front of Beau at brunch, I was going to fill my own shoes with concrete and jump into the lake.

Beau Fontaine would *not* see me bleed...or barf. I had to get my shit together.

"Don't worry, Granny!" Kierra shouted from the porch. "Your cooking smells great! Aunt Livvy is just having a baby!"

5

Beau

Brunch was an idiotic concept, but a fine excuse to day drink.

The sun glistened across the water of the nearby pond as I sat at the small table beneath the covered porch. A gentle breeze made thin silver wind chimes sing above me. I checked the time on my phone—Olivia was ten minutes late.

I frowned and tapped the heel of my boot against the porch deck. Olivia had always been obnoxiously early to every event in school—as if waiting outside the locked building before sunrise earned her bonus points—so either she had gotten lost on the way to brunch or she figured out that I knew she was lying.

I should have seen the con coming a mile away. She hadn't seen me or spoken to me in ten years, but wanted to fuck me? Her IUD was probably just as fake as her pregnancy was, but I had been so wrapped up in my own plan for revenge that I fell right into her trap.

But if Olivia Adams thought she was dealing with the same eighteen-year-old boy who didn't want to make waves to preserve the peace, she was in for a rude awakening.

The screen door to the restaurant creaked open and Olivia stumbled onto the porch. I held back a laugh at the pinch of her brows as soon as she laid eyes on the catfish pond.

After a bewildered blink, she tore her big brown eyes from the pond and found me at the lone table on the covered porch.

"Oh…" she breathed. "I didn't expect to find you out here."

What, didn't expect that your mark would ask you to meet him at the Bait N' Bites off the highway?

I figured my location choice would throw her off, but I didn't think she would show up to brunch in an ankle-length velvet dress and silver heels.

My eyes dropped to her lower stomach for only a moment. I couldn't tell if the swell beneath the twisting pattern embroidered into the purple velvet was an actual baby bump, but my mother raised me better than to study it for too long.

Olivia wobbled on her ridiculous silver shoes across the creaking deck and sat in the chair across from me. She tapped her pumpkin-colored fingernail on top of the laminated menu in front of her, sucked her lower lip between her teeth, and finally looked up.

"So, what made you choose this place?" she asked.

I shrugged. "I take all my important business out here. Can't have someone overhearing us and then all of Elren knows about our situation before I can even get back to my truck."

Olivia glanced at the old man fishing at the dilapidated deck over the pond. "What about him?"

"That's just Uncle Joe, he can't hear shit," I answered. "I could shoot a hole through the porch roof and he wouldn't even turn around."

She looked back at Joe and her brows furrowed again. "That man is your uncle?"

"I never said that."

The screen door smacked open and Olivia nearly jumped out of her skin.

Dad always said that only liars needed to be nervous…

"Here's your mimosas, baby," the waitress said as she plopped plastic cups of orange juice onto the gray laminate table.

"Thanks, Kathy," I said.

"Um, could I have regular orange juice please?" Olivia asked.

Well, well. She was clever enough to pass the first test.

"Sure thing, hon," Kathy responded. "Are y'all ready to order?"

I handed her my menu. "Get me Uncle Joe's special."

Kathy grimaced. "You want *that* much grease this early? I thought you were on a health kick."

I glanced at Olivia, who kept her lips tightly pursed. *If* Olivia was telling the truth, she would be at the height of morning sickness by now. The smell of meat from a griddle that hadn't been cleaned since cars still had built-in phones was sure to reveal a real pregnancy.

"Oh, you know I'm sore after that on-field massacre at the Thanksgiving game," I said innocently. "I need some comfort food."

"You and me both, sweetie," Kathy replied. She turned to Olivia. "What about you, fancy shoes?"

Olivia's eyes dropped to her menu. "Just the short stack of pancakes."

Kathy took up Olivia's menu and left us on the porch. The faint sizzle from the griddle inside told me that she was going to be occupied for the next fifteen minutes—plenty of time to expose a liar.

Olivia reached into her large black purse and pulled out an aluminum blister pack. She dumped a small white pill into her palm and then popped it into her mouth, probably thinking I wouldn't notice.

I raised an eyebrow. "What was that?"

She swished her tongue in her mouth for a few seconds before answering. "Anti-nausea medicine. Dr. Copeland hooked me up after Thanksgiving dinner."

Fuck. She really thought she was slick, didn't she?

She blinked and tilted her head slightly. "You know, Dr. Copeland? Tyson's dad? Owns the pharmacy?"

"I know who he is," I responded.

I pushed the sleeves of my Lindsay University crewneck up to my elbows and then leaned on my forearms. "OK, cut the bullshit. How much do you want?"

She quirked a brow. "Excuse me?"

"I'm not playing your game, Adams. Do you want your fake-pregnancy extortion money paid in a lump sum now? Or do you want it in installments over the next eighteen years?"

Her mouth fell open. "You...you...complete jackass! I'm not lying!"

"You might be loath to remember, but I got an A in Calculus just like you." I balanced the table knife on the blade's edge and spun it once. "So I know your story doesn't add up. Which was the lie, Adams? The pregnancy or the IUD?"

She slammed her palms on the table so hard that the knife fell from my hand. "I want *nothing* from you. In fact—"

She reached into her bag again and pulled out a wad of dark fabric.

"Here!" she snapped as she tossed the fabric at me.

I caught it before it could knock over the mimosas—my jacket, the one I had worn to the class reunion. I dusted off the shoulders and found a hot pink sticky note pasted to the edge of the sleeve. I peeled it off and examined the bubbly script written in black marker.

"Work until your name is on the building?" I read.

"Ignore that." Olivia folded her arms and her cheeks flushed beneath her layers of makeup. "Your jacket has been in my backseat for weeks…it must have gotten tangled up with the boxes of stuff from my office."

I folded the note in half and slipped it into the pocket of my jeans. Wait, she wouldn't have boxes of office junk in her car unless…

A smile crept up my face. "They fired you, didn't they?"

She tightened her arms across her chest. "My career is none of your concern."

I shook my head. "Come on, Adams. Don't play coy when I know what you taste like."

Her cheeks burned red and she turned away, pretending the catfish pond was suddenly very interesting.

What was the sense in being embarrassed now? Besides, she had tasted *damn good*—gave me the same feeling as wearing flannel and eating a cinnamon roll after dinner.

But exposing her deceit would taste even sweeter.

"It was a sudden…parting of ways," she finally admitted.

So that was the why behind the lie. She got pregnant from some random hookup, her horrible law firm fired her for it, and she was desperate for security.

If I thought prudish Olivia Adams begging me for more sex would be a satisfying revenge, watching her crawl back to me because she fucked up her life gave me a high better than anything I had ever tried in a club bathroom.

I just never imagined she would be this pathetic.

"But I thought you were a lawyer," I said as I leaned back in my chair. "Can't you just sue them since they fired you for being pregnant?"

She let out a slow, tense breath. "The firm didn't know about my pregnancy. They told me I had too many client complaints over the last quarter, but—"

"Oh, I don't believe that for a moment." *God,* listening to her admit failure was too fucking good. "Who would ever complain about having Miss Perfect represent them?"

Her glare sharpened. "They were about to pay me a big bonus. I suspect they took advantage of the termination clause in my employment contract so they could keep the money."

"You got fired because you achieved too much. *Sure.* "

Keep lying, Adams. A lawyer through and through.

Her lower lip trembled only once. "My bonus was $2.9 million, you *asshole.* "

A laugh burst out of me. "Now *that* I believe. Let me guess, they worked you like a dog for years, promised you a corner office if you followed orders, and as soon as you made your bag, they stole it all from you?"

Olivia held her glare as I laughed, her hard silence confirming my suspicion. I could always read her like a fucking book and she still thought she could deceive me?

I closed my eyes and held my fist against my lips to try to tame my laughter. "And you think *I'm* evil."

She took in a stiff breath. "I don't recall ever saying you were."

The screen door smacked open again and Kathy set our plates in front of us. My stomach rumbled as I surveyed my oval plate piled high with sizzling bacon, glistening sausage, two fried eggs, and hash browns that were drowning in the grease from the meat.

I took a bite out of the bacon and sipped the mimosa—it was a screwdriver that Kathy called a mimosa, but it was delicious nonetheless.

"So," I said after a swallow, "when is your next doctor's appointment? I want to see my growing baby."

Olivia paused mid-chew to look up at me. She let out a tense breath from her nose and swallowed. "I don't have an appointment yet. I have to apply for government insurance and then find a provider who accepts it."

I dug my fork into my egg. Absolute bullshit—she just didn't want me going to her appointment and finding out the baby she's carrying was conceived a month before our class reunion.

I took a bite and then pulled out my phone. "That won't do. No baby of mine is going to be on government insurance."

"What are you doing?" she asked.

I pointedly refused to answer. After a few moments of silence, she turned her attention back to her stack of pancakes. While she stuffed her face, I looked up the most reputable OB-GYNs in the city, read reviews, and most importantly, found out who had immediate availability.

My thumb tapped a pink button confirming the plan. "It's done. You have your first appointment Tuesday at 10 a.m."

Her brows flew to her hairline as she dropped her fork. "You can't do that! I'm not on your insurance!"

I scoffed. "Insurance is a scam for poor people. I just put it on my credit card."

Olivia's face blanched. "I…I already told you that I don't want your money."

But she wasn't exactly refusing it, now was she?

"If the baby really is mine, contributing to its medical care is the least I can do." I slid my phone back in my pocket and flicked my eyes up to meet hers. "And if the baby *isn't* mine…well, we can just call it a bit of holiday charity."

She stiffened, breathless, with her garish orange nails digging into her velvet sleeves.

I glanced at her empty plate. "I don't know what kind of man you think I am—but I'm not one to let a single mother go hungry."

She launched from her chair and yanked up her purse. She furiously dug around in it while her whole face turned red.

I grabbed my mimosa. "What are you doing?"

She pulled out a black leather wallet. "Paying for my fucking food."

"You can't afford it," I said before taking a sip.

She snapped her head toward me and I swore her eyeballs were about to pop right out of her skull. "You ass! If you think I can't afford an eight dollar stack of pancakes—!"

I pointed at her plate. "That is not an eight dollar stack of pancakes. You have no idea how much the price of silence is in this town."

She stared at me mouth agape, her chest heaving with her furious breath, while I simply took another drink.

"Fuck you," she finally said before sliding the straps of her bag onto her shoulder.

I pulled my lips from my cup. "Isn't that how we got here in the first place?"

She shook her head and stomped toward the door.

"I fucking hate you," she mumbled. She pulled open the creaking screen door and shot me a glare. "You piece of SHIT!"

She slammed the screen door behind her so hard I thought it might pop off the hinges.

I raised my mimosa. "See you next Tuesday, sugar!"

I had never been more excited for a doctor's appointment in my whole life. I couldn't wait to see the look on Olivia's face once she realized I caught her in a lie.

6
Olivia

I couldn't wait to see the look on Beau's face once he realized how much of an asshole he is.

The silence of my apartment's parking garage amplified my anticipation for the doctor's appointment. I drummed my fingers on my steering wheel, ignoring the painful rumbling in my stomach.

Not even when I was poor did I have such a long streak of bad luck. Not only did I drop my contacts down the sink drain this morning, my car wouldn't start when I tried to grab breakfast before the appointment. I texted Beau about my car trouble, but he responded that he would meet me in the parking garage and jump my dead battery.

He probably thought I was lying to get out of the appointment, just like he thought I was lying about having an IUD and about him being the father of my baby. The only thing stopping me from murdering the next person I saw out of sheer hunger was the thought of Beau's embarrassment once he learned I was telling the truth. Maybe he'd even apologize. Oh, how I would love to see him grovel.

Once I got that bit of satisfaction, I would walk out of the doctor's office and never see him again.

The low growl of a diesel engine echoed through the parking garage and a huge white truck pulled into the empty spot next to me.

I rolled down the window as soon as Beau stepped out of the truck. I met his eyes and then gave a pointed glance to the behemoth he had just driven up in. "I thought you didn't have to compensate for anything."

"It's a farm truck—a rolling tax deduction," he responded dryly. He tapped the hood of my Jaguar. "All right, open her up for me."

I pulled a latch and the hood popped. As soon as Beau lifted the hood, white smoke billowed out.

"Get out of the car!" he shouted.

I fumbled with the door handle and flung myself out of the driver's seat. He grabbed my hoodie's sleeve and dragged me a few steps across the garage.

As soon as we were safely away from my car, the smoke thinned until it finally stopped.

My eyes dropped to a large puddle below the front of my car. "The hell was that? Is my car going to blow up?"

Beau silently walked over to my car and peered under the hood. "No, but you're gushing coolant…and oil. The battery is the least of your problems."

My stomach dropped. I wasn't sure what that meant, but it didn't sound good. "I swear to God, Beau, if you think I messed with my car just so I wouldn't have to go to this appointment—!"

"I don't think that." He shut the hood and looked back at me. "You're a lot of things, Adams, but you're not stupid. This car is toast."

I suddenly felt dizzy. "T-toast?"

He shrugged and tossed a glance at the car. "If you're still under warranty with the dealership, they might be able to fix it without costing you five figures."

Five figures. I was going to throw up. "I-I don't have a warranty. I bought the car from a guy off the internet."

He pinched the bridge of his nose and took in a deep breath. "*Mon dieu.*"

"Wh-what?" I asked. "Was that French?"

He looked up at me. "Do you know French?"

I hated the snobbish undertone of his question. "No. Not all of us got to go to Paris for the summer."

"I summered at an island resort, not Paris." He flashed me a cocky grin. "But now I know what language to use when I don't want you to understand me."

I flipped him off, but he ignored me. He pressed a button on his key fob and unlocked his truck. "Get in. We're going to be late."

Beau walked around to the driver's side of his truck, but I stayed frozen as I stared at the front of my car. I pulled up a spreadsheet in my mind, calculating the cost to repair the car versus buying another one and weighing the need for a car against my monthly rent, and groceries, and bills, and...and...

The heavy slam of Beau's truck door jolted me back into the moment. I couldn't panic, not when I was about to go to my first prenatal appointment and *definitely not* when Beau was relishing in my despair. I took a breath and mentally gathered all my worries and put it in an imaginary sack, tying it shut with a pretty satin bow of denial.

With that imaginary bow double-knotted and secure, I silently climbed into the passenger seat of Beau's truck. As I settled into the leather seat, I stared out the window and a strange sort of numbness settled over me. I was suddenly reminded of when I stared down at the city from the window of my mom's hospital room, submerged in that paradoxical state of being both empty and too heavy all at once.

The darkness of the parking garage turned into daylight as Beau drove, but my eyes stayed fixed on the same nondescript location as we passed by revolving doors and the darkened voids of storefront windows. Two voices from some podcast played over the truck's speakers, but I couldn't really listen.

At the doctor's office, I sat silently on the pink couch in the lobby as Beau checked me in. I wrung my hands on top of the swell of my belly, using all my strength to hold my feelings behind that imaginary satin bow.

Someone handed me a plastic cup to pee in. I followed instructions.

I stepped on a scale and didn't bother to read the measurement. I felt the squeeze of a blood pressure cuff on my arm.

A woman in purple scrubs asked me the date of my last period. I mumbled that I couldn't remember.

When she left, I finally realized that I sat in a small examination room on a strange table beneath a circular golden lamp. The table was positioned diagonally in the corner of the room, making me look like a specimen about to be studied and the star of a miniature stage show all at once. My one spectator, Beau Fontaine III, sat in a nearby chair and scrolled through his phone.

I balled my hands into loose fists on top of my lap and heard the soft crinkle of paper. Oh, I supposed I had taken off my sweatpants and underwear at some point. Maybe I should have felt embarrassed since Beau would have been in the room, but what dignity did I have left to preserve?

The door opened and the same nurse from before wheeled in a tall machine with a big screen and a wand attachment. A woman in black scrubs followed her and sat down on a small circular stool. She introduced herself as Dr. Ornelas and asked me some questions that I vaguely remembered already hearing from the nurse.

Dr. Ornelas glanced at the laptop she balanced on a counter near a small sink. "You're not sure of your last menstrual period, but you're confident the date of conception was September 26th, right?"

"Yes," I answered.

"Allegedly," Beau added as he lounged in his chair.

I slowly turned from Dr. Ornelas and gave Beau a look, silently begging him to not be a dick for once in his life.

Dr. Ornelas glanced up from her laptop at Beau. "Are you the father?"

"Allegedly," Beau answered with a smirk.

Dr. Ornelas waved a hand vaguely in the direction of my left side. "Well, Mr. *Allegedly*, go stand over there if you want to see."

Beau slowly rose from his chair as the nurse flicked off the lights. I reclined back on the cushioned table and Dr. Ornelas warned me of an incoming uncomfortable pressure.

My brows pinched together as she inserted the ultrasound wand, but my eyes were too glued to the flickering gray lines on the screen to care.

There was the head, the body, the tiny hands and feet—my baby. *My baby.* The baby fluttered its itty bitty limbs as it swam around its little bubble inside me.

Dr. Ornelas shifted the wand ever-so slightly and the screen shifted, revealing a bright white "T" shape above my baby's bubble.

Dr. Ornelas pointed a gloved finger at the white shape. "There's your IUD."

She shifted the wand again, but I pulled my eyes away from the screen and looked up at Beau. Where I had wanted to catch him in a state of contrition as he realized he had been wrong all along, I instead found a man who looked like he was falling from a hundred feet.

His wide eyes made something behind my ribs flutter, so I turned back to the ultrasound screen.

My heart stopped. I blinked to make sure I was reading the screen correctly but...two. Two heads, two bodies, two sets of hands and feet.

"Well," Dr. Ornelas said with a smile, "would you look at that."

Twins. I was carrying twins.

The satin bow of denial broke and all my worry spilled out of that imaginary bag. My heart raced as spreadsheets monopolized my brain, each calculating the cost of two cribs, two daycare tuitions, and two sets of clothes. Double the diapers, double the jars of baby food, double the doctor visits, double the school supply lists…

The lights flicked back on but my internal calculator didn't stop. I stared up at the golden lamp as my brain ran through all the data of how badly I was fucked. My hands shook as they rested on top of my belly.

Dr. Ornelas explained that I had to get my IUD removed immediately, and all I remembered was heavily nodding my head. A quick pinch and it was over. I could barely feel it. I could barely even breathe…

I mentally traced the edges of that golden lamp in a counterclockwise spiral. I heard Dr. Ornelas talking to Beau, but the sound hit my ears as if I were stuck inside a glass fish bowl. I could only process bits and pieces of their conversation as my internal system whirred with numbers on a balance sheet and sorted through the acronyms of all the government assistance programs I could remember.

"…measuring at eleven weeks gestation," Dr. Ornelas said.

"…never done this before, but…with twins?" Beau asked.

Twins. Twins. Twins. The word was an echo in my fish bowl as I drowned.

"…needs more help," Dr. Ornelas replied. "…mobility concerns…more water…rest…"

Rest? Who could rest in my position? I needed to get another job, needed insurance, needed a babysitter, needed two cribs, needed to call the county health department, needed my mom—

I closed my eyes, listening to the memory of my mother's voice echoing through my mind as if she were crying out to me at the end of a long, dark hallway.

"I can do hard things," she had always told me. I had always listened to her, I had always succeeded because of her, but why could I not believe her now?

"Adams? ADAMS!"

I jerked my head to my left to find Beau glancing at me as he drove. I looked down and plucked at the seatbelt cutting between my breasts. Somehow, I had made it back into the passenger's seat of Beau's truck. The tall buildings of the cityscape passed us on either side as we made it through downtown.

"Christ, Adams," Beau snapped as he shook his head. "You're white as a sheet. If you're going to get sick, warn me to pull over so you don't ruin the leather upholstery."

I frowned and pulled the bottom of the seatbelt below the swell of my belly. Of course he was only worried about his precious upholstery. Twins weren't a financial death sentence for him.

"When was the last time you ate?" he demanded.

I shrugged. "Can't remember."

He scoffed and flicked his turn signal. "I'm finding the nearest smoothie place so I can at least get something in you. No wonder your blood pressure was so low."

"It was?"

He shot me a quick, disbelieving look. "How do you not remember?"

I hissed out a breath but kept my eyes on my belly. "Maybe if you had the slightest bit of emotional intelligence, you might understand how this situation could be quite overwhelming for a person."

"Damn it, you're not taking care of yourself!" he said. "First you let your IUD expire, then you let your car go to shit, and now you're not keeping up with your nutrition. Neglecting yourself is bad enough, but now you're carrying my babies—"

"*YOUR* babies?" I snapped.

"Yes, *my* babies." He pointed at my belly as he took a turn down another street. "They are the only heirs to the company, the family land, the Fontaine name—"

"Heirs? What century are you living in? And don't you think they're getting your name because—!"

"My point is that neither of us can just think about ourselves anymore." He glanced toward my belly. "They need us."

I folded my arms across my chest and leaned away. "Us? There is no us! I don't need or want you to—"

"*Somebody* has to remember what the doctor says—so, yes, there is an us," he argued. "You can't do this alone and I won't let you try."

Heat flared across my face. "Don't you dare say that I can't do this. I *will* get through this pregnancy and I'll do it without you!"

"Oh yeah? Do you know what you can and can't eat? What about how much water you have to drink every day? And how are you going to get it all without a car or a job?"

I clutched myself tightly and stared out the window. "I'll figure it out. I always do."

The truck slowed down as we reached the beginning of the suburbs.

Beau let out a long, tight sigh. "Adams, for once in your goddamn life, don't be so fucking stubborn. Dr. Ornelas said that twin pregnancies are much harder than normal ones, and from what I hear, normal pregnancies are already awful. You can't win this."

How many times had men just like him told me I couldn't win? I tightened my grip on my arms, ready to scream at him.

"You're going to hurt the babies if you don't accept help," he added.

My chest deflated, as if my iron constitution had instantly turned to marshmallow. Maybe he had a point. After all, Ashley's parents were divorced but her dad had still played a small part in her life. He at least paid child support, which kept her from knowing what 11 p.m. hunger pangs felt like. Beau was an insufferable ass, but I could let him help a little.

"Fine," I said in a low breath.

I wasn't going to rely on him. I wasn't going to let him have access to any part of me ever again. I was still going to be completely independent and—

"You're not going back to your apartment," he said. "You're moving into the manor so I can keep an eye on you during your pregnancy."

I snapped my head toward him.

"The hell I am!" I shouted. "Just because you got me pregnant doesn't mean you own me!"

"I didn't say that! Quit fucking putting words in my mouth—"

"You called me a liar and an extortionist to get away from me, and now you're suddenly doing the opposite because of the babies you didn't even believe were real? This isn't about the twins, this is about control."

He shook his head. "Before you villainize me, take a look in the mirror. Maybe then you'll see just how selfish you're being."

"*Selfish?*" I turned to glare at his profile. "Let me be very clear, Beau Fontaine, I don't want your money, I don't want your time, and I don't want *you.*"

A cruel smirk flicked up the side of his face. "You should have thought about that before you wrapped your legs around me and made me finish inside you. You can't get rid of me now."

My hands balled into fists at my sides. "Why can't you just accept that I'm giving you what every man wants—the opportunity to just walk away!"

The seatbelt slammed into my sternum as Beau hit the brakes and I gasped. The truck came to a sudden stop in the middle of the street.

My hands flew to my belly and I looked up. "Beau, what the fuck are you doing?"

He didn't answer. He stared straight ahead, his hands wrapped around the steering wheel so tightly that his knuckles turned white. Cars honked around us, but he didn't even blink.

My heart pounded. "Beau...? Beau! Get out of the middle of the street you jackass!"

His voice was low and tight. "Adams, I'll make you a deal... right now. If you can name one person, one single fucking soul in this city, who can help you through this pregnancy, you will never hear from me again."

"Done," I agreed.

"But if you can't..." Those blue eyes gleamed and too late I realized that I had sprung a trap. "...we're packing your shit and going back to Elren. Today."

I clenched my jaw. Ashley could help me...but she had Miss Kaye's house to renovate, her own kids to take care of, and Elren was an hour and a half away from my apartment. Beau said my person had to live in the city. All the attorneys I used to drink with wouldn't drive me to a 10 a.m. doctor's appointment. I could dredge up some men from my dating apps…but that was too dangerous for me to even consider.

I gritted my teeth and held my arms tighter. Anybody else in my position had parents, or grandparents, or even a cousin to help them out. But me? I had no one.

I had dealt with years of empty seats at graduation and silent apartments at holidays, but never had the absence of family felt more like a slap in the face.

But I could still beat Beau at his game. I could make up a half-sibling that I could rely on, he'd never know. I bit my lip, silently inventing a fake name and a fake address when Beau let out a low laugh.

"That's what I thought," he said with a smug smile. He took his foot off the brake and started to drive as my heart sank. "Figure out what kind of smoothie you want. I suggest getting something with protein—you're going to need your energy for all the packing ahead."

Olivia

Mom once told me to never drive past a covered bridge when a tornado was coming—always take shelter as soon as you can.

She was wrong, a covered bridge was actually the worst place to be in a tornado. You were better off leaving your car and hiding in a ditch until the storm passed.

My temple pressed against the passenger window of Beau's truck as he drove into Elren. The sunset-kissed gray December sky showed no sign of a tornado, but I was forced to seek shelter from a storm nonetheless.

Would I much rather wallow in a ditch than live with Beau Fontaine? Absolutely, but I couldn't make decisions based on what I wanted anymore.

Moving into the famous Fontaine Manor for the ease of my pregnancy was just like when Mom and I had to move in with

Grandma after my dad left. Mom and Grandma didn't see eye-to-eye, to put it lightly, but Mom put up with her for my sake.

"Pride doesn't keep your stomach full or your bed warm," Mom had said.

That advice I had to agree with. Accepting Beau's charity felt like I had spiders crawling beneath my skin, but my babies deserved the best I could offer.

And right now, all I could offer them was a rich father.

As the men on Beau's podcast droned on about the discovery of a new sea urchin, I weakly lifted my arm and my lips caught the edge of my straw. I sucked down the last dregs of my extra-large peanut butter smoothie and listened as my suitcases slid around in the bed of Beau's truck.

I had left most of my decor and books in my apartment, but I stuffed all my blankets, candles, and sweatshirts into every piece of luggage I owned. They were heavy as all hell, but that was Beau's problem.

If I was carrying his babies, he could carry all the suitcases he forced me to pack when he strong-armed me into moving in with him.

Well, except for my purse that rested at my feet. No one was touching it but me.

Beau turned the truck and suddenly the cracked pavement of the highway smoothed into dark asphalt. Since Ashley and I weren't too keen to get drunk in fields or smoke blunts in the grocery store parking lot, we spent hours of our teenage years cruising all over Elren in her rusty beater sedan. Even though I swore Ashley and I had explored every back road around Elren's city limits, I had never been down this country road before.

After a few minutes of driving, I saw it on the horizon—Fontaine Manor. I had always heard that Fontaine Manor was a creature borne from the pages of a leather-bound gothic horror and dropped into the middle of the prairie. With its stone walls, mansard roofs topped with copper spires, and corners rounded out with ostentatious turrets, I understood where people could have gotten that idea.

Though if anyone had asked me, I would have described the massive house not as a dark fairytale dream, but with a mere two words—gaudy and imposing.

The truck headed up the long driveway to the manor that circled around a large, three-tiered fountain before parking in front of the mahogany double doors.

Beau got out of the truck as I examined the front of the manor. The brickwork that made the base of the manor suggested that it was built in the early 20th century, but I couldn't find any architectural cues that would connect the manor to any other building in Elren. From the small iron bars that formed diamond window panes to the perfectly square hedges that guarded the foundation like a moat, everything about the manor screamed old money.

A shiver went up my arms—this was nothing like moving in with Grandma. Still, the stay at Grandma's house was temporary, just like my stay at Fontaine Manor.

Granted, we only left Grandma's because she died and the bank took her house…but it was still just a temporary stay!

Beau opened my door just as I pulled my purse onto my shoulder. He held out his hand, but I squeezed my purse closer to my body.

"No, I've got it," I protested.

Beau stood aside with his arms folded as I carefully shimmied and slid my way out of his giant truck. My pelvis didn't want to cooperate for whatever reason, so I had to escape my seat like an oversized penguin.

And I thought nausea was going to be the most humiliating part of pregnancy.

I ignored the pointed eye-roll Beau gave me as I struggled. Maybe I would move faster if he had a normal vehicle…or if he knew how to pull out.

My legs were a little wobbly as my feet planted on the perfectly smooth concrete near the front steps, but Beau didn't wait for me before turning to the front door. He pressed his thumb against a pad on the handle. A lock clicked and then he pushed the door open.

I raised an eyebrow. "So only you can get in and out? Are you planning on locking me in here to keep your precious heirs safe?"

He scoffed. "I'll get you added to the system after you settle in, but don't tempt me."

I followed him inside, but my feet froze as I took in the interior.

The foyer was papered in veridian green and stretched two stories high, leading to a circular mural of Baroque-style dolphins on the ceiling. Hanging from the ceiling was a wrought-iron chandelier that was dripping with…strands of pearlescent beads from a craft store.

Black and white marble tile stretched all the way to the back doors of the manor. The curved stairs lead to the second story landing where…chartreuse suits of armor stood guard. My eyes darted around, finding a raspberry pink frame on the wall featuring a portrait of peacocks in top hats, a gilded mirror that flipped its reflection upside-down, and a standing iron candelabra fashioned with two of its arms on its "hips" to appear as if it had been impatiently waiting.

Beau stuffed his hands into his pockets and I followed him through the foyer, my head turning to examine the wall full of mounted heads of an antelope, a gazelle, and even a giraffe that stretched up to the dolphin mural.

"Dad likes to shoot things," Beau casually explained.

I froze in front of a rhinoceros head that had been spray-painted gold and had hot pink eyelashes glued above its black glass eyes.

Beau followed my eyes and sucked in his lip. "And…Mom likes to get creative."

I turned from the poor animals to face him. "Do your parents live here?"

He glanced away. "No, just me." Soft clicking noises suddenly echoed through the foyer. "Oh, and my roommate."

I clutched my purse closer to my body. I pictured sharing a living space with one of Beau's rowdy friends from college, but then a big white dog appeared from behind a set of sponge-painted columns.

Beau held his palm out and the dog came right over.

"This is Titus." He gave him a big scratch behind his floppy ear. "He's absolutely useless."

"Poor boy—Beau is so mean to you." I gave Titus a gentle head-rub. "Next he'll say you're broke and have a shitty car."

"Nonsense, Titus wouldn't be caught dead in a Jaguar." Beau turned toward a closet with a gilded cage door near the stairs. "Come on, I'll show you to your cell, *prisoner.*"

I rolled my eyes and followed. On the wall next to the closet was an awkward rectangular gap between the decorations like a large frame had just been removed. I bet Beau commissioned an oil painting of himself and then threw it away in a tantrum because it didn't flatter him enough.

He pressed a button near the closet door. "I normally take the stairs, but since you're likely going to need this in the future…"

The gilded closet door split in half and opened. Only then did I realize it wasn't a closet but an *elevator*.

Beau stepped inside the elevator and I carefully followed. The elevator was small and I was too damn close to him, but Beau was the least of my worries.

I turned my head to all my reflections on the mirrored walls, half-expecting to see the face of a family ghost in the glass. Both the birdcage style of the door and the filigreed frame around the column of buttons suggested that the elevator was *very* old.

"Quit freaking out," Beau said. "This elevator is ten times safer than that death trap you used to drive."

He pressed the button labeled with a hand-painted "2" and his arm accidentally brushed against mine. I sucked in a breath at the sudden warmth of his touch.

Nope—that was how I got into this situation. I wasn't going to entangle myself deeper with Beau Fontaine and his haunted house of oddities. I was his temporary roommate and nothing more.

Thankfully, Beau moved closer to the wall as the elevator ascended.

He cleared his throat. "The media room, kitchen, and gym are on the first floor. The study is in the east wing next to the library—if I'm at home working, that's where you'll find me."

I ignored the third floor button and focused on the lowest button in the column. "What's in the basement?"

"A dungeon for sexual torture."

The elevator doors opened to the second floor and Beau casually stepped out, but I was stone still as heat pooled beneath my cheeks.

He turned to face me, hands in his pockets and that damnable smile on his face. "That was a joke, Adams. Never thought you would be so gullible."

I gripped the strap of my purse and hurried out of the elevator. "You have half a safari on the wall downstairs, why wouldn't I believe you?"

He led me down a dark hallway and let out a small disappointed sigh. "The basement is a tornado shelter that functions as a den. God, I hope my twins don't inherit your terrible sense of humor."

I scowled. "Call them your twins one more time and I'll turn that basement into a real torture dungeon."

He took a few more steps before hooking his long fingers onto a crystal doorknob to his left. "Here you go, inmate. This is where you'll finish out your nine-month sentence."

He opened the door and I peered inside. A king sized bed sat against the wall with a mahogany nightstand on either side. A wide dresser rested on the opposite wall with a large TV mounted above it. Lace curtains hung from the long windows, filtering the soft evening light onto the shining wooden floor.

I hummed. "Not bad, warden."

Beau retreated down the hallway to bring up the first of my bags. I let out a breath before stepping inside my new room.

I passed a set of upholstered armchairs and resisted the urge to set my purse on one—I couldn't surrender even a little bit until I had a full lay of the land. I turned the knob of the first door I found and discovered a deep walk-in closet, perfect to store the three outfits that could currently fit me.

I chewed on my lip and put my hand on the swell of my belly. With twins, I'd outgrow my hoodie and sweatpants before I knew it. I'd have to figure out how to fill my wardrobe with what little savings I had left, but that was tomorrow's problem.

I crossed over to another door and found a bathroom. Tiny opalescent tiles covered the floor and a large shower took up the entire back wall. The shower featured a mural of a voluptuous sea goddess because *nothing* in Beau's house could be normal, but the shower did have a solid bench and an antique brass handrail. Practical.

In fact, the same handrails were installed all over the bathroom, blending in seamlessly with the vaguely Art Nouveau design.

Curiously, I walked over to the gigantic bathtub on the opposite end of the bathroom and pressed my foot on the bottom step leading into the tub. Solid construction. The large window over the bathtub caught my eye and I looked out at the vast expanse of the Fontaine ranch.

The sun was disappearing over the horizon, leaving the small black silhouettes of a herd of cattle grazing in the distance. I held my breath as I counted five pumpjacks sprinkled across the land. During the Herringbone case, I had gone down a rabbit hole researching how much each pump produced per day, and my heart thumped as I calculated how much money was being pulled from the earth with only the pumps I could see from my bathroom window.

The numbers were dizzying, so I dug into my purse for my anti-nausea medicine and left the bathroom.

As the little white pill settled my stomach, I gently rested my purse on my bed and pulled out that precious pewter canister full of ashes. With a heavy heart, I placed my mom on the nightstand and quickly set two framed pictures around her. My eyes moved from the photo of graduation day to my debut as Miss Kaye at the history fair.

"I hope you're still proud of me," I said to the canister. "I know you told me to never rely on a man, no matter what, but—"

I glanced past those lacy curtains, taking in the silhouetted peek of the land where the Fontaine fortune—*my children's* future fortune—was growing by the second. A quick spark of exhilaration drowned in the deepest shame in an instant.

"But it's not about the money," I reassured my mom's remains. "I can't make it about the money. I worked so hard for so long because I thought money meant freedom, but…"

I picked at my fingernails before reaching into my purse, pulling out the last of my prized possessions. The soles of my red-bottomed stilettos were smooth in my hands, never having the opportunity to earn scuffs.

My breath left my lips in a sigh. "But money is more like cotton candy in the rain—gone in an instant. Temporary."

I looked from my shoes to my mother's smiling face in my history fair photo, then the photo from graduation, until I was blinking away tears at the sight of the person I loved the most reduced to a can on my nightstand.

"Everything is just…temporary," I whispered.

The faint sound of suitcase wheels in the hallway grew louder, so I quickly switched my heels to one hand and dried my eyes with the other. I sniffed away my tears right as Beau walked in with two of my suitcases.

He gave me a brief quizzical look before dropping his gaze and clearing his throat. "This used to be my grandparents' room. We took up the rugs because they were a tripping hazard for Grandpa's cane." He looked back up at me. "I can put them back if you'd like, but you'll still probably trip if you insist on wearing those."

I glanced down at my stilettos.

"Oh," I breathed as I sucked down a sob. "I'm not going to wear these anymore. I'd just be all dressed up with…nowhere to go."

The end of my nose prickled and tears gathered in the corners of my vision, but I quickly blinked them away. I would not cry in front of Beau Fontaine, damnit!

Beau abandoned my suitcases and stepped over to me. He laid a comforting hand on my shoulder and I held my breath. His hand was so big and so warm, and his eyes were soft as he looked down at me.

"I know today's been a hard day, but don't be sad about the shoes," he said gently. "Mom always said shoes like that were *horribly* tacky."

He smiled and gave my shoulder a quick pat before turning to collect my other bags. I clutched my shoes as I watched him walk away, regretting with every fiber of my being that I had been too shocked to gouge out one of his pretty blue eyes with a stiletto.

I glanced at my mom as I let out a heated, tense breath.

"This is only temporary," I promised.

As soon as my twins were born, I was *gone.*

Beau

"You're...you're going to be a father?"

I clicked out of my inbox and closed my browser window before getting up from my desk. "Yeah, that's what I just said in my email."

"Sure, but I had to call to make sure you weren't hacked," Chuck said through the phone. "You said that you wanted nothing to do with women when I called about those galas, and now you're emailing me saying you have babies on the way? Forgive me for being skeptical."

I let out a short laugh as I spun the giant antique globe next to my desk—the one my mother had glued googly eyes all over. "I pay you to be skeptical. If this were a test, you would have passed with flying colors."

I grabbed the water bottle that I had drained after my run and walked out of my study. "And I never said I wanted nothing to do with women."

"Could have fooled me," Chuck said as I entered the kitchen. "Anyway, it's pretty early to be doing everything in the list you sent me—trust funds and the like. Do you even know what names the babies are going to have?"

"No." I set my water bottle by the sink and grabbed the handle of the first brightly-colored steel cup from the line of tumblers I had bought last night. "Their mother thinks the twins are getting her last name, but she's not going to win that fight."

I set the phone on the kitchen island as I opened the freezer drawer.

"I don't know," Chuck groaned through the speaker. "My mom didn't give me my dad's last name, but he also wasn't a Fontaine."

I dropped a couple pieces of daisy-shaped ice out of their silicone molds into the steel cup. "Exactly. If your dad was going to have you inherit a generations-old family business one day, maybe your mom would have seen things differently."

"She gave me his first name, but I don't go by it," Chuck said. "Not that it mattered. He walked out on us when I was five, so he wasn't around to call me anything. "

I opened the refrigerator door and swallowed the lump that had suddenly formed in my throat. "I...I didn't know that about you, man."

I silently grabbed the first of four pitchers of water out of the fridge.

"Eh, it doesn't bother me," he said, and I could almost hear him shrug through the phone. "It happens a lot more often than people think."

The ice in the cup cracked as I poured the water over it. "Yeah."

"As far as the kids go, I can at least look into making trust funds for the little beans. You have enough capital to play around with, so I'll see how I can make their money grow the fastest."

I put the pitcher back into the fridge. "Speaking of which, I need you to make an account for child support. Open up a card for Olivia Adams."

"You know you don't have to legally pay child support until the babies are born, right?"

"Do you think I give a shit?" I screwed the lid securely onto the cup and walked out of the kitchen. "This is the best way to make sure my babies are taken care of without their—"

I stopped in my tracks as soon as I entered the foyer and looked up at the second floor landing to check for movement. Even though I found none, I still dropped my voice to a whisper. "—without their *stubborn ass* mother fighting me on it. You can't imagine just how prideful this woman is."

"You picked her."

I scowled at the phone. Olivia Adams was the last person I would have ever picked to be the mother of the only Fontaine heirs. Thanks to their mother's genes, my poor babies would probably be born with miniature encyclopedias in their hands, have horrible eyesight, and I would hear *"Did you know...?"* in stereo for the rest of my life.

"What can I say," I replied cooly. "I'm a man who honors my obligations regardless of the circumstances."

I crossed the foyer and headed up the stairs. "And on that note, put ten percent of my monthly income in the child support account."

"T-ten percent?" Chuck replied. "Are you insane?"

My feet hit the carpet runner of the second story landing and I paused in front of one of the green knights.

I considered just how much ten percent of my monthly income was. "You're right. I'm having twins—make it twenty percent."

"But—!"

"Gotta go, Chuck. Try not to have a heart attack when you move the funds over. It would be a real pain in the ass to replace you."

I ended the call and my feet softly padded across the wooden floor of the wing where the family bedrooms were. Though the hall was quiet, the usual morning silence was less hollow with another person occupying the house. The unease in my stomach from her sleeping across the hall might go away after a few days...but I wasn't that lucky.

I knocked on Olivia's bedroom door. "Room service, Adams."

A noise between a whine and a groan filtered through the door. I took that as permission to come in.

I opened the door to find that Olivia had wasted no time settling in. Every single one of her suitcases were on the floor with their maws open, their contents spewed about the room. A white fluffy throw blanket was draped over Grandma's green armchair. Photos littered the nightstands. A fat candle on the dresser was likely responsible for making the room smell like...gardenias, I think.

Just as I was about to question if the princess had made herself comfortable enough, she decided to wake up. With a very unladylike groan, she slowly lifted herself from the tangle of ivory sheets and the emerald down comforter.

Seeing someone after just waking up was an under-appreciated kind of intimacy. It wasn't like the intensity of fucking her raw in an attic or the overlit exposure of her doctor's appointment, but a quiet level of vulnerability that carried its own truths.

Despite being horrendously uptight when fully conscious, Olivia *clearly* wasn't the type to wear a bra to bed. Instead of normal pajamas, she wore a faded pink college shirt over her baby bump and a pair of shorts with a pattern of little white cats. She didn't even bother to brush away the wisps of chocolate brown hair stuck to her forehead as she pawed at the nightstand for her glasses.

I could almost admit she was cute. Almost.

I walked across the room and set the forty-ounce cup on the nightstand. "Drink up, buttercup."

She slid her glasses onto her face and blinked in surprise at the lemon yellow cup I had just placed in front of her. "The hell is this?"

There was the Olivia I had expected.

I folded my arms across my chest, preparing for the fight that was surely coming. "You have to drink at least a gallon of water a day—doctor's orders. You can't rely on the lawyer diet of black coffee and bourbon anymore, so now you have to actually hydrate."

She picked up the cup but tossed me a dirty look. "I never drank bourbon."

I held down a smile as she took a sip—the first of many small victories. Maybe pregnancy would make her less of an argumentative pain in the ass.

Olivia's eyebrows knitted and she pulled her lips off the straw. "What's in this?"

"That's your 'wake-up water,'" I explained, "infused with oranges so the citric acid helps with nausea. It's in the yellow cup so you know to drink it first thing in the morning."

She blinked once, glanced at the crown logo on the side of her cup, and looked back up at me.

What wasn't she understanding? "You know—yellow, like the risen sun."

"I know what color the sun is!" She shook the cup, making the ice rattle against the steel. "If this one is yellow, how many others are there?"

I let myself smile that time, proud to show off my hard work. "The pink cup is for mid-morning and it's infused with raspberries for a vitamin boost. The green cup is for early afternoon—it's a fun mix of cucumber, lime, and coconut water to restore potassium. Your last water of the day is in the blue cup, infused with camomile and a bit of powdered fiber."

Her mouth hung open, as if she had to process information by looking like a catfish.

I gestured to her yellow tumbler. "The powdered fiber is to help with the consti—"

"Damnit, Beau, I know what fiber is for!" she snapped. "This tumbler brand costs fifty dollars a piece, and you bought *four* of them? Are you too stuck-up to know that a dishwasher exists?"

I scrubbed my hand across my face. I did not go on a late-night grocery run in town for her to be this much of a bitch over a fucking cup.

But research had also told me that Olivia was just under the influence of pregnancy hormones, and with twins it was worse. Double the babies, double the crazy.

"The cups are for your convenience, Adams," I replied with the calmness of a pot of water that was *just* under boiling. "The articles I read last night said that drinking a daily gallon of water can get boring, so I wanted to make the water a little fun—"

"You really think I would be *bored* of clean water?" She swung her legs to the edge of the mattress and stood up. "Do you have any idea how disgustingly privileged you sound?"

I bit my tongue to stop myself from asking her if she had any idea how insufferably *ungrateful* she sounded. There was no winning against the hormones, so I had to switch tactics.

Back in college, I read a book that challenged the idea of any retreat being a surrender. Like leading in a waltz, taking a step backward was the ideal way to force your opponent in the right direction. I had no idea how educated Olivia was in dance techniques or classical warfare, but I'd let her think she won this round if it gave me a peaceful morning.

"Yes, yes, I am both disgusting and privileged." I turned to the door. "Now if you'll excuse me, I just got back from a run and I need to shower off with pure mountain snow melt and baby seal tears."

"Is this how you're punishing me for getting pregnant?" She was just getting louder and louder. "To lock me in your house and rub your money in my face? Do you have a humiliation fetish?"

Hormones. It's the hormones, Beau. Don't take the bait.

I walked toward the hallway. She could scream at a closed door if she wanted to.

"Or are you controlling me and everything I put in my body because of some deep-seated daddy issues?"

A stake of ice speared me in the spine and I stopped before I could reach the doorknob. I chewed on the inside of my cheek before turning back around with a smirk.

Olivia glared up at me like she was about to grab me by the sweatshirt and drag me into a dark alley to fight, but she was in *my* house. She didn't fully understand the dangerous territory she had just walked into, but I was about to give her a taste of something even more bitter than her own medicine.

I casually shoved my hands into the pockets of my joggers. "Fine, I'll admit it. I do enjoy humiliating you."

I slowly walked over to her, her cheeks reddening as her chin tilted higher to glare up at me with each step I took.

"After all the shit you gave me back in high school, I greatly enjoy seeing you now," I said. "No job, no car, no friends who can help you in your time of need. Oh, you acted like you were crowned queen of the universe when you got that stupid gold valedictorian medal, but now..."

I looked down at the swell of her belly and then met her furious brown eyes. "...now your greatest accomplishment is trapping a rich man with a pregnancy. I hope you're proud of yourself."

She held her glare, but her face paled. Maybe she needed to vomit. Whatever it was, I didn't care. I turned on my heel and started to walk out.

"Oh, and by the way," I said over my shoulder. "You'll be getting a new credit card soon. It benefits my babies to not grow inside a mother who only wears sweatpants, so buy yourself some new clothes. Hell, maybe buy some books so you don't completely atrophy your brain while you lounge around my house for the next few months."

Her bicep trembled once—she was fighting the urge to slap me.

That's it, Adams. Learn some damn self-control.

I pushed a little more to see what I could get away with. "The credit limit is higher than any bonus those demons at your old law firm ever gave you, so shop until your dark little heart is content."

She shook her head once. "I'm not spending a *dime* of your money."

I flashed her a purposefully patronizing smile. "Oh, you will. Everyone does when given the opportunity." I carelessly waved my hand in the direction of the door. "The fridges, the freezers, and the butler's pantry are completely stocked—gorge yourself until you puke, for all I care. I'm going to lunch with my mother today, so I won't be monitoring your every bite. Don't be alarmed if you see a red corvette out front, that's just Margot. She cleans."

She scoffed. "Of course you can't pick up after yourself. I'll ask her to blink twice if she needs help."

I shrugged. "Go ahead. She only speaks French."

Olivia's clenched jaw and tight fists softened. A feline smile crawled up her cheeks and she cocked her head. "My, a man who gives out credit cards like Halloween candy and pays his little French maid enough to afford a corvette. I'm so lucky I *trapped* a man like you."

The poison-tipped sass was gratingly juvenile—but also a clear concession.

I won again, Adams.

My fingers wrapped around the doorknob as I looked back at her. "The corvette was my dad's, actually. I gave it to her." I smirked and shook my head. "Happy men don't own corvettes, even if they are rare vintage models."

Olivia picked up her cup and held it in both hands like a child. She looked back at me with big eyes and a fake-ass smile. "I'll be sure to drink my water while you're away, master."

I clenched my jaw. If she weren't the mother of my children, I would have grabbed her by the hair and put her sassy mouth to better use.

"Aren't you a good girl," I teased, and then I shut the door as softly as possible so I didn't slam it into splinters.

I let out a long, shaking breath as I stood in the hallway. Olivia Adams was an even bigger pain in the ass than I remembered. Petulant. Ungrateful. Blind to her circumstances.

But she was the mother of my children. *Mother of my children.*

And I would wear condoms lined with sandpaper for the rest of my fucking life before dooming myself like this ever again.

I loosened the tension in my jaw and walked away before I could wonder if getting rid of that damn corvette actually made me a happy man.

Beau

Santa Claus—my old nemesis.

In any other context, I had no qualms with the jolly old elf. But the seven-foot-tall plastic statue with the faded red suit that stood in Aunt Liz's backyard? Never had I wanted to burn a beloved holiday icon in effigy so badly.

"Twenty-seven years old and you're still terrified of that thing," Mom said from across the table.

I turned my head from the Santa statue to look at my mother. "Don't confuse terror for sustained contempt."

The wrappers and grease-stained paper bags from our lunch still rested on the iron patio table between us. The outdoor thermostat painted with cardinals read that it was 48 degrees out. The burgers were soggy and grease on the fries had cooled before we could even eat them, but lunch indoors wasn't an option for Mom.

With a flick of her lighter, Mom lit her second cigarette. She inhaled and blew a curl of smoke out into the gray December sky. Her phone lit up with an email notification, but she quickly flipped it face-down before I could see who had contacted her.

Whatever. It was probably a random promotional email from one of the luxury stores she liked to shop at, anyway.

Mom flicked her blue eyes to the Santa statue and her filler-stuffed lips stretched into a smile. "You really need to learn to let things go, baby."

My eyes narrowed. Had *she* been trapped in the snow beneath that abomination of a Christmas decoration when she was four, she might understand. Though my real grudge was with Uncle Rick, who kept the statue up past Easter and Fourth of July solely because I was scared of it. The damn thing never went into storage because Uncle Rick thought tormenting the only child in the family was the funniest shit in the world.

And since that asshole was finally dead, the tacky giant Santa would be a permanent sentinel in Aunt Liz's brown, overgrown backyard. Grief was an odd animal.

Mom leaned back in her patio chair, her cigarette trapped between her ballerina pink nails.

"All right," she sighed. "I've got a belly full of grease and lungs full of nicotine. Let's talk."

I rubbed the back of my neck and my stomach twisted, as if Santa's cracked-paint gaze had suddenly turned judgmental. "Well, the timeline adds up, so I'm fairly certain they're mine."

"*Fairly* certain?"

My eyes narrowed. "You were the one who warned me to never get DNA tested—that's the only way to be sure."

"But you *saw* them?" she stressed. "This isn't just a repeat of what Gold Digger did?"

I shifted in my chair and my eyes dropped to my lap. "Don't call Katie that."

"She broke my baby's heart, I'll call her whatever I want." Mom took another drag of her cigarette. "Although there's two gold diggers now. I should call the old one GD1 and this one GD2…"

"Mom, come on," I groaned. "This is serious."

Her fingers clutching her cigarette made her right hand look like a smoking pistol as she pointed at me. "I *am* serious. You called me last night about your new *problem* and now you're shocked that I have concerns?"

I folded my arms. "Olivia Adams is many things, but she's not a gold digger. She does wear those shoes you hate, though."

Mom grimaced. "The ones that have 'new money red' paint slathered on the sole?"

"The very same."

Mom flicked ash off her cigarette and sighed. "To tell you the truth, I just about fainted when you told me you got someone pregnant, but I'm not surprised it was her. You were obsessed with her in high school."

I wouldn't have been more shocked if Mom had slapped me across the face with a large mouth bass. Obsessed with *Olivia?*

"Did you and Aunt Liz hit the sauce this morning?" I asked. "I was never obsessed with Olivia!"

She gave me a look that I still recognized under all the plastic surgery and dropped her voice to imitate mine. *"I hate Olivia Adams so much. Why did Olivia Adams have to join the debate team? Olivia*

Adams is so fake. I got grouped with Olivia Adams for a project and I want to jump off a bridge. Olivia Adams, Olivia Adams, Olivia Adams."

A vein throbbed in my temple. "What you're describing is annoyance, not obsession!"

"Regardless..." She waved her hand, twisting the trail of smoke from the end of her cigarette. "We are the last Fontaines at a crossroads of the family legacy, so you have to be honest with me."

Her eyes suddenly turned deathly serious. "Are you getting rid of the problem?"

I stiffened, returning her frozen-faced stare with an even colder one. "No."

Mom leaned back in her chair and sucked on her cigarette until all that was left was an impossibly long cylinder of ash. Though I was resolute on seeing the pregnancy through, I couldn't ignore the pang of guilt as I watched my mom cope.

After everything she had covered up, after everything *generations* of Fontaines had kept under wraps, I was going to be the first person in the family to have a real scandal.

I was having twins out of wedlock, there was a real doubt they would even bear the family name, and the woman I picked as their mother could barely function. What would Grandpa have said if he were still alive? He certainly wouldn't have been proud of me.

I looked up at my mom as she smashed her cigarette into the ash tray. I couldn't imagine my mother, who still had her blonde hair styled perfectly and wore her pearls to just lounge around the house, was proud of me either.

Yet she was still going to clean another mess up.

Her phone vibrated with another email notification and she quickly shut her phone off. "God damnit, does *everything* have to be on fucking fire right now?"

She lit a third cigarette and the sudden burst of tobacco in the air burned my eyes. She used to never smoke—said it would give her wrinkles—but that was before what happened with Dad.

Mom puffed out a cloud of smoke. "Who else have you told?"

"Just you and my finance guy," I replied. "Not sure who all Olivia has been blabbing to, although she doesn't appear to have any friends outside of Ashley Copeland and her husband."

Mom scoffed. "Those two are all over the internet sharing their business. What makes you think they won't share yours?"

I picked at the edge of my sweater sleeve. "Word was going to get out eventually. Olivia's already showing *and* she's living in my house. I know the average Elren citizen isn't the most educated, but surely people will put two and two together."

Though...it wouldn't be fair if everyone in Elren found out before the rest of the family.

I swallowed, but my mouth had suddenly gone dry. "I'm...I'm figuring out a way to tell Dad."

Mom sucked on her cigarette and looked away. "Just send him an email, like you always do.'"

My hands balled into loose fists on top of the patio table. I hadn't sent anything to Dad's work email in a few months—I was past that.

Although, maybe he'd respond for once. Maybe parents change when they're about to become grandparents.

I cleared my throat. "You could come back to the manor, you know. I never moved into your old suite." I looked up at her and tried not to sound too hopeful. "Neither of us know what we're doing with the pregnancy. We could use some help."

Mom blew out a puff of smoke and tapped her nails on the back of her phone. "You know I have to support Aunt Liz."

I scoffed. "She has half of Mawmaw and Pawpaw's inheritance *and* Uncle Rick's military retirement. She could hire a team of maids and butlers if she wanted."

Mom narrowed her eyes and flashed me a smile. "Liz is terrified of burglars and I'm a good shot—how about that?"

I leaned back in my chair and suppressed an eye-roll. As if burglars would come all the way out to Aunt Liz's house—miles away from civilization. Unless someone just really wanted to steal a couple of decrepit horses or some tacky Christmas decor, Aunt Liz's house was the safest place in the world.

The Santa statue would melt in the summer sun before Mom ever told me the truth of why she hid out here, so why bother asking?

Mom caught her reflection in a window and gently stretched the skin near the corner of her eye—or, at least, as far as it *could* stretch.

"I'll have to run to the city for a touch up," she said as a wave of smoke washed over her teeth. "One bad habit begets another, unfortunately."

I rested my forearms on the tabletop. "Did you know scientists recently discovered a new sea urchin? Its venom contains neurotoxins that rival the effectiveness of your current injections."

"If the venom can reverse the effects of a son who stresses me out," she said as she put out her cigarette, "I'll rub six of those fuckers across my face."

Mom dusted the leftover ash off her hands. "How much does the girl know about your father?"

My chest tightened. "Same as everyone else—nothing."

"Good." The iron patio chair screeched across the concrete as Mom stood up. "Start the truck—I want to see her."

My stomach was in knots the instant I turned onto the manor's driveway. I had been horribly nervous the first time I introduced my mother to a girlfriend, but this was so much worse.

I had texted Olivia before we left Aunt Liz's to warn her that we were coming, but I never got a response. I had no idea what state she would be in when we entered the house. Was she even dressed?

God, I hoped she had at least eaten something.

Titus greeted us in the foyer, but only Titus.

I gave my good boy a scratch behind the ears before calling out, "Adams, we're here."

No response.

I cursed under my breath and Mom trailed behind me as I searched for Olivia. She wasn't in the kitchen, or the back patio, or the media room.

"She probably found the safe," Mom said as I walked out of the empty gym. "She raked up all the family jewels while you were gone and drove off into the sunset."

I crossed into the foyer and mashed the call button on the elevator. "Don't be ridiculous, Mom. She's probably in her room."

"*Her* room," Mom repeated with a smirk. "Well, that was fast."

Her eyes glanced to the wall. "The old family portrait is finally gone, at least."

I entered the elevator. "I didn't want to risk Olivia asking questions."

"Good boy," Mom said as she joined me in the elevator.

We ascended to the second floor and I almost turned toward the bedrooms, but stopped when I noticed Titus sitting in the middle of the opposite hallway. He looked at me, his tongue flopped out as he panted. Poor boy was exhausted from taking the stairs.

Before I could wonder why he was randomly in the guest wing, I caught a glimpse of a traffic-cone orange sleeve peeking out from the hallway alcove. I quietly walked over to Titus and found him sitting with Olivia.

Olivia was stretched out on the cushion of the alcove bench with an e-reader in her lap, but her eyes were fixed on the hazy sky outside the window. I nearly made a remark about her wearing her bright orange Plains State hoodie to meet my Lindsay University superfan of a mother, but Olivia's blank stare made me pause.

I could see my own reflection in the window pane, and yet she didn't turn to greet me. Titus's panting was anything but quiet, but she didn't acknowledge him either.

She was just like she was at the doctor's office...there but not.

"Adams, my mother is here," I said.

Olivia turned so quickly that her e-reader slid off her lap. She didn't even try to catch it as it clattered to the floor and instead jumped to her feet to shake my mother's hand.

"H-hello," Olivia said with a sheepish smile and a growing flush. "Pleasure to see you again, Mrs. Fontaine."

Mom's face was unreadable as she lightly shook Olivia's hand. "We're all adults now, just call me Cheryl."

Olivia looked down at the striped socks on her feet as her cheeks grew red. "I'm not sure if you know, but I'm—"

"Up in the duff, as our friends across the pond like to say?" Mom interrupted. "I'm well aware."

Olivia paled and curved in her shoulders, as if Mom were about to send her to a proverbial time-out corner.

Instead, Mom reached into her purse. "Here, I have something for you." She pulled out a black and white striped notebook—as if *that* would help Olivia's prisoner complex—and held it out. "It's a pregnancy journal."

Olivia gingerly took the journal. "What am I supposed to write in it?"

Mom shrugged. "Everything—the good, the bad, and the ugly. You have a long road ahead and a journal will help you process."

I smiled. Though I was certain Mom wanted to wring my neck for getting someone pregnant, she still had grace for the situation. The journal was a very thoughtful gift.

Olivia turned the journal over in her hands and furrowed her brows. "Am I supposed to write like a diary? Or write as if I'm speaking to the babies? Do I write every day? How long should the entries be?"

The constant questions stabbed me in the temple. "Damn it, Adams, it's not an assignment."

Olivia sucked in her lower lip and Mom tossed me a look—a look that told me she was about to send me to a *real* time-out corner.

Mom turned back to Olivia. "It doesn't matter what you write as long as it's the truth."

Olivia nodded and an awkward, heavy silence followed. Her brown eyes darted around beneath her glasses frames. "Um…I love how you decorated."

The wainscoting in the hallway was painted a glossy maroon. The dusty pink wallpaper looked like random filigrees at first glance, but was actually repeating images of writhing nude women. A long collage of disembodied blue eyes and colored beetles was pasted along the ceiling.

I made it a point to rarely go into the guest wing.

Mom glanced at the horror show on the ceiling. "I was on a coke bender when I did this, but I'm glad someone around here appreciates a strong message."

She clapped me on the back. "Come on, Beau. Make me a drink so we can let the poor girl nap."

Before she walked toward the landing, Mom gave my hand a sharp squeeze. The wordless command was clear: *Tell her nothing.*

I glanced back at Olivia as she retrieved her e-reader and settled back into the alcove. Staying in the manor made her way too close to our secrets. Mom was right to be concerned that Olivia could pass along whatever she learned to her big-mouthed friend. Scandal gets attention, and who knew what Ashley and Tyson would do for even more social media fame?

I might have believed Olivia when she said she wasn't after our money, but everyone else always was.

Bringing Olivia to the house was a risk, I knew that from the very beginning. Weighing the well-being of the Fontaine babies against the security of the Fontaine legacy was a tough decision, but the babies had won. The babies would win every time.

I would just have to keep Olivia at arms-length to mitigate damage. No, further than arms-length. She was both an obligation and a liability, like a dormant fire bomb that could destroy everything.

And I had already been destroyed too many times to risk it happening again.

I shoved my hands in the pockets of my jeans as I headed down the hallway after Mom, hoping Grandpa would still be proud of me even though I put the entire family legacy in jeopardy.

10

Olivia

The second trimester began without fanfare.

I wasn't expecting a "You survived!" banner to unfurl over my bed as confetti rained from the ceiling, but I was still surprised that very little had changed by the thirteenth week of pregnancy.

I still had to take my anti-nausea medicine twice a day. I still slept between ten and fourteen hours. I still had to suck down my water regardless of how I felt.

Each morning, I rolled out of bed and lumbered downstairs to report to the kitchen. Like the manor's foyer, the kitchen was decorated like it was the product of a fever dream brought on by expired cough syrup. The counters were made of white stone sprinkled with small colorful inclusions that might have been sea glass. Shining magenta glass balls hung from the ceiling. The cabinets were all painted bubblegum pink. The glossy floor tiles were the exact color of blue cotton candy.

Though the decor was saccharine enough to give me a cavity, the actual cooking appliances were all business. The range was a cast iron behemoth with eight burners and shining gilded handles. Every pot and pan was made from gleaming copper. The sink was big enough to be a bathtub.

Beau, of course, was also all business.

As soon as I sat at the long kitchen island that looked like a large piece of birthday cake, Beau would wordlessly present me with my yellow cup and a stack of pancakes. I could no sooner pick up my fork for breakfast before he would mix his protein shake, make an excuse of needing to work, and leave.

The silence made mealtimes awkward, but I had to admit Beau was a good cook. He could make just about anything from the groceries he had delivered to the house. Pasta primavera. Filet mignon. Beef Wellington. I once asked him why he didn't hire a personal chef if he was so rich and he curtly replied that he didn't like people being in the house.

He was being so cagey that I stiffened every time he walked into the room. The only time he broke our strange parallel existence was when he gave me food or checked on my water intake—making me feel rather like a toothless lion in a zoo.

Hell, the manor felt like a zoo, or at the very least an odd museum. I had wandered around the manor for exercise and each room I explored brought more questions than answers. The formal living room had a bookcase that was really a door into a small bar. An upstairs half bath was decorated floor-to-ceiling with mirrors and had a clear acrylic toilet. I ignored the third floor, too afraid of what oddities could exist in the attic.

Attics had become bad luck for me, anyway.

The most puzzling room of all was an unfinished nursery in the family wing. Squares of cornflower blue and delicate pink paint samples were still taped on the walls. A teddy bear sat abandoned on the floor. The cushioned wooden rocking chair appeared to be a family heirloom, but the white crib looked like it was fresh out of those inch-thick luxury furniture catalogues the partners at my old firm would get.

I might have asked Beau if he had been working on a nursery for the twins if he weren't so icily aloof.

His room, I discovered, was always locked.

The only breaks in my monotonous existence were my doctor's appointments, now scheduled for every two weeks. For my most recent appointment, I had struggled to climb into Beau's truck, we spent an hour and a half wordlessly listening to his podcast as we drove to the city, and I got to see the babies on the ultrasound.

They were moving, but I still couldn't feel them yet. Apparently, they didn't want anything to do with me either.

I never realized how much I missed working in the hustle-and-bustle of a law office until the only living beings around either couldn't or wouldn't speak to me. Sometimes, I would write in my pregnancy journal as if I were talking to my only friend.

Luckily, Ashley would sometimes resurface from the dust of Miss Kaye's house renovation and we would go on a date. Two days before Christmas, she let me use her buddy pass at the gym on main street to sweat out our frustrations.

"So, John Whitecloud is doing our electrical, right?" Ashley huffed as she conquered the stair-stepper. "He said he'd have to rewire the whole house or else we're risking a fire with all the outlets we want to install. I wanted to preserve the wallpaper in the foyer at least, but now we're having to take everything down to the studs!"

I slowly walked on the treadmill next to her and took a sip from my pink cup—I was behind on my water schedule, but Beau wasn't around to bully me about it. "The stained glass on the stairs is staying though, right?"

Ashley whipped her head toward me, sweat beading on her temples as her green eyes turned murderous. "If *anyone* touches that window, I'll hit them with my car!"

The rectangular stained-glass window at the top of the first landing of the stairs was the crown jewel of Miss Kaye's house. The window wouldn't have turned many heads when it was installed a century ago, but now it was a rare specimen of craftsmanship. The design was a perfect marriage of the natural, sinuous curves of the Art Nouveau era and the geometric structure of the early Art Deco era. The glass was a harmonious mixture of marbled greens, golden amber, and a hint of lavender.

It was simple, but I loved it.

"Maybe I can find new wallpaper to complement the window?" I suggested. "I need an activity."

"Yes!" Ashley cheered. "You're so good with historical crap and the donors will *love it.* Tyson posted a how-to video recreating one of the dowels for the front porch railing and preservation enthusiasts ate it up. We're getting more donations by the day!"

I laughed. "I can always donate more, you know."

"Babies come first, not us," Ashley chided. "By the way, I love your new workout set."

I smiled, feeling confident in my icy lavender maternity leggings and matching longline bra that was nursing compatible.

Paired with new walking shoes that cushioned my sore feet, I felt almost human.

Was it a practical, useful purchase? Yes. Was it expensive as all hell? Indeed, but I considered it part of Beau's reparations for every time I vomited until my body shook.

Since my only job was gestating my twins and processing my ever-changing emotions alone, I started giving into my more destructive urges. I cycled between refusing any of Beau's help, even food, or burning through my "child support" card out of spite.

I hid my turmoil about using Beau's money in my pregnancy journal. I had promised myself I would never rely on a man to survive, and yet…

Guilt rained down my back when the packages from my first shopping haul came in, but at least I knew my new credit card was a well I could never see the bottom of. I might as well have kept some of my promise to fund the Kaye house renovation. My donation wasn't hundreds of thousands of dollars like I had originally planned, but Ashley still almost fainted when I transferred her some of that sweet Fontaine money.

"Oh! The kids' Christmas presents are in the back of the car," I said. "Remind me to grab them before we leave."

Ashley groaned. "I wish we weren't going to my dad's for Christmas, I hate leaving you in Elren alone. When is Beau coming back?"

I shrugged. "No idea. He just told me he had to travel for work and then he got on his plane—"

"He has a *plane?*"

"And a helicopter too, apparently." I took a short sip of my water. "But I don't know where he's going or what he's doing. The man tells me *nothing*, Ash."

She pushed a button to slow the stair-stepper as she began her cool down. "I once heard a rumor that his family was part of some weird rich-person sex cult. Maybe he's on his way to a cult meeting where they drink blood and have masked orgies."

I started my cool down too, taking the speed of the treadmill from slow to extra slow. "I shower with a mural of a naked woman and spit my toothpaste into a clamshell sink. Anything about the Fontaine family is plausible at this point."

After our workout, I slipped on my new dove gray sweatshirt that read "Twin Mom," gave Ashley her stack of Christmas presents and a big hug, and got into the car to drive back to the manor.

The Christmas lights lining main street warmed the twilight sky and guided my way back to Fontaine Manor. Titus was waiting for me in the cold, empty foyer when I returned.

I looked around the foyer and frowned. A house that big without a strand of greenery or a single glimmer of tinsel at Christmas was a crime. I supposed it would have been illogical for Beau to decorate if he was planning to travel, but I was still here!

And I wasn't alone either. I had the twins…and Titus.

My thirty-minute walk at the gym had energized me instead of exhausting me for once. For the first time since I could remember, I felt a little like my old self again—productive, inspired, and, dare I say it, capable.

I had to take advantage of it.

I smiled and jingled my keys. "Get in the car, boy. We're going shopping."

On the morning he left, Beau dropped a set of keys on the kitchen counter and said, "Hope you can drive stick." As much as I hated to admit it, the blue 1969 Mustang that had once belonged to Beau's grandfather was a much better ride than my old Jaguar.

I secured Titus in the Mustang's front seat and dialed the radio to a holiday station so we could take the town in style.

We listened to classic Christmas songs as we cruised past the retro neon lights on the downtown shops. The drive-thru of the local coffee place was our first stop. I enjoyed my peppermint milkshake and Titus scarfed down his cup of whipped cream as I slowly drove around the neon-soaked town square, letting the Christmas lights sparkle in Titus's dark eyes. He joined me in the grocery store as I filled the cart with wired ribbon, greenery, beaded garland, candy canes, ornaments, and a small Christmas tree.

I even grabbed a Christmas present for Beau, since he was the one paying for it all.

Once we were back at the manor, I set up the Christmas tree in the media room. The media room was offensively decorated in Lindsay University pennants and jerseys, so Titus and I spent all of Christmas Eve covering the snooty-school paraphernalia with holiday cheer. I even made a salt-dough ornament with Titus's paw print.

When Christmas morning came, I arranged boxes of treats and toys beneath the tree and "surprised" Titus with the haul. With a lot of bribing, I got him to wear a Santa hat and sit perfectly in front of the small tree for a picture.

I smiled wide and called him a good boy, the *best* boy, as I snapped photo after photo. When Titus had enough and wanted to lie down in front of the fireplace, my heart was so full.

I couldn't help but picture my babies in Santa hats in front of the same tree a year from now, surrounded by all their beautiful, but *educational,* toys. Maybe they would sit with Titus for a picture. Maybe I would let them try a taste of a candy cane.

I chose the best of the photo of Titus and texted it to Beau. He responded with nothing more than a thumbs-up emoji.

I spent the rest of the day in the media room flopped on the leather couch like a rag doll, watching all the Christmas classics on the massive flat screen while Titus gnawed on his new chew toy. Since I had spent the past two days playing Santa, I subsisted solely on milk and chocolate chip cookies.

If Beau had wanted to enforce my diet and water regimen, maybe he should have stayed home.

I sucked on the end of a candy cane as the credits rolled from the fourth movie of the day. Titus whined and nudged the edge of my slipper with his nose.

"OK, boy," I sighed. "We can go outside."

I hauled myself off the couch and shuffled to the back door with Titus at my side. I stood on the patio with my hands in my pockets as Titus scampered off to do his business. I blew out a breath as my head fogged and I swayed uneasily on my feet—maybe I should have eaten more than just sugar. At least we wouldn't be out for long.

The weather wasn't frosty enough for a white Christmas, but it was still so cold that I was grateful for my new fleece-lined slippers and thick maternity joggers. Despite giving myself new comfort clothes for Christmas, I still had on my tried-and-true PSU hoodie. Margot had washed all my clothes with scent beads that I thought were wasteful, but they made my hoodie smell delicious and feel even more cozy.

Titus ran up to the patio from the grass with his tail wagging. It was just half an hour until sunset and neither of us had really moved all day—I probably should change that before all the daylight burned out.

I spied a wire basket full of tennis balls and carefully walked over to pick one up. I rolled the fuzzy yellow ball in my hand and showed it to Titus, waving it back and forth to make sure he was tracking the movement of the ball.

When I was sure he got it, I turned and threw the ball off the patio as far as I could—which, apparently, was only a few yards. The ball rolled to a stop in the grass just before dropping off a steep hill that sloped down to the cattle pasture.

Titus, apparently uneducated in the game of fetch, had stayed put on the patio.

I rolled my eyes and slowly walked over to the ball. "OK, we'll try this again."

I widened my stance and bent down to pick up the ball.

"But this time, you have to—"

Blood rushed to my head and my vision swam as soon as the ball touched my fingers. My side gave out, I lost my balance, and I went down.

I hit the grass and rolled, and *rolled*—faster and faster until I came to a sudden stop.

For a moment, I couldn't breathe. I just stared in shock at the orange sky as I gulped in dry gasps. When my lungs finally filled with air, I grabbed the swell of my belly. The twins weren't moving, but they hadn't moved before. Were they OK? How would I even be able to tell?

Oh *God,* what had happened?

I turned my head to find that I had hit the metal fencepost at the bottom of the hill that marked the beginning of the pasture. A sharp pain suddenly flared through my side where I had hit the post and I cried out.

My scream echoed, but no one was around to hear.

Titus started barking above me and I rolled my head through the grass toward the noise. I had lost my glasses in the fall, so his large white body was little more than a blurry speck at the top of the hill. The manor looked like a dollhouse from where I sat in the grass—I might as well have rolled down the side of a mountain.

I checked my hoodie pocket, then the pockets of my joggers. My heart dropped into my stomach as I realized I had left my phone on the couch.

Shit, shit, *shit!*

Titus barked again and disappeared back toward the manor, where he barked some more.

A shiver went down my arms. Light was fading and the temperature was about to plummet. I had to get up the hill.

I rolled onto my hands and knees and tried to stand, but my vision went sideways again. I pushed myself up with all my might, but my body refused to cooperate.

I gritted my teeth and crawled upward, one fistful of grass at a time. Titus ran down the hill and bit my hood, pulling me up as hard as he was able. He gave my arms a little reprieve, but I was too heavy for him to drag me to the house.

Titus dropped my hood from his mouth with a booming bark. He ran back up the hill and barked over and over at the patio.

"Beau isn't here, boy!" I shouted. "Come here, don't leave me alone!"

But Titus kept barking.

I groaned and slowly kept working my way up the hill. The sun disappeared behind the horizon and soon I could only see the white skin of my hands reflecting the moonlight. My arms trembled with exhaustion and my belly dragged against the ground, but I couldn't give up. I *wouldn't* give up.

My foot found a small ledge, so I stretched my leg against it to raise myself a few inches. Instantly, my calf muscle exploded with pain and I screamed. The muscle still throbbed with pain as I gripped the grass. My left leg twitched, utterly useless. My arms were about to give out, but I had to be close to the patio...I had been crawling for so long.

Tears filled my eyes as I looked up, finding only the faintest yellow glow of the Christmas lights from the window of the media room. The manor was still so far away...and I couldn't move.

"Titus..." I cried weakly. "Titus!"

Instantly, the barking stopped. Grass crunched beneath his paws as Titus bounded down the hill. He plopped down next to me and I wrapped my shaking arms around him. I buried my face and chest against his soft fur, taking in his body heat. If I held him tightly, I wouldn't freeze through the night. Once the sun rose, I could try to make it up the rest of the hill. Margot would come in the morning if I failed. I might not have known any French, but everyone screams in the same language. Hopefully, she'd find me.

My back muscles shivered as I clutched Titus, but then he suddenly sprang to his feet. He ran up the hill, barking all the way.

"Come back!" I cried. "Titus, come back!"

Titus's barking at the patio got louder. A light from within the manor brightened the night.

"Olivia?" Beau shouted. "OLIVIA?"

My heart skipped a beat. He couldn't have been there, it wasn't possible.

Titus ran through the grass and the silhouette of a man who could be no one else but Beau Fontaine sprinted down the hill behind him.

Beau's large hands wrapped around my arms and flipped me onto my back. He grabbed my face and made me look at him. His face came into a soft focus and I caught his blue eyes darting around as they examined me.

His breath came out in a curl of mist as he spoke. "Breathe for me, OK?"

My heart raced, but I managed to nod.

"Where does it hurt?" he asked.

My throat shook as I answered, "E-everywhere."

His hands slid beneath me and I wrapped my arms around his neck as he lifted me like I weighed nothing.

"Come on," he huffed, "I'm taking you to the emergency room."

I buried my face in his neck as he sprinted up the hill. He smelled like barbecue and cheap beer. I had no idea how he had known I fell, or how he had arrived at the manor, or even where the hell he had been.

I only cared that he was finally there.

Beau

Never had I been more grateful for that ugly orange hoodie—so bright, I could find it even at night.

Never had I been more grateful for Titus, who protected my babies and their mother. Never had I felt more validated in installing sound-sensitive cameras that send alerts to my phone the instant Titus barks. Or for hiring a pilot who was always sober so he was ready to fly at a moment's notice. Or for buying the fastest plane on the market so I could get back to the manor in just over an hour and a half.

And though I should have enjoyed the flood of euphoria from finally reaping the benefits of good fortune, I was too fucking angry to consider any of it.

I sat in the stiff gray chair next to Olivia's bed in the emergency room, softly tapping the heel of my boot against the tile as I glared at the closed white curtain that separated us from the rest of the ward. I was embarrassed enough to be back at the Elren hospital after what had happened last time, and I would only get angrier if anyone recognized me.

We had spent four hours in that curtained coffin of a room. First, the nurse checked on the babies. Olivia had reported no signs of internal bleeding or miscarriage, but the doppler on her belly reporting two perfect heartbeats was still music to my ears.

As Olivia got diagnosed, I had to chew on my tongue and stare at the tile to keep from exploding.

Light-headedness from lack of nutrition. Muscle cramps from dehydration.

She had completely neglected herself. Again.

I clutched her discharge papers in one fist when we finally left that hellhole. Olivia had already developed the damn pregnancy waddle, so I had her wait in front of the sliding glass doors while I brought the truck around.

The only sound in the truck was the heater blowing fog off the windshield. I hadn't bothered to turn on my podcast when I had sped to the manor and I was too pissed off to listen to the Bored Bros yap about some bullshit on the drive home.

I gripped the leather steering wheel as Olivia struggled to get in the truck. Any other night, I would have gotten out and helped her. Any other night, I would have breathed a sigh of relief that the babies were just fine.

But it was three in the morning and she had made me go back to that damned hospital.

With a small grunt, she closed her door and clicked her seatbelt. I threw the gear shift into drive and left the parking lot faster than I was legally able to.

Once the Parkland Hospital sign disappeared from my rearview mirror, I spoke to Olivia for the first time since we were admitted to the emergency room.

"Five days," I said, my voice gravelly and hoarse. "I'm gone for *five days* and you do this."

"I just fell," she said quietly. "It was an accident."

"An accident that could have been completely prevented had you just eaten," I argued. "Or if you had just drank your *fucking water!*"

My temple throbbed from the volume of my own voice. I took a deep breath and slowed the truck down, even though no one else was on the road.

"I thought we were past this," I said calmly, but strained. "You told me you could put aside your pride and accept help. I provided you with a roof over your head. A private gym. A limitless credit card so you don't have to work a stressful job. A fridge full of food that you barely eat. Customized water that I bring to you *four times a day.*"

My teeth ached and my skin stretched across my knuckles from how hard I gripped the steering wheel, but I kept driving at a steady pace.

"And all I ask in return is that you take care of the twins," I stressed. "All I ask is that you try. You're high-risk. Twin pregnancies aren't just difficult, they're *dangerous,* and you don't even care!"

I held my breath as I waited for Olivia to respond, hopefully to apologize for how stupid and selfish she had been. I glanced over at her and found her staring out the passenger window with her arms folded. Even if she had her glasses, it was too dark out to actually fucking see anything.

Stay stubborn, Adams. Keep it up and you'll like me even less.

I let out a short breath and turned onto the road to the manor. The silence was near strangling, but I still calmly pulled into the garage and parked next to the Mustang.

I left the car and went around to open the door for her. As gentlemanly as the gesture seemed, I was done waltzing to guide her in the right direction. Oh no, I would *yank* her across a metaphorical dance floor if it meant keeping my twins safe.

"Kitchen, *now*," I ordered.

To Olivia's credit, she awkwardly slid out of the truck and walked into the house without protest. Though if exhaustion had made me more irritable, it could also make her more compliant. She probably wasn't even sorry for the stress she caused me, or that I had to leave my work duties, or that she had put the babies in danger.

She used to be the most obnoxious over-achiever, but now she couldn't even fucking *try*.

I walked into the kitchen to find her climbing onto her usual stool at the island. I filled her yellow cup with her wake-up water and set it in front of her. I wasn't about to make pancakes at three in the fucking morning, so I grabbed one of my plastic shake cups and started scooping protein powder in it.

After pouring some oat milk into the cup, I shook the mixture way too vigorously, but I was too pissed off to give a shit.

"Here," I said as I slammed the shake onto the countertop. "Won't taste great, but it'll keep you from ever going to *Death*land Hospital again."

She finished her sip of water before popping the cap off the shake cup. "What about when I give birth?"

I scoffed. "You aren't giving birth there. It's horrible."

"I was born there."

I gripped the edge of the counter and swallowed a comment I just knew she would take the wrong way. "You're giving birth in the city so Dr. Ornelas can do a scheduled c-section."

She furrowed her brows. "Scheduled c-section?"

I might have taken her more seriously if she didn't have remnants of the protein shake on her upper lip, but I tried to stay calm nonetheless. "Yes. Had you listened at your first doctor's appointment, you would have heard Dr. Ornelas explain that caesarean deliveries are the safest way to give birth to twins."

"But vaginal deliveries are cheaper!"

I pushed myself off the counter and raked my hands through my hair. Why the fuck did she care about the cost? Was she trying to spite me? At the expense of the babies?

She was willing to risk bleeding out during delivery over something as frivolous as money?

I dragged my hands down my face and let out a breath. "Fine. You want to save money so badly?" I turned and gestured to the large bay window that overlooked the pasture. "I'll call the ranch hands and get a set of chains. They'll pull the babies out like it's just another day in calving season!"

I caught a projectile in the corner of my vision and ducked. The protein shake hit the cabinet behind my head and exploded all over the kitchen.

I whipped around. "What the hell, Adams?"

Olivia jumped off her stool. "I've always just been a damn cow to you, haven't I? Graduation was one thing, but even when I'm carrying your babies you still—!"

"What the *hell* are you talking about?" I gestured to the remnants of the protein shake grenade that dripped down the cabinets. "Have you gone insane?"

"You're treating me like an animal!" she yelled. "Between the scheduled meals and the water—"

"You won't take care of yourself!"

"YOU WON'T TALK TO ME!" she screamed. Her eyes turned glassy and her chest started to heave. "I've lived in your house for three weeks and you still won't speak to me like…like I'm a person. You ignore me like I'm…I'm just another weird piece of furniture in this God-forsaken manor! You've always acted like I'm beneath you, but now—"

"When have I ever acted like you're beneath me, Adams?" I challenged. "Have you considered that I don't talk to you because when I do—"

"You treat me like I'm the biggest mistake of your life!" A tear rolled down her face. Then another. "When *I'm* sitting here, having lost everything! I lost my job, my car, my peace…the life that I *worked* for is gone and it all happened because you came back into the picture…and…and…"

She tightened her fists and intensified her glare. "This…this pregnancy is a prison sentence…and my only crime was *you!*"

Her rant broke down into incoherent sobbing. Her whole face turned red before she covered it with her hoodie sleeves and sank to the floor.

A fucking prison sentence.

I turned on my heel and walked out of the kitchen before anything else could explode. My feet took me in any direction that would get me away from her fucking sobbing. I found myself at the bar in the media room, gripping the edge of the marble counter like I was about to crack it. Whatever movie was playing on the TV was nothing more than garbled noise in my ears.

Hissing out a breath, I grabbed the nearest bottle and took a pull. My face twisted in a grimace as the familiar taste slid down my throat—one of Dad's old bottles of bourbon.

I abandoned the bottle on the counter and retreated to the center of the room. I sank onto the center cushion of the leather couch and let my head fall into my hands.

I massaged my temples as I listened to whatever was happening in the movie.

"Wowie, Mom!" cried a boy with an obnoxiously high-pitched voice. *"How did Santa know I wanted the Cowboy Jones quick-draw pistol set?"*

"Well, Timmy, Santa is Father Christmas," cooed a woman with a mid-Atlantic accent, *"and Father always knows best."*

I picked up the nearest object—a plate—and threw it at the TV. The plate shattered into bits against the screen, sending bits of porcelain and cookie crumbs to the floor. The screen was covered in black rectangles, but the speakers were still perfect.

"I can't wait 'till Dad comes back from the war," said the stupid boy. *"Then we can shoot bad guys together!"*

I launched up from the couch, yanked the TV out of the wall, and threw it to the floor. I held my breath through the initial crash, but let out a long, soothing exhale in the silence that followed.

When I opened my eyes, I took in what Olivia had done to the media room. She had strung multi-colored lights on the dark paneled walls, lined the cabinets of the bar with plastic evergreen garland,

and taped a fat, glittery golden bow right on top of the framed poster listing all of Lindsay University's national championship wins.

I walked over to the little Christmas tree and admired the cherry red and bright gold ornaments. I wrapped my hand around an odd, lumpy disk hanging off a high branch to find that it had Titus's paw print stamped on it.

A flash of green beneath the tree caught my eye. Wrapped in shining emerald paper and gold ribbon was a present with my name on the tag.

Olivia had…bought me a present?

I carefully tore through the tape and unwrapped the paper to find a set of pajamas in the box. Well, it wasn't exactly a set. Olivia had paired blue plaid flannel pajama bottoms with a navy "Elren Oilers" cotton long-sleeve. I couldn't remember the last time I wore an Elren Oilers shirt and I couldn't remember the last time I had exchanged Christmas presents with anyone, either.

Maybe I was too quick to accuse Olivia of not trying.

My eyes moved from the Christmas decorations to the ruined TV on the floor—yeah, I was definitely too quick to point fingers.

I blew out a breath as I rested the back of my head against the wall. I was tempted to blame Olivia's outburst on her hormones, but that felt too simple. She had always gone the extra mile because she had a chip on her shoulder about needing to prove herself for whatever reason. Creating a Christmas explosion all over my media room was proof that she still had that drive in her, but why couldn't she just care for herself?

I would have thought Olivia would have been grateful for the easy days I had given her, but maybe it was too easy. She had always run around like her feet were on fire between study hall or whatever new club she had signed up for, so I could only imagine how busy she would have been as a lawyer in a big firm. Losing that lifestyle must have felt like being a racecar crashing into a brick wall.

How…sad. That was it. Between the shock at the initial doctor's appointment to refusing to care for herself, Olivia was just sad. If I were spending weeks alone grieving a life that I had lost, I might also count down the days until the pregnancy was over.

I looked down at the box in my hands. And yet, she had still bought me a Christmas present.

I groaned. Keeping Olivia at a distance made me look like an asshole, but I didn't have much of a choice. If she had only known what had happened in my past, she'd give me a little grace.

Or she'd run to her gossipy best friend and ruin me.

God, Olivia was a fucking conundrum. I didn't trust her, but that didn't mean I thought of her as a cow. Where had that even come from? And why had she brought up *graduation,* of all things?

She was the one who had been a terror that day. As if her valedictorian medal hadn't been flashy enough, she had to wear all the medals from debate team and the fucking marching band, making them all clang together when she walked like a…

My eyes widened as ice trickled through my veins. Oh…oh *God.*

I ran a hand down my face, wishing I could brick up the door to the media room and stay there, but I couldn't just hide. I could almost feel Grandpa's spirit whacking me with his cane to steer me in the direction of the kitchen.

I had to fix this, for the sake of my babies. If that meant I had to let a couple of the skeletons out of my closet to get her to understand, so be it.

So, against all my self-preservation instincts, I went to the kitchen. As I moved through the house, the sounds of Olivia's sobbing got louder until I found her in a heap on the floor by the kitchen island.

A younger version of myself would have loved to see the smug, proud Olivia Adams cry on my kitchen floor—to witness her finally knowing what it feels like to lose.

The present Beau, however, watched Olivia's tears drench her sleeves and felt like the smallest man on Earth.

Olivia looked up at the sound of my approaching feet and her eyes traveled up my body. I had put on the pajamas she had given me as sort of an olive branch. Though the flannel was cozy, I couldn't feel comfortable just yet.

"I've been an asshole," I admitted.

She nodded and looked down. "I...I barely cried when my mom died. I didn't even shed a tear when I got fired from my dream job, or when I found out I was pregnant, b-but here I am now."

She wiped the glistening tear tracks off her face with the heel of her palm. "I...I *hate* what you've done to me."

My stomach filled with lead. I would have rather she stood up and slapped me than say something that loaded. I wasn't sure if she meant that she hated that I made her cry, or if the sentiment went deep enough that she hated me for making her a mother.

I rubbed the back of my neck. My lifetime of horrible luck had transferred to her as soon as we left that attic at our class reunion. I couldn't restore her old life, but hopefully I could try to repair what I had broken.

Slowly, I sat on the floor across from her. My throat twitched as I worked up the nerve to speak.

The truth was dangerous, my mom had always said. The "Fontaine facade" was a decades-old trick—we hid our feelings, our thoughts, and our plans to protect ourselves from the leeches of the world. We kept people away. We ran from problems and covered up everything we couldn't escape.

But I couldn't escape Olivia. I had to face my old rival once again, but this time I hoped we could both leave the kitchen with at least a small victory.

And first...I had to start with an apology I should have said a decade ago.

"I was pissed off at our graduation," I admitted. "Your medals sounded like you were wearing a cow bell when you walked so that's why I..."

I couldn't say it. I knew I was being a little shit when I actually *mooed* at her when she crossed the graduation stage, but I never thought it would bring me so much shame after all this time.

I swallowed. "That's why I did what I did. I never considered how it would have come across...or how it would have made you feel. I'm sorry."

She looked up at me and sniffed. "You were that upset about coming in second place?"

No, but I wasn't ready to tell her the real reason.

I ran my hands down the flannel pants. The back of my neck warmed and I chewed on my lip. It was exactly as Mom had warned—as soon as I opened up a little bit, more would come flooding out. I couldn't stop what was coming, but maybe I could limit what I admitted to.

"And...I was a jerk at the hospital, but it wasn't because of you," I said. "Grandpa died there, Christmas break of my sophomore year of college. It was…" I swallowed, trying not to remember what the doctors had done to Elren's greatest man. "…horrendous. I was by his side when…when it happened. Clear case of medical neglect."

She blinked away a tear. "Did you sue?"

I almost laughed, because of course she would ask.

I rested my head against a lower kitchen cabinet, not caring that I was getting protein shake in my hair, and let my eyes wander up to the white enameled ceiling that resembled clouds of icing. "I did, but we settled. All I got was money, there was no justice."

I still remembered the sound of the paper sliding against that overly-lacquered table at the law office. I had wanted to throw the settlement offer back in my lawyer's face, but Mom held me back. My lawyer had explained that Grandpa's medical records would be made public if we went to trial. Mom gave me a pointed look and shook her head, so I clenched my teeth and picked up the pen.

My hands gripped my knees as I remembered that lawyer's eyes lighting up like a fucking cash register as I signed my name on that settlement.

If that wasn't the moment that solidified that I was just big game in a money-hunting world, then…

I closed my eyes, wishing I could cover my mouth with tape instead of admitting what was about to come out. Though if Olivia was hurt because of how I reacted to her pregnancy, I needed to tell her why I had done it. The last thing I had wanted to do was rip open that scabbed-over wound, but I would do it for my babies.

I pried my eyes from the ceiling and looked at Olivia. She stared back at me, her eyes soft with fatigue but dry. Her face was splotchy and her shoulders were slumped forward. She was completely and utterly pathetic—harmless.

Yet I was still terrified.

With a silent gulp, I swallowed my cowardice. Though I couldn't open the iron vault and let all my secrets out, I would let Olivia Adams have just one more.

"I was engaged once," I said.

Her eyes dropped to the floor. "Oh."

I ran a hand through my hair. "Her name was Katie. I met her freshman year at Lindsay and we were together all through college." My tongue suddenly felt too heavy in my mouth, but I couldn't stop talking. "Right before spring break of our senior year, she told me she was pregnant."

Olivia's eyes met mine. "The pregnancy wasn't real, was it?"

Damn it, Olivia. Always smarter than me.

My eyes prickled with heat and I held up my hands before dropping them back into my lap. "I proposed as soon as I found out. I even took her to Paris so she could pick out a ring. I remember she would choose one and I'd keep telling her to get a bigger diamond." A hollow laugh escaped my lips and I shrugged. "Most guys would have panicked but I was just...so excited to be a dad."

I let out another shallow laugh. And I was an idiot, a fucking idiot.

Shaking my head, I met her eyes again. "I...didn't take it well when I found out the truth."

I held back the gory details of the explosive breakup—tossing a whole box of wedding invitations into the firepit, blinking away cold tears as I shut that nursery door for the last time, and spending years trolling clubs as I tried but failed to numb the pain and paranoia Katie fucking caused me.

"She never had a reason to lie," I said. "She wanted my money, but I would have given her a glass jar full of stars if she had asked. All I wanted, all I *needed* from her, was to trust her, and…"

I swallowed and nearly collapsed under the weight of the moment. Olivia merely looked at me—not mocking me, not chastising me for being foolish, not even pitying me, really—but still I felt completely naked as I sat on the kitchen floor.

With little else to lose, I released the last confession I could bear. "…and now I can't trust anyone. No one but my mom and my finance guy, of all people."

"I'm sorry," Olivia softly responded.

"It's not your fault, I just—" I reflexively opened my hand and closed it, as if I were trying to catch something.

I pursed my lips and gently tapped my closed fist on top of my knee. Fuck, might as well say it.

"I'm sorry that I…disrupted your life," I said. "I approached you at the reunion because I wanted to mess with you—to get some vengeance after we were so shitty to each other in high school. I never thought we would end up here but…"

Her hands moved over her belly. There they were, real as could be. My babies.

I let out a breath, but then forced myself to look up at her. "I might be the biggest mistake of *your* life, but you're not a mistake to me."

"Beau…"

"I regret how I did it, but I don't regret what I did." I chewed on my tongue. God, I sounded like an asshole. "I never thought I would get to be a dad again and…"

"*Beau…*"

"Thank you," I said in an exhale. "Thank you for letting me disrupt your life so I can finally be a father."

Her hands stayed on her belly and she gave me the softest smile. Maybe that meant she accepted my pathetic ramble of an apology.

"OK," I sighed as I slumped backward against the cabinets. "I'm done. What is it?"

Olivia's eyes shined with tears. "I feel the babies."

My heart stopped. "Y-you do?"

She poked near the pocket of her hoodie. "Here." Then her other hand poked at a lower spot. "And here."

Now it was my turn to be speechless.

Her face grew serious. "I think it's obvious that neither of us would have picked the other to have a baby with—much less two of them."

I nodded.

"But I'll make *you* a deal this time, Beau Fontaine III." Her smile returned, but only a little bit. "I can accept your help, but not if you ice me out. You don't trust me to not hurt you and I can't trust you to not hurt me, but…"

She flattened her hands against her belly and looked down. "…we have to try."

"I'll try if you try," I promised. "But, hey, the pregnancy will be over before you know it, then everything can go back to normal."

"Only five months left—law school was longer than that." Her smile grew bigger. "I'll get to go back to my apartment and get a new job…and never have to wake up to you shoving a giant yellow tumbler in my face."

I laughed. "And I'll never have to dodge flying protein shakes. I'll finally have my peace and quiet back."

The earliest glimmers of sunlight streamed in through the kitchen window and stretched across the floor. Slowly, I stood and extended a hand to Olivia. She raised an eyebrow, but finally let me help her up.

As soon as her hand met my palm, a rush of warmth shot up my arm. I blinked and held my breath.

Five months. Five months and then everything goes back to normal.

The instant Olivia was steady on her feet, I let her go and shoved my hand into the pocket of my pajamas.

And then I made her as many pancakes as she could eat.

12

Olivia

Pink.

When Beau ripped the canvas cover off the car that had sat in the corner of the cavernous garage, pink was the last color I was expecting. I held back a squeal of delight as I admired the cotton candy paint of the 1957 Chevrolet Bel Air.

"It was my Grandpa's," Beau said bluntly. "The truck is in the shop, get in."

I carefully eased my way into the passenger seat. My hips were still achy and stiff, but getting into the pinkmobile was much easier than forcing myself to climb into Beau's giant truck.

Beau drove out of the garage and we headed to the city for my sixteenth week prenatal appointment. The mid-century car hadn't been updated to have a stereo, so we would have to spend the next hour and a half listening to FM radio instead of the Bored Bros podcast. The car didn't even have cup holders, either. I had to secure my giant pink water cup between my feet as I held my yellow cup in my hands.

Hints of orange washed over my tongue as I drank. Divorced dad music played from the local alt-rock station, but I preferred it to silence.

Beau might have opened up on Christmas, but he had clammed back up in the days afterward. We had both promised each other that we would try, but emotionally the man was still cowering in an imaginary treehole like a frightened squirrel.

I let him lick his self-inflicted wounds in peace, though. I was too busy to deal with him. As soon as a new pair of glasses was shipped to the manor, I spent days researching historically accurate decor for the Kaye house.

Just the night before, I had emailed Ashley an entire file of different wallpaper samples, tile, and paint swatches that would complete the Kaye house renovation. Ashley had been so ecstatic with my findings that she had replied to my email with the famous clip of her shaking me with glee.

After the singer finished crowing about how he wished the devil in red heels had never walked into his garage, a commercial blasted through the speakers.

"Like lightning from the heavens, it's TYSOOOO—"

Beau quickly switched off the radio.

Weird. Maybe the man had a personal affront to advertising? Rich guys probably got access to ultra premium packages that blocked all ads except for commercials for buying private islands or whatever.

I put down my water. "Was that Tyson's toothpaste sponsorship or the car dealership one? Both commercials start out the same."

"Don't know," Beau said, keeping his eyes glued to the highway.

I hummed. "I wonder how much companies pay to use that clip from the national championship game?"

"Too much." He flicked the turn signal and steered toward an exit ramp.

Did Beau have something against Tyson? No, he couldn't— no one had anything against Tyson. Tyson certainly didn't have a problem with Beau, either. He would even shut Ashley down when she would bring up a rumor about the Fontaines— always saying Beau was a decent guy and not a foreign spy or a crime lord.

I decided to poke Beau a little more to get to the truth.

"His Tigerade sponsorship was the best one," I said innocently. "Tyson kept my fridge full of those six-packs for months. Blue was my favorite flavor."

"Blue is not a flavor," Beau said curtly.

I cut him a glance. "You sound like a cop."

He rolled his eyes in response, clamming up yet again. Beau bled crimson and ivory just like all Lindsay University worshipers, so he probably just hated Tyson for winning the championship for Plains State when we were seniors.

How petty. Lindsay couldn't win *every* championship. Get over it, loser.

Beau pulled up next to a pump at a gas station and got out of the car.

"Want any snacks or drinks?" Beau asked through the open door as he clicked the nozzle in place. "If you do, give me the name of an actual flavor—not a color."

I finished the last of my wake-up water. "I'll stick to the waters for now, officer."

He rolled his eyes. "I'll go grab some food just in case. Just sit tight, Jenny here takes forever to fill up." He gently tapped the hood of the car. "Like Dad always said, Jenny sucks down gas like a Plains State girl sucks…"

I glared at him through the open door. Thankfully, Beau knew when to shut up.

"Anyway," he said with an awkward second tap on the hood. "Snacks. I'll be back."

I concentrated on hydrating so I wouldn't have to look at him. Once he disappeared, I watched the numbers on the pump climb and climb. Since he was a modern oil baron, I couldn't imagine Beau was too concerned with buying the most expensive gas possible. Hell, Fontaine Energy probably supplied the gas.

Of course, that would depend on which gas station we had stopped at.

I rolled down my window and stuck my head out to get a better look at the sign. I spotted a green dinosaur on the sign—StegCo. I didn't know much about them, not like…

I turned my head and instantly scowled. I knew my old nemesis was near. Just across the street was that ugly red geometric logo that some shitty focus group had thought made an acceptable "H."

Fucking Herringbone. Their station was advertising prices that undercut the StegCo station by ten cents because *of course* they were. A $98 million verdict wasn't enough. I should have asked that jury for *much* more.

Fueled by the hatred in my heart, I flipped off the Herringbone station just as the driver's side door shut.

Beau settled in the driver's seat and set the plastic bag of snacks on the console. "Is that for me?"

I put down my middle finger as a hot flush crept across my cheekbones. "No! That was for Herringbone. My verdict against them was what my $2.9 million bonus came out of."

Beau raised his eyebrows and started to drive away from the gas station. "You sued Herringbone and won? What happened?"

A little yellow butterfly in my chest fluttered its wings. I could have talked for hours about everything that went on in the Herringbone case, but this was the first time Beau wanted to really speak to me since Christmas and I didn't want to risk annoying him.

"Long story short," I said, "Herringbone made a bunch of contracts with smaller companies they never intended to fulfill. Enough of the smaller companies got together and sued for the money they were owed, money from lost business due to the non-payment, and…"

Oh, might as well brag.

"I pissed off the jury enough with Herringbone's history of shady business deals that they awarded a few million extra as a 'fuck you.'"

Beau laughed. "Damn, sugar. You kicked them in the teeth."

I took a sip of my water to keep from blushing. "Well, one of the partners did most of the trial. I did the grunt work before and after…but I still got to get up in front of the jury and yell about how shitty Herringbone was."

Beau changed lanes and sped up. "That's what happens when a company is publicly traded. When you promise your stock holders continuous growth quarter after quarter, a lot of businesses will do anything to raise profits. It's why Fontaine Energy is still family-owned. We can take some losses every now and again for the ultimate health of the company because we have no one to answer to but ourselves."

Made sense why Beau was so concerned about heirs, then. I imagined our babies in matching pinstripe suits, sitting at tiny desks and…doing whatever Beau does.

"Where did you go at Christmas?" I asked. "You've never actually explained what you do for the company."

His jaw clenched and I studied the passing billboards on the side of the highway as I waited for him to answer. Maybe he really was attending that masked orgy like Ashley had suspected.

He cleared his throat. "So, my dad runs the company as the CEO, but he doesn't get out much. My grandpa used to go out to the oil fields and offshore rigs to meet with the managers and shake hands with some of the workers. I started going in his place during the last year of his life and I've been doing it ever since. It builds unity and loyalty to the brand when you can put a face to the Fontaine name."

We passed a Lindsay University billboard, featuring their goofy felt Crimson Knight that danced on the sidelines at games. "So… you're like the company mascot?"

"No, I take important business matters into consideration and…" He sighed. "Yeah. I'm like the company mascot."

Well, that's a little embarrassing.

I rattled the ice in my cup and took a drink. "Mascots are good for morale."

"Exactly, and that's what I was doing at Christmas," he explained. "I flew down to the gulf and met with all the managers of our offshore rigs so they could air out all their concerns. And for all the rig workers who didn't get to go home for the holidays, I rented out this huge dance hall on Christmas day and threw a massive party. Every year, I pay for an open bar, grazing tables full of barbecue and seafood, and tons of door prizes that the company gives out through the night."

He rubbed the back of his neck. "It's...a good time—like I'm fraternity president again and everyone likes me. We have low turnover on our rigs compared to everyone else and I like to think the Christmas party is a big reason why."

"But then I had to fall down a hill and spoil the party this year?"

He shrugged. "I had already made my big 'thank you for working for us' speech. Everyone had their alcohol and food by then, so they probably didn't miss me too much when I had to run out."

My stomach growled a little at the mention of food. I dragged the plastic bag from the gas station into my lap and inspected the snack haul—carrot sticks and beef jerky. Was he joking?

"Can we pull over at the next gas station?" I asked. "I have to use the bathroom."

He raised an eyebrow. "Can't you wait until we get to the appointment?"

"You really want to test that?"

With a quiet sigh, he merged onto an exit ramp and pulled into another gas station—one that luckily didn't have Herringbone pumps outside of the store.

After visiting the bathroom so I wouldn't have completely lied, I grabbed a bag of chocolate mini donuts and walked up to the register.

As I paid, the clerk glanced at my belly.

"Six months, right?" he said.

This motherfucker.

"No, I'm only four months along," I replied dryly. "I'm having twins."

The clerk's eyes widened. "No way!"

I bit my tongue to stop myself from pointing to the big white letters that read "Twin Mom" on my sweatshirt. The machine pinged that it had accepted payment from my card, so I snatched my precious donuts before that *man* breathed any more of my air.

When I got back into the car, Beau tossed a look at my bag of donuts.

"Say anything and I'll put you in the trunk," I warned.

He rolled his eyes, but pulled out of the parking lot.

"You remember Anthony Dauphin?" Beau asked as he drove back onto the highway. "He graduated two years before us."

"Wasn't he quarterback before you were?" I asked as I pulled out a donut.

"Sure was," Beau responded. "He was valedictorian too."

I savored the pillowy bite of my donut instead of asking any follow-up questions. The conversation reeked of "sore loser" and I had already dealt with *one* jackass before noon.

"The morning of his graduation," Beau continued, clearly not taking the hint that I wasn't interested in his high school soliloquy, "he made a post bragging that he plagiarized his valedictorian speech. He wrote, 'I cheated all through high school, why stop now?'"

I hummed as I chewed my donut. I had never followed Anthony on his socials, but I would have never guessed he would have fully admitted to cheating his way to the top.

"I never had a problem with the guy until then, but the post really pissed me off," Beau said. "So, I got a bunch of the ranch hands together and we egged his truck during the graduation ceremony."

I swallowed my bite. "Well, did you get vengeance for your precious morals and values?"

"Not until today," Beau replied. "From what I heard, Anthony never faced any repercussions for being a deceitful shit. He graduated from college just fine and then got himself a *big* fancy job..."

I caught the twinkle in Beau's blue eyes in the rearview mirror. "...securing contracts at Herringbone's corporate office."

My donut was halfway into my mouth when I gasped. "That was *him?*"

Beau held up a finger like he was an old man about to give a lecture. "A dishonorable person is mold in a mansion's walls. Unless you scour them out of your life, they will destroy everything you have."

I couldn't say Herringbone was destroyed...yet, but Anthony Dauphin did cost them $98 million. Now I wanted to egg his truck too.

"Grandpa raised me to believe that honesty and honor were more important than anything else, but…" Beau took a deep breath. "…I had still wanted to take Katie back after she lied about the pregnancy. Does that make me a hypocrite?"

My stomach dropped. Why was he asking me?

I pretended to intensely search my bag for the perfect donut. "Um, I don't think so."

"I almost unblocked her number and called her last year," Beau said. "But then I just thought of when we went shopping for nursery furniture. She held her lower stomach the whole time, knowing *nothing* was in there, and…" He sighed. "Even after all that, I just…couldn't let go of her."

My gaze dropped to the floorboard as I ate another donut. Watching him sit on his kitchen floor and nearly cry over a woman he had once deeply loved had been hard enough to witness. I understood why he had told me about Katie, but listening to him talk about her again sent a horrible prickle crawling down my neck and I had no idea why.

Maybe his pain made me uncomfortable. Broken hearts have barbs—anyone close enough can feel them.

"I never had another girlfriend after her," Beau said pensively. "You're the first person I've slept with in years who knew my real name."

I couldn't help but laugh. "You had a fake name for fucking around?"

I instantly felt bad for laughing at him, but luckily he gave me a little smirk back. "Go to any club in the city and anyone there will tell you my name is Jake."

"Jake, rhymes with fake."

His smirk softened into a real smile. "Never thought of that."

I picked up my pink water cup and set down my bag of donuts. "Did you know that I've never had a boyfriend?"

Beau took his eyes off the road for a split second to toss me an incredulous look. "You serious?"

I nodded as I took a sip of raspberry water. My dating apps were for hookups only, not commitment. After my dad left and the string of Mom's boyfriends that followed, I was forever put off on the idea of being completely vulnerable to someone.

Mom had fallen for so many men and none of them ever did us any good.

"I never wanted anything serious and anything serious never wanted me," I answered. "Besides, I'm not Ashley."

He made a face. "What do you mean?"

I was about to ask him if *he* was serious. Ashley had been pretty and charming since junior high. All the boys wanted her, but she only had eyes for the shy running back who had helped her with her math homework.

I might have never wanted a relationship, but it still didn't feel good being invisible next to Ashley.

"You remember me from high school," I answered. "I was a potato in a hoodie! No boy wanted anything to do with me."

He sucked in a long breath and drummed his fingers on the steering wheel. "I'm going to say this as politely as I can…"

My fingers clutched my cup. "What?"

"We were teen boys, Adams. *Everyone* wanted something to do with you."

"Explain."

Beau held his fist over his lips, staring ahead as if a billboard with the correct response was just over the horizon.

"Your hoodie couldn't hide what was underneath it," he finally responded.

Oh.

Back in high school, I had strangled my growing chest with sports bras because anything that would fit me properly was out of our budget. When cooler weather came around, I figured I could get away with only wearing a tight tank top and a hoodie over it.

Guess not.

I scoffed. "Well, if my tits were that great, why didn't I have a date for prom?"

He rested his elbow on the console between us. "Any guy was probably too scared to ask you. You were, and still are, very intimidating."

I crossed my arms. Good. I could never stop men from leering at my big tits, but at least my resting bitch face kept them from invading my life. Beau was my one slip up, but he was just the father of my children. He wasn't a partner, or a boyfriend, or even in that nebulous zone of being a friend with benefits.

Hell, I didn't even consider us actual friends. We were merely two people irrevocably yoked by circumstance. Just because we could be civil on one car ride didn't make us anything more than co-parents.

"I was never scared of you, though," Beau said with a smirk.

I rolled my eyes. "I'm clearly not trying hard enough."

"I remember sitting behind you in English class junior year," he said. "You used to go off about all the macabre shit that some dead poet wrote about and gave everyone the creeps. I was only annoyed, but I never wanted to move because you smelled good."

"Glad to know you're still a douche—wait, what did you just say?"

I turned to him, but he responded with only a shrug. "Whatever soap you used back then…I don't know, it was really strong."

"My Island Passion body wash?" I asked. "I got it from the *dollar store.*"

"I always thought it smelled like summertime," he said. "Sometimes I would lean forward to flick you on the head so you would shut the hell up, but then I would smell that fruity, tropical scent and just…"

Slowly, Beau's hand that rested on the console rippled into a fist, as if he were grabbing an imaginary ponytail.

Heat flooded my cheeks in an instant. I squeezed my legs together, as if to trap the tension that had suddenly built there. I stared at the approaching city skyline, but I couldn't stop the rush of mental images of his fist in my hair, of me taking his cock into the back of my throat, and of him gasping and pleading for mercy as I sucked his soul out.

Oh, no. Oh, no no no *no.*

I took a gulp of my icy water to try to douse the dirty thoughts out of existence, but my growing libido was becoming a powerful itch I had to scratch. Scientifically, it made no sense that I was so horny when I was already pregnant, but I couldn't keep ignoring the problem.

Thank God I had my vibrators back in my room.

After a silence that was so tense Beau had turned the radio back on, we had finally made it to the appointment. The babies were fine. I was gaining weight at a good rate. Dr. Ornelas even praised me for keeping up with my water intake.

And as soon I was back behind the locked door of my bedroom, I took care of my urges—over and over.

Though the thought of Beau and his big hands and his little whimpers kept creeping into my fantasies, I refused to cross the hall and knock on his bedroom door.

But one night…the temptation to break down the "we're only co-parents" wall called to me. Instead of giving in and risking losing myself in his sheets, I pulled out my phone and did a deep dive of Beau's socials.

And I found Katie.

He hadn't deleted any of their photos from college, not even their engagement shoot.

And just as I suspected, Katie was an Ashley. She was thin and perky with a pearly white smile and long blonde hair down to her waist. Her ruffled floral dresses mad her look *perfectly* delicate. She probably came from a good family that went to Europe at least once and wanted to be a veterinarian when she grew up. And the way Beau looked at her in each and every photo…

I slammed my phone onto my nightstand and rolled over in bed.

Katie was his type. I was the high school rival he wanted to *mess with*.

Beau was not my boyfriend. He was not my lover. I would not fall into the trap of believing we were anything more than temporary roommates.

Even when he had texted me to meet him in the garage to get the onion fried burgers I had been craving, I had refused to consider it a date. He was doing the bare minimum to provide for the woman he knocked up, nothing more.

Beau's giant truck had finally come back from the shop and was waiting for me in the garage, so I mentally prepared myself for the struggle of climbing in. Before I could even grab the door handle, Beau ordered me to stop and back up.

Reluctantly, I did as he asked, even though my growling belly was making me homicidal.

The truck's engine started with a roar, as expected, but then the truck slowly lowered closer to the ground and a step on the passenger side unfolded—a step just for me.

Beau rolled down the window of the passenger door and gave me a soft smile. "OK, now get in."

I returned with a little smile of my own, just to be grateful, and put my foot on that first step.

Just because he could be nice sometimes did *not* make him my boyfriend. Beau had wanted a Katie and got stuck with an Olivia. He could live in my fantasies when I had to take care of my pregnancy libido, but I wouldn't let him in anywhere else.

I couldn't risk it.

Beau

The pregnancy had taken up so much of Olivia's energy that she could only do one activity per day. On the morning of January 9th, she decided her activity was…going to the dollar store.

I didn't even listen to my podcast during my run because I was wracking my brain to figure out why Olivia was still so hell-bent on saving money. Why was she not satisfied with what I had given her? Was *abundance* not enough for her?

Desperate for a key to unlock the female mind, I called Mom and asked her.

"It isn't about money, it's about control," Mom said through the phone. "She thinks the more she depends on you to survive, the more control you have over her."

I set the ingredients for my post-run water on the marble bartop in the media room. "Doubt it. *No one* can control Olivia Adams, you don't know her."

"And *you* don't know women," she argued. "Your endless money pit isn't impressing her, it's freaking her out."

I mixed my water and scoffed. "How would you know that? A month ago, you were calling her a gold digger."

"So she's a different type of dangerous, then," she said dismissively. "A tiger has stripes and a leopard has spots, but both will still maul you."

I took a slug from my water and walked toward the study. Might as well spend thirty minutes answering emails before I figured out what to do for the rest of the day.

A tense sigh left my lips and I kept my voice low in case Olivia was home. "If I'm attentive, I'm wrong. If I keep my distance, I'm wrong. Do you have any other creative ideas for how I can be completely useless in this situation?"

"Fulfil your obligations as the father of those twins, that's all you do," Mom said. "Don't involve yourself with her any more than you already are. She might be growing the next Fontaines, but she clearly doesn't want us to bring her into the fold."

I pulled open the study door and stepped inside. "She doesn't even want to give them the Fontaine name. I'm just hoping I can get her to see reason and she'll give up the ridiculous notion that *my* babies will carry the name Ada—"

The sight of a tall coffee cup placed on my desk stopped me in my tracks. I set down my water and picked up the cup—the coffee was still warm.

"She...got me a coffee from the place downtown," I said into the phone. A neon blue sticky note on the side of the cup caught my eye. "And a note."

"What does it say?"

I read the message written in purple marker. "Of course you're a Capricorn."

"Great," Mom groaned. "She's one of *those* women."

I put the note in my pocket. "How did she know? What does this mean?"

"It means she snooped through your socials and got information," Mom said. "Worse, it means she's suspicious or she's bored—either way it's dangerous."

I weighed the coffee in my hands, as if testing to see if it would explode. "So, do I need to make myself even more uninteresting so she doesn't go digging?"

"Nothing about you is uninteresting," Mom said. "But if Olivia doesn't want to be part of this family, she *can't* learn anything else. Understand?"

Though she couldn't see me, I still nodded.

Mom wasn't happy that I told Olivia the bare-bones story of what happened to Grandpa, or even that Katie and I had a bad fallout instead of just spinning the "amicable breakup" lie. She could be as mad at me as she wanted, but Mom didn't understand what it was like at the manor.

"You know I'll do anything for this family...what all is left of it." I examined the coffee cup and then tossed a glance to the framed ultrasound photo that sat on my desk. "But the family includes the babies and the babies are relying on their mother. Olivia is...fragile right now, and sometimes I have to share bits of my life to get her to take care of herself. I'm doing my best to be discreet, but this is a tough balancing act."

Mom took in a long inhale, likely taking a drag of her cigarette. I anticipated a lecture, but instead she sighed and said, "You're going to be a good father."

My heart warmed as I kept my eyes on that blurry black-and-white photo of my little babies. "Thanks, Mom."

"You have a good rest of your day," she said. The soft patting of her carton of cigarettes against a table echoed through the speaker. "And happy birthday, baby. I love you."

"Love you too," I replied.

After she hung up, I examined the seemingly innocuous note. The blue note had come from a pack in my desk drawer. Had Olivia been snooping? Did she find the keys to the filing cabinet that were hidden in a box behind the pens? Did she drug the coffee to make me collapse on the study floor so she could make copies of my thumbprint to use on the family safe?

I let out a breath and glanced at the googly-eyed globe on the other side of the desk. Mom was making me paranoid, but was it unjustified? I hadn't been this close with anyone since Katie, and even though I couldn't say Olivia and I were anything resembling romantic, she made me feel very...exposed.

I was a defanged rattlesnake when it came to the mother of my children. We could hiss at each other all we wanted, but I could never risk inflicting strife on her as she grew the babies. She could hurt me a hell of a lot worse than I could ever hurt her, but I couldn't let her know that.

As exposed as I felt, the real question was if I actually craved the opportunity to let her hurt me. Was the pendulum swinging in the other direction after years of isolating myself? Did I want to find out if Olivia Adams was the type of woman I could hand a gun to and trust her not to pull the trigger?

Swirling the coffee in my hand, I dared to test my theory. I took a sip, just a little one, and let the warm coffee trickle down my throat.

Carmel vanilla latte. Delicious.

After sipping the coffee and thinking too much, I shut myself in the gym and made my body work through the turmoil so my brain wouldn't have to. I wore only my gray sweatpants as I cycled through a body weight circuit, grounding myself with the feeling of my feet and palms on the floor as I did push-ups.

I shot Olivia a text to check up on her in the middle of my workout. Close to the end of my final set, she responded.

"I'm in pain."

My brows furrowed as I looked at my phone. I asked her to specify what kind of pain and finished my set as I waited. Olivia had been complaining about her hips being stiff for the past few weeks, so maybe that was it.

Or maybe it was worse.

I got up from the floor and texted her again. No response. I toweled the sweat off my neck and chest—still nothing from Olivia.

My heart started racing. Pain could mean one or both of the placentas detached. She could be hemorrhaging. I shoved my phone into my pocket and left the gym.

"Damnit, Adams," I called from the foyer as I quickly headed up the stairs. "You're scaring me."

I had hoped for a sassy response, but was only met with silence when I made it to the second floor landing. I hurried down the hall to her bedroom door and knocked. "Olivia?"

No response. I turned the knob—locked.

She had fallen again. She couldn't reach her phone. She was bleeding, unconscious, on the bathroom floor. I had only seconds to spare.

"OLIVIA!" I shouted as I shoved my shoulder into the door, popping the lock open. The door gave way and I stumbled into the room, my chest heaving as my head whipped from side to side. She wasn't in bed. Or on the floor.

I only took a few quick steps into the bathroom to find her. She was in the bathtub, her hair piled into a bun and her face frozen in shock. She was awake and not bleeding, but the relief washing over me didn't stop my pounding heart.

"Beau, what are you—?" she whispered.

I threw down my hands. "You can't just text me that you're in pain and disappear!"

"I'm sorry, I…I left my phone on the dresser," she said. "It's my pelvis again. I thought taking a bath would help."

I forced out a sigh. She was fine. It was a simple misunderstanding. The babies were fine.

I rubbed my shoulder to soothe the ache from hitting the door. "Well, next time could you tell me—"

A low vibrating noise hit my ears. I looked at Olivia and she looked back at me. Her eyes were the size of baseballs and her cheeks grew redder by the second. Though the bath was full of bubbles, covering everything below Olivia's shoulders, it couldn't hide the very mechanical trembling beneath the surface that made the water ripple.

So *that's* why she wasn't answering my texts.

I leaned against the doorframe and gave her a little smile. "Pain, huh?"

She furrowed her brows. "OK, big strong man—you got to bust open my door and now you know I'm just fine. Now if you will please just—"

The vibrating noise softened until it fizzled out. The bathwater went completely still and Olivia looked down at the bubbles and cursed under her breath.

As if there couldn't have been a more perfect time for a battery to die.

I held back a laugh. "Serves you right for scaring me like that."

She turned back to me like she was about to spit venom, but then her eyebrows raised and her face softened. I tracked her gaze and suddenly became hyper-aware that I wasn't wearing a shirt.

"I didn't know you had a tattoo," she said softly.

I lifted myself off the doorframe and looked down at the tattoo of an angel spearing a python on my right arm.

"I, um, got it while traveling a few years ago." I rotated my arm toward her so she could get a better view. "Didn't hurt as bad as people say."

"It's pretty."

Badass was the term I would have used, but I'd take the compliment. That might have been the first compliment Olivia had ever given me, actually.

Olivia's eyes dropped to the bubbles as the flush creeping along her cheeks deepened. She bit her lower lip in a way that made me want to swallow my own tongue.

"I have a tattoo on my back." Her eyes flicked back up to meet mine. "Want to see?"

My heart started to pound. I put all my willpower into keeping my eyes on her face and not giving into the temptation of taking a quick glance into that thinning layer of soap bubbles.

Her tattoo wasn't all I wanted to see.

If I were a rational creature, I would have left the bathroom. Unfortunately, I was instead a mere man. The bathtub siren was calling and I had no choice but to answer.

She turned around. As I stepped forward to get a better look, the scent of the soap hit me like a punch to the nose and I had to grip the bathroom counter to keep my knees from buckling. The tropical scent flooded my brain like a tidal wave and unlocked dozens of shameful high school fantasies that I had repressed.

I couldn't even breathe as I thought of weaving my fingers through Olivia's hair, or shutting her up by shoving my cock in her mouth, or fucking her on top of her desk so I could watch those big tits bounce.

The fantasies replayed like flashbangs over and over in my head as the blood drained from my brain. I needed to get the hell out of that bathroom, but my feet were stuck to the tile.

Olivia looked at me over her bare shoulder. "Are you OK?"

I tightened my grip on the counter's edge and cleared my throat. "You bought that soap at the dollar store, didn't you?"

She quickly glanced to the side. "Yeah, um…I thought it would put me in the right mood."

She looked back at me and her eyes widened. I dipped my chin to follow her gaze—I was hard as a fucking diamond and my sweatpants hid nothing.

My mouth went dry as I remembered to be embarrassed. "I…I'm sorry. I'll leave."

"Don't."

I swallowed, trying to form a response but failing to even form thoughts. "What?"

Her face sharpened a little. "You interrupted me, so you should take over."

My hand ran through my hair. "How do you want me to—?"

"Get in the bathtub."

I nodded as my thumbs slid beneath the waistband of my pants. I pushed down, freeing my aching cock to the air, and kicked off my pants and boxers.

I stood before her, my body as naked and vulnerable as I felt. The imperious look on her face softened as she moved forward in the bathtub, silently inviting me to sit behind her.

My eyes stayed on the tops of her breasts peeking out from the bubbles as I eased into the tub with her. The water warmed my legs as I positioned myself around her body. She moved into me, her ass pressing my cock into my stomach as I bit back a groan.

I looked down at her bare back—*there* was her tattoo. Between her shoulder blades was a rose, tattooed all in a single line. I lightly traced the stem of the rose on her spine and felt her skin prickle.

"Is that really where your hands should be?" she said in a breathy exhale.

I dropped my hands just beneath the surface of the water and grazed my knuckles along her sides. "You tell me…"

Slowly, I dragged the backs of my hands along her ribs until I cupped the undersides of her breasts. She let out a sweet moan and leaned into my chest, freeing her breasts from the thin layer of soap bubbles.

I cut a glance to the mirror on the opposite wall and caught the reflection of soapy water running down her breasts. Her nipples were dark and rosy. My hands were big enough to wrap around a football, but her massive tits were spilling out of my hold.

I slowly traced my thumb around her right nipple as I stared hungrily at our reflection.

"Fucking gorgeous," I breathed. "Better than I ever imagined."

She let out another moan that heightened into a whine as I lightly pinched her taut nipple.

"Lower," she ordered.

I let myself have a final, greedy squeeze of her right breast before letting my fingertips wander down her side.

She stiffened. "Don't touch the belly."

My hands paused. "Wasn't planning on it."

Moving my fingers down her ribs, I found the crease where her thigh met her belly and followed it down. Slowly, I traced circles against that sensitive flesh. *Fuck,* her pussy was just as soft as I remembered.

"I...I didn't shave," she whispered. "I can't see down there anymore."

As if I gave a fuck.

My lips grazed the side of her temple as I said, "If you're thinking about that, then I'm not doing my job."

I pressed two fingers into her and she melted back into me. Her head rested against my shoulder and her thighs opened beneath the water, giving me full access.

I took in our reflection. The soap bubbles had thinned, leaving Olivia fully on display. Finally, *she* was the vulnerable and helpless one.

My heart pounded as I took advantage of the moment, my fingers pressing up against that magical spot inside her as my other hand enjoyed the weight of her breast. She squirmed as I stroked, her ass rubbing against my shaft. I bit my tongue to keep myself from coming as I fought to make her unravel.

My thumb rubbed her clit and she let out the most beautiful little sob. She started to shake, I worked my hand faster and faster, and then—

"Fuck!" she cried, long and drawn out, as her body tensed.

"That's it," I rasped against her skin. "Come for me, Adams."

The bathwater quivered as Olivia's body quaked under my hands. A surge of triumph rushed through me. I wasn't helpless with her, not when I could command her body like this. This was *my* house. I was still in control.

When her climax faded and her sweet little noises softened into gentle panting, I slowly took my fingers out of her and rested my hand on her hip. With a sigh, she collapsed into me.

I looked in the mirror, relishing the sight of her resting on my shoulder. Her lashes had fluttered closed and water gleamed off the curves of her shoulders and her breasts.

I let out a very satisfied hum at our reflection. "See? Good things happen when you just let me take care of you."

Olivia's eyes popped open and her eyebrows furrowed. She sat upright in the tub and turned around.

"Get on the ledge," she ordered.

My cock twitched, but I was frozen as she sat on her knees in front of me.

She shot me a commanding look. "Now."

Without hesitating, I gripped the edges of the tub and pulled myself up to sit on the tile ledge. My back was flush against the wall and I held my breath as she moved to sit between my legs. Her hand broke through the surface of the water, her skin dripping wet as she wrapped her fingers around the base of my shaft.

I held back a moan as she stroked me once and let out an appraising hum. Then, her eyes locked with mine as she leaned forward. The afternoon sun from the window lit up Olivia's eyes like bronze as she opened her mouth and licked the underside of my cock, her tongue tracing a line from base to tip.

A spark of pleasure flicked up my spine, but it wasn't enough. My head fell back against the wall as she lightly licked me over and over, deliberately avoiding the sensitive head.

She was getting her revenge for what I had done in the attic, no question. I didn't dare look down to catch her delighting in my misery. I wasn't going to beg, but *fuck* I ached to be fully inside her again.

As if she heard my silent plea, she took the head into her mouth and sucked.

Relief and pleasure washed through me, like she had released a pressure valve deep within my body. I closed my eyes and groaned as she took me in deeper, deeper, until her hand let go and her lips wrapped around the base of my cock.

I opened my eyes and looked down in pure disbelief. Her hands gripped my thighs as she took me in all the way to the back of her throat.

The scent of the soap filled my nose and made my head hazy as Olivia blew me. I wasn't going to last much longer, and I couldn't let the opportunity pass me by, so I slowly worked the pink scrunchie out of her hair to unravel her bun. As soon as her hair was loose, I tightened my fist around it and used the leverage to guide her at the pace I wanted.

Olivia moaned at the pressure, sending an incredible vibration around my cock that nearly made me blow. I gripped the edge of the bathtub's ledge even harder than I held her hair as I fucked her throat, letting myself indulge in the real-life fantasy as long as possible. My heart jumped when the points of her teeth scraped my shaft, but I couldn't fucking stop, I *wouldn't* fucking stop.

But then my balls tightened and I let go. I released her hair, but Olivia's lips tightened around my cock as I pumped cum onto her tongue.

Fuck, that was good.

I let out a breath, beginning to come down from the high, but then she gripped the base of my cock *hard.* My eyebrows shot up and I gasped, and then she sucked harder than ever.

My vision blew out into white lightning. Every single one of my nerve endings fried at the intense sensation. I gritted my teeth, but I whimpered as my muscles jerked. Her nails bit into my thighs as she furiously sucked me down. It was too much, *too much.*

I opened my eyes as I tried to ride through it and found her staring up at me, her cheeks hollow but her eyes full of malice.

She really was a sadist.

"You fucking *demon,*" I bit out. "You bitch from hell!"

She released her mouth and stroked me. Her hand worked slower and slower, softening the blaring intensity into a quiet ecstasy.

Then she gave me a pointed look and swallowed.

I released a shaking breath. My hands trembled as they gripped the bathtub ledge. Even after all the hotel suites and club bathrooms I had frequented through the years, I never had a blowjob that compared.

Olivia sat on her knees in the bathwater and gave me a very satisfied, very feline smile. Any trace of the bubbles was long gone.

My cheeks grew hot as my blood circulated back to my brain. "Um...I'm sorry. I probably shouldn't have called the mother of my children a demon...or a bitch from hell."

She shrugged. "Other lawyers have called me worse."

I swallowed and glanced out the window. "Th-thanks for the coffee, by the way. I was more surprised you knew when my birthday was than anything."

"I make it my business to know things. I am a Virgo, after all."

I had no idea what that meant, but it scared me.

My heart skipped a beat as I looked back at her, but she was already getting out of the tub. She slowly stepped onto the bathmat and I sat breathless as I took her in. She was nude, voluptuous, and pregnant with my babies. God *damn*.

The image of her curvaceous silhouette burned into my memory just before she wrapped a fluffy green towel around herself.

She tossed me a look before glancing at the bathwater. "Remember *that* the next time you think I'm just going to lie back and let you take care of me."

She stepped out of the bathroom and left me there, my legs soaking in the tepid water. The vibrator was still at the bottom of the tub—useless and abandoned.

I let out a sigh and released the edge of the bathtub. A tough balancing act—that's what I had called whatever Olivia and I were. Could I really only look at her as the mother of my children after seeing her, all of her? Or after watching her suck five years of my life out of me?

But those eyes... *God* she knew what she was doing. She wanted to make me squirm, and she did. She wanted to make me helpless, and she did.

No, I was worse than helpless—I was weak. If I wasn't careful, that woman would have me collared and leashed like a dog. I was worried about the family legacy crumbling if Olivia Adams knew too much, but now *I* was in danger of crumbling.

And I couldn't. Not again.

Most importantly, I couldn't allow a woman who wanted nothing to do with me to have me under her control.

Olivia

Under normal circumstances, I never would have done it.

No matter how many books I read or true crime documentaries I watched to distract myself, I couldn't stop thinking about what Beau and I had done in the bathtub.

Only my pregnancy journal saw my confession of self-betrayal. I had promised that Beau would never access me again, but I couldn't resist.

I blamed my indiscretion on the unfortunate timing of my vibrator dying and my nearly unmanageable pregnancy libido… and the fact that Beau had barged into the bathroom with a look of crazed concern in those pretty blue eyes. What woman would have told him to leave? He wasn't wearing a shirt, his tattoo gave him a certain edge, and his gray sweatpants showcased just how big and hard he was because of me.

Despite being a frequent rider of the dick carousel in the past, I was certain I wouldn't have just invited any man into the bathtub. Beau was the father of my babies, he was…safe, somehow. I was used to him. Maybe living with him for nearly two months had just dulled me to his presence.

My senses hadn't dulled to him, though. If anything, I noticed more of his little quirks. Sometimes I would catch him pacing and muttering to himself in French. He had a scar on his lower back from a Christmas decoration falling on him. His hair curled at the nape of his neck when he had gone too long without a haircut. If he stood in front of the window in the late afternoon, the sunlight made his blonde eyelashes glow.

I realized I was getting in too deep when we watched the "Murder in the Heartland" documentary. I hadn't wanted to leave bed, so Beau found the remote to start the miniseries. He made a snide comment about my macabre taste in entertainment, but then silently stood at my bedside and watched the first twenty minutes of the initial police investigation. I was too eager to rub it in his face that I had a superior taste in entertainment, so I invited him to get in bed to watch it with me.

It wasn't until we were three episodes into our binge that I realized what I had done. Not only had I been spending more time with him, I was enjoying it. Except when Beau brought me food in bed, we ate every meal together. We drove to every doctor's appointment together. I had even ventured downstairs to join him in the gym a few times when I had a burst of energy.

I hadn't even tried to find contract work to earn my own money because I was just so damn comfortable. My constant fatigue made it easy for me to snuggle into the mattress and be at peace with being taken care of, but comfort was a trap.

If I let a man feed me, I gave him the power to starve me.

Also, I had a lingering suspicion that Beau only tolerated me because of the babies. He had never liked me before and I certainly wasn't his type, so there was a real chance Beau was going to discard me once I gave birth. I couldn't trust him to still make me pancakes in the morning, or debate me on endless "who-done-it" theories, or flash me that cutting little smirk when he thought he had won an argument.

"Until I know what he wants," I had written in my pregnancy journal, *"I can't trust him at all."*

And I wouldn't know until the babies were born.

So, as I'd always done, I mentally prepared for the worst. No more bathtub forays. No more stalking him on socials. No more relaxing in bed where our shoulders almost touch.

Even during my 20-week anatomy scan where lying on my back made me feel like I was slowly drowning on my own lungs, I had refused to grab Beau's hand for support.

But the pain and discomfort of the ultrasound had been worth it. Other than the fact that the twins were measuring a little big thanks to their six-foot-two father, Dr. Ornelas confirmed that my babies were absolutely perfect.

Even better, I found out that Twin A was my daughter and Twin B was my son.

After the appointment, Beau and I had faced-off across the kitchen island, negotiating names. I wouldn't budge on last names and he also dug his feet into the mud on the issue.

Only after hours of debate did we reach a compromise—I would choose first names and he would choose middle names, with either of us having veto power if the names didn't roll off the tongue or wouldn't look good on a resume. The last name issue was tabled to keep us—OK, to keep *me*—from burning the house down.

Whether they would bear the name Adams or Fontaine, we at least knew what to call our babies.

Our daughter would be Annie Cherie and our son would be Brady Louis.

Ashley had lost her mind when we told her the good news. She gave me the biggest hug, covering my entire front in sawdust, and promised that she would throw us a huge baby shower in Miss Kaye's house as soon as the renovation was finished.

Even though I trusted Ashley to come through on showering me with gifts, my nesting instincts had kicked in and I wanted to go shopping.

I had Beau drive his truck to the city in case I saw something on sale that I wanted to haul back. Only when Beau and I walked through the sliding doors of the store and I was assaulted with the sight of heart-shaped mylar balloons and legions of flowers did I realize it was Valentine's Day.

Beau, on the other hand, didn't appear to notice.

We walked past dozens of frantic husbands buying armfuls of gifts and camped out in the baby section of the store. I let Beau get lost in the pastel clothing racks while I studied the more important baby gear to figure out what I wanted to add to the registry. The choices were dizzying, but all my prior research from online blogs and Ashley's tried-and-true expertise had helped me narrow down what I wanted.

Even though I had perused the aisles for cribs, double strollers, carseats, and even sheet sets, Beau only happened to find me when I was comparing breast pumps.

He gave a discerning eye to the row of display models and wrinkled his nose. "Please tell me you aren't looking into these torture devices to save money. You know we can afford formula."

His use of "we" made my skin crawl.

"My boobs, my business," I said plainly. I took a wearable pump off the display shelf and examined it. "The Aspen model 9 is *nice*. I can just pop these into my bra and pump while I work."

He let out a short sigh. "You don't have to work, you know."

I cut him a glare. "I *want* to work."

Beau shifted the green basket full of clothes from one hand to the other, but still gave me a little smirk. "Well, I suppose it would be a tragedy for society if you were no longer around to bully Herringbone."

Finally, he was starting to see things my way.

The basket of clothes caught my eye and I reached down to pick up a blue sleep-and-play with brown puppies on the feet.

I shook my head as I held up the little footed onesie. "No, these have snaps. Ashley said we will hate ourselves unless we go with zippers."

He rolled his eyes as I inspected the rest of the clothes he picked. I silently approved the texture and design of a few pieces, but recoiled as soon as my fingers touched slippery crimson fabric.

I yanked two tiny Lindsay University jerseys out of the basket. "Absolutely not. Put these back, or better yet, burn them!"

He snatched the jerseys back. "Every Fontaine has gone to Lindsay dating all the way back to my great-grandpa Louis! You won't deny the twins their legacy just because you prefer obnoxious orange!"

I scoffed. "Fine. You can put my precious babies in that ghastly crimson on *your* weekends."

"*My* weekends?"

"That's how it works when parents share custody," I explained. "Once I move out of the manor and start working, you get every other weekend and a big block of time in the summer when they start school."

A muscle feathered in his cheek, but his eyes stayed cool. "And when they're too young for school, Miss Lawyer?"

I swallowed. "Well…you wouldn't get them overnight until they're three—especially if I'm breastfeeding."

He cut a cold glance to the shelf of pumps. "So that's why you want to do it."

"That's not why," I protested. "Did you know that breastmilk can strengthen a baby's immune system—"

"Bore someone else with your titty trivia," Beau said as he walked away. "Now if you'll excuse me, I have to purge my basket of all your dreaded *snaps.*"

I hissed out a breath as I watched him disappear behind the aisles, but turned back to add the Aspen model 9 to my baby registry app.

Beau could be as pissy as he wanted—Annie and Brady needed their mother. I would never keep the babies away from him, but I had to be independent, I *wanted* to be independent.

Did he expect that our arrangement was going to end differently? That I would suddenly turn blonde, wear Lindsay crimson, and become the perfect Fontaine wife that stays at home all day to take care of the babies?

If he did, he was delusional. We were always meant to part ways after the babies were born. Besides, we weren't even together!

I didn't suck his dick because I liked him, I did it to prove a point—he *couldn't* control me.

Listening to him whimper as I made him suffer was just an unexpected bonus.

I leaned against the shelf to take some pressure off my aching back as I scrolled through my registry list. I wasn't going to register for double of everything—Beau could put in some work to figure out what diaper bags or other bullshit he wanted for his house.

What he did with the twins on his time was not my problem. He could dress them in Crimson Knight onesies with snap-fasteners if he wanted. Nothing he would do in that creepy manor would have anything to do with me or my life.

I finished adding the last item to my registry and looked for Beau. When I found him, the pile of clothes in his basket had only gotten taller. I was too tired to go through his likely ill-informed selections, so I merely waddled to the front to check out.

Beau batted my hand away when I tried to use my child support card to pay for the clothes, but I rebelled by buying myself a chocolate bar.

He pulled the truck around to the front of the store so I wouldn't have to traverse the parking lot. When I climbed into the passenger seat, I caught a burst of red in the rearview mirror.

I turned around and my heart skipped a beat when I found a vase holding a dozen red roses in the backseat.

I blinked, wondering if I had imagined it, but no—the flowers really were there. He must have snuck away and bought them while I was adding items to the registry.

Not counting the construction paper and glitter cards that everyone in fourth grade had put into my decorated shoebox, I never had a Valentine's Day gift from a boy before.

"It's tradition," Beau explained as he drove out of the parking lot.

Heat crept across my cheeks. "W-what's tradition?"

Beau reached behind him and grabbed two teddy bears, one pink and one blue, and set them on the center console between us. "My parents always got me gifts on Valentine's Day, so I wanted to get gifts for the twins. The flowers are for you, technically, as a thank you for carrying them."

I glanced at the flowers in the rearview mirror. For the twins. Just a thank you.

"Oh, right," I breathed. "Who could forget Valentine's Day in middle school when your parents sent a limousine to take you to lunch."

He let out a short laugh. "That was a fun year—something I'd like to repeat with my own kids. Provided Valentine's Day happens on *my* weekend, of course."

I folded my arms on top of my belly and looked out the window. "We would alternate holidays, you know." I sighed softly. "But I'll let you have Valentine's Day every year."

I caught his little smile out of the corner of my eye. "Always a pleasure negotiating with you, Counselor Adams."

I grabbed my green water jug out of the cup holder and took a big sip, letting the cool cucumber banish the heat that had built in my cheeks.

Tears fogged my vision as I stared at the passing buildings. I used to be so tough, but I cried over everything lately—lasagna that was cold in the center, losing the drawstring in my pants, or the sight of my mom's ashes on the nightstand.

God, I wished I could just talk to my mom. Maybe she could make sense of what I felt.

Slowly, I picked up the pair of teddy bears and crushed them to my chest as I looked out the window. Hopefully, Beau would believe I was crying over the memory of my mom and not because the roses in the backseat were only *technically* for me.

Beau

Sophomore year, Olivia argued with me about the use of a semi colon so ferociously that she snapped a pencil in half. Junior year, I accidentally almost ran over her in the school parking lot and she threatened to slash my tires. Senior year, she clocked Zach Wilson across the face with her binder because he pinched her ass.

The last word I would have ever used to describe Olivia Adams was docile, yet she had started agreeing with me, giving me quiet smiles, and letting me have only the briefest moments of eye contact.

She had to be hiding something.

Maybe it was my own paranoia or a hunter instinct that I never knew I had, but I was determined to track down exactly what was making her so squirrelly. Any time I asked her if she was all right, she brushed me off or only complained about her pelvis hurting.

On the rare occasion she was happy, like when I brought her the exact chips and queso she had been craving, she still wouldn't talk.

She still napped, read her lurid books, and watched people murder each other on TV, but she was a grayer shade of her normal rosy pink.

My concern was building, but I was too afraid to confront her and upset her like at Christmas. When she walked into the gym during my arm day, my heart pounded a little faster as I did bicep curls. She was out of her normal routine, so maybe I could finally catch her off-kilter and figure out what was wrong.

Olivia unrolled her squishy purple mat to do some yoga, but then walked over near my weight rack to examine herself in the mirror wall.

I couldn't help but watch her as I finished my set. Her hair was in a neat braid that ended just between her shoulder blades. She had one hand on her back to brace herself and the other running over her protruding belly.

Watching her triggered a caveman instinct in the base of my brain. Only a few feet away was a full-figured woman that was pregnant with *my* babies, wearing a pink maternity workout set that *my* money paid for, and exercising her body in *my* gym.

I did that—*me*.

She rolled down the high waist of her leggings and frowned. "My belly button is gone."

I put down my hundred pound weights and reached for my drink. My mouth had already watered before I took a sip from my bottle.

Her belly button was indeed completely flat—and I had done *that* too.

Olivia's hands ran down the smooth slope of her round bump, right over the newly-formed stripes of her stretch marks. She kept that dissatisfied frown on, but I was suddenly very jealous of her hands. Despite our bathtub rendezvous weeks ago, she still hadn't let me touch her belly.

I swallowed my water. "You're twenty-five weeks in and you're measuring eight weeks bigger than a singleton pregnancy—your body is doing exactly what it's supposed to."

She scoffed and tugged her waistband back over her bump. "Don't say bigger."

I watched her reflection as she waddled to the yoga mat. "You have *two* in there, sugar. Bigger is better."

I expected her to flip me off, but instead she quietly turned the TV on and played her prenatal yoga video. I swallowed my disappointment and went to work on my triceps.

During the middle of my set, I glanced up at the mirror to find her kneeling on her mat and staring at me. As soon as I caught her, she quickly looked away and got down on all fours like the video instructed. I ignored her for a few minutes, but felt a prickle on the back of my neck and looked up. Sure enough, there she was staring at me like a brown-eyed barn owl again.

If I hadn't been wearing a shirt, I might have thought she was ogling me.

With a sigh, I put down my weight and sat on the end of the workout bench to face her. "Do you need me?"

Her nose wrinkled with distaste. "*No.* My hips are just aching again, so I'm letting them rest."

I leaned on my knees. "The problem probably isn't your hips, you know."

"Oh really? I invite you to trade bodies with me and try to get out of bed every morning."

"I minored in physiology, Adams," I said with a smirk. "It's probably your glutes that are disrupting the whole system."

She hummed. "I thought you would have studied business, or something equally as douchey."

I actually *majored* in business, and had a whole douchey diploma hanging in the study to prove it, but that wasn't important at the moment.

"The human body is a machine and I wanted to know how it works," I answered with a shrug. "If you're up for it, we can try a massage and see if it helps."

Olivia got on all fours again. "I don't care if you beat me with a tire iron as long as I get some relief."

I left the bench and knelt behind her on the mat before my brain caught up to realize what I was doing. I quieted the damn caveman in the back of my mind that was way too excited to see Olivia prostrate with her voluptuous ass in the air.

She was just wanting me to ease her pain, that was it.

I used all my willpower to look past the cute dimples in the thick pink spandex and envision the muscles beneath. Carefully, I placed my hands on either side of her ass and started a deep tissue massage.

Every part of a woman was a gift, but Olivia's ass made my inner caveman feel like he had just discovered fire. I bit my tongue and mentally recited the names of the muscles I was massaging to stay focused.

But my focus instantly broke when Olivia let out a little moan.

My cock jumped, but I tore my eyes away from her round rear and stared at her face instead. "That doesn't hurt, does it?"

"No," she murmured, the left side of her face smushed against the mat. "Blood is rushing through my legs. My hips are opening. I think you were right."

I wished I had cameras in the gym so I could play that "you were right" over and over. I'd even make it the sound for my morning alarm.

She shifted her knees and widened her stance. "Get closer to the center."

My heart rate spiked. I took a deep breath and pictured textbook illustrations of human anatomy as my thumbs moved across the expanse of her ass. As soon as I touched her pelvic floor muscles, she let out a deep moan.

"*God,* don't stop." She melted into my touch. "It feels so damn good."

My breathing turned shallow as my cock instantly stiffened. I had been smart enough to wear black sweatpants so my arousal wouldn't be immediately obvious, but if she backed up a couple inches or even took a glance in the mirror wall—

"Harder," she breathed as she leaned into my hands. "You won't hurt me, I promise. Just *let me have it.*"

A short sigh escaped my lips. "It's really hard to be clinical about this when you keep moaning."

She gave me a wicked look. With a tiny push, she pressed her ass into my aching cock.

She hummed. "It *is* really hard, isn't it?"

I bit my tongue. This woman, I swear to God.

My hands rested on either side of her hips and I held in a tense breath. "Do you want me to be *less* clinical with you?"

Olivia coyly avoided my eyes and stayed silent, but that naughty smile on her lips remained.

Even with her ass smashed into my hips, she was still playing keep-away. Fed up, I reached down and tilted her chin to face me.

"When are you going to tell me what's going on in that head of yours?" I demanded.

Her eyebrow quirked in a challenge. "I'm not."

Olivia's stonewall defense was frustrating, but I never faced a defense I couldn't penetrate. If she refused to talk, I'd make her scream.

I hooked my thumbs beneath the waistband of her leggings. "You said you didn't care what I did back here as long as I gave you relief. Is that still true?"

She nibbled her lower lip ever-so slightly and locked eyes with me. "Yes."

"Good." I gave her ass a gentle push. "Scoot up on the mat."

Slowly, Olivia crawled her way up the yoga mat until she rested on the very top edge. As soon as she was steady, I pulled down her leggings and panties and yanked them off her legs. She was completely bare save for her pink nursing bra and her pussy was already glistening and swollen.

What a gorgeous sight to behold.

I turned around so I could get on my back beneath her. Once my shoulders were pressed against the squishy yoga mat, I wrapped my arms around her thighs and guided her onto my face.

Olivia let out a tortured whimper as I ran my tongue along the slickness at her core. *Fuck.* She had tasted good before, but the pregnancy had only made her essence stronger.

I tilted my chin up and got another taste, then another. The second I started *really* enjoying myself, Olivia eased off me.

"Um, Beau, are you sure?" she asked with an infuriating waver in her voice. "I'm getting really big and I don't want you to—"

"Damnit, Adams," I bit out. "I can bench more than whatever you think you weigh. Come here."

I yanked her back down, the muscles in my arms tensing as I locked her legs against my cheeks. Olivia drew in a breath like she was about to complain again, but I flattened my tongue against her and shut her up. She was so fucking delicious that I groaned low in my throat as I ate her out. Her hips wiggled as she rode my face, and then the mother of my children let out a whine that made me harder than I thought possible.

Olivia's legs started to turn to jelly, so I strengthened my grip on her thighs to keep her upright.

As soon as she was good and steady, I sucked her clit into my mouth. She jumped forward a little, but I held her fast.

"You can't get away from me," I teased before I folded my tongue around her clit again. A shiver went down my spine as Olivia screamed and shook.

Not so quiet anymore, now was she?

She was close to the edge, but I wasn't going to let her off that easily. I gave her a soothing little lick before I slipped out from under her and rolled onto my knees.

I positioned myself squarely behind her and lowered my waistband to the tops of my thighs.

My cock rested between her ass cheeks as I grabbed her hips. "Do you still want that relief?"

Her cheeks burned red and her eyes were squeezed shut, but she nodded eagerly against the mat.

I carefully pushed inside her and a miserable groan escaped my lips. Though she was dripping wet, she was tight as hell. Despite all the massaging, her body wouldn't let her muscles relax fully.

"Easy," Olivia pleaded.

I gritted my teeth as I went in slowly, unlocking her inch by inch. Her walls gripped me like an iron fist, but she gradually softened. I couldn't get myself fully seated, but I fucked her at a steady enough pace to watch her whole body jiggle with every thrust.

Desperate for more, I reached forward and quickly unclipped each side of her nursing bra so her delicious tits spilled onto the yoga mat.

Though I had stripped her, bent her over, and was buried inside her, that possessive instinct in the back of my mind wasn't satisfied. She was still guarded, still holding back.

I grabbed the base of her braid and turned her head so she faced the wall of mirrors. Her eyes widened as I forced her to see that I had her.

"You can't hide from me, Adams," I said between breaths as I thrusted. "I know something is up with you, so tell me what you want."

Her face turned venomous. "Shut up and just fuck me!"

So dismissive. So demanding.

And all she wanted from me was *just* to fuck her.

Fury washed over me. "That's what you want? You want to use me, just like everyone else?"

"I never said—"

My hand dove to her clit and she screamed instead of finishing her bullshit excuse. I gave her no mercy as I forced her to come. Her walls clamped down on my cock as she cried, dragging me over the edge with her. I gritted my teeth as I came, but I kept playing with her so she was still coming.

Olivia's keening sobs echoed around the gym. Her body shook as I made her come over and over, forcing her to take her pleasure past her limit. Pride filled my chest as her miserable little face flushed red.

Have a taste of the agony you choke me with, Olivia.

When she finally flopped to the mat, I withdrew and pulled my pants back on. My head cleared and a flash of shame burned the back of my neck.

What…what had just happened? Why had I suddenly gotten so angry? What had made me lose control like that?

Disgusted with myself, I rose to my feet and looked down at the mess I had made.

Olivia was on her side, eyes closed and panting. One hand rested limply beside her while the other cradled her belly. Her calves twitched in the aftershock of her climax as trails of my cum glistened on her thighs.

"That's mine," my instincts whispered.

My shoulder muscles quivered as I tried to shake off that possessive masculine urge. I grabbed a rolled-up gym towel from a nearby warmer and gently cleaned Olivia as she rested, biting back a string of curse words as I mentally pieced together what had happened.

I was hunting down her secrets and forgot that I was the real prey.

I was playing with fire when it came to that iron-hearted woman. I had made it six months into the pregnancy without spilling all the Fontaine family secrets, but Olivia knowing me was no longer my concern.

Olivia *had* me, plain and simple. Maybe it was merely paternal instincts temporarily clouding my judgment, but I couldn't deny that Olivia made me *feel*. I wanted to buy her a castle to keep her away from me, but hold the key in my pocket so she could never leave. I wanted her sleeping silence in the morning and her screams on my sheets in the evening. I wanted her to confess her ugly truths and then tell me pretty lies.

Not since Katie left had I experienced such a messy splatter of emotions one right after another. Olivia had made me so weak that she could crumple me like paper. It wasn't fair, but if I stayed calm and made her think I had the upper hand, maybe I could keep her from knowing.

I quietly knelt just behind her back. Gently as a whisper, I hooked a loose strand of hair behind her ear and leaned in close.

"Playing cool won't work anymore, not when you bare yourself like this," I said softly against the shell of her ear. "I *will* find out what you're hiding. Enough with the games, Olivia, you won't win."

My lips moved down and I placed a lingering, claiming kiss on the side of her neck. I looked at the wall of mirrors as soon as my lips touched her skin, and I caught those beautiful brown eyes popping open in horror.

Hopefully, I had made her feel just as scared as I was.

With that possessive itch at the base of my brain satisfied, I calmly rose to my feet and walked out of the gym.

I went upstairs and hid beneath the foggy steam of my shower as the hot water beat against my back. I had no idea how I was going to navigate the rest of the pregnancy, nor was I any closer to knowing what was going on in Olivia's head, but I was certain of one thing…

Olivia Adams was finally making me lose all control.

16
Olivia

What had this damn pregnancy done to me?

I gnawed on my nails as I confessed the mortifying truth in my pregnancy journal. Beau was turning me into glass—if he could see through me, he could shatter me.

Running away with my feelings of growing comfort with him had only made him chase them. Even days later, the skin on my neck still tingled with the memory of Beau's kiss. And the way he kept his eyes open, just so he could watch my face as he did it...

Someone started a rumor in junior high that Beau and his family were all vampires, and that searing, possessive kiss on my neck made me think there was some truth to that theory.

Beau being a blood-sucking monster would have made my situation easy—black and white, good against evil—but Beau was keeping his intentions a mystery. Even if what had happened in the gym was just a weird humiliation ritual for him, at least it was clear he was trying to get in my head.

I would rather he actually drain my blood and make me sleep in a coffin before he had any access to my thoughts.

And if that wasn't bad enough, that damn man had made me need his hands. I couldn't even look him in the eye when I asked him to massage away the pain in my hips mere days after he had bent me over on my yoga mat. To his credit, Beau quietly met my needs like an obligation even though our massage sessions had coin-flip odds of ending in sex. Of course, he usually dropped a smug line like, "Always a pleasure to sate your voracious appetite, Adams," before he dropped to his knees, but he wouldn't be Beau if he wasn't a little bit of an asshole.

We both silently agreed that we should resist each other, but neither of us could help it. I kept at least one boundary up by refusing to kiss him, making it clear that my roving hands were after carnal gratification and nothing more, but Beau didn't make it easy.

When that golden tongue of his traced little French words between my legs…*mon dieu.*

As much effort as I spent enforcing physical boundaries, I spent even more effort dismantling my emotional ones. The strategy might have seemed counterintuitive, but it was ultimately very simple. If pulling away from Beau had only made him suspicious of my deeper feelings, then leading him to safer emotional territory might take him off the hunt for my soft spots.

Talking about college was a good neutral ground for the both of us. I found out he would have been a doctor had he not been the only heir to the family business. To my surprise, he apparently had been a bit of a party boy too.

But when he brought up Katie, *repeatedly*, I struggled not to squirm.

So, as we were on our way to meet Ashley at Miss Kaye's house, I moved on to a slightly riskier topic so I could avoid Katie all together.

"You said at Christmas that one of the only people you trust is your finance guy," I said from the passenger seat of his truck. "Why?"

He chuckled as he drove. "I met Chuck on a spring break trip in the mountains when I was in college. I had gotten into extreme skiing—the kind where a helicopter takes you to the summit."

I shivered as I pictured flying that high, but of course Beau would be a thrill seeker. "So, Chuck skis?"

"Not at all," Beau responded. "He was the helicopter pilot. He flew during his time in the military and decided that shuttling rich kids in the air was a decent hustle. Got to talking to him and found out he was really good with numbers too. Figured that if I could trust him to not crash into the side of a mountain, I could trust him with my money."

I gave him a skeptical look. Any other rich guy would have gone to one of the big finance firms in the city. Beau still kept mum on what his finances actually were, but they seemed more complicated than what a single helicopter pilot could handle.

Regardless of Chuck's financial ability, Beau may have just unwittingly revealed another pillar of his core persona. Beneath a cool and snarky exterior was someone who cared deeply about honor, veracity, and—as I had just discovered—trust.

"Where does Chuck live?" I asked.

"In the mountains, but he can be in Elren at the drop of a hat," Beau answered as he made a turn. "I pay him to fly my helicopter too."

The truck slowed down to park and I gasped as I looked out the window. Ashley had told me they had finished the exterior paint refresh, but I hadn't expected Miss Kaye's house to look so stunning. The once faded green siding was now a bright veridian, the chipped gingerbreading on the wraparound porch was a buttery yellow, and the trim framing the windows and lining the columns of the porch were all painted a bright raspberry red.

She was like a butterfly fresh out of the cocoon.

"Oh!" I cried as I fumbled with the truck door. I didn't even wait for Beau to lower the truck and extend the step before I jumped onto the curb. I held my belly and quickly waddled up the freshly-laid brick pathway to the house.

"Use the handrail, speedy!" Beau called after me. "Don't test Ashley's insurance coverage by falling before you can even get in the door!"

I rolled my eyes, but gripped the railing as I took a step onto the stairs. To my delight, Tyson had replaced the rotting wood with sturdy pine and the red paint on the rail was glossy to the touch. My baby bump heaved as I pulled myself up the four steps to the porch.

Though I nearly started panting as I ascended the steps, Beau effortlessly climbed the stairs and met me on the porch at the same time. He held my green cup in his hand—I guess I had been so excited to see the house that I had forgotten it.

"We have a ramp, silly!" Ashley said as she walked around from the side of the porch. Her blonde ponytail swished as she tossed her head to the right, gesturing to the ramp with sleek steel handrails that wove around the front of the house. "'Course we're still waiting for the sign that directs people to it..."

I wrapped my arms around her shoulders and squealed. "Her house looks so good, Ash! Better than the pictures you sent!"

Ashley walked to the deep purple door and wrapped her hand around the shining brass handle. "Just wait until you see the inside."

I tried to peer through the door's oval window to get a sneak peek, but I still gasped when Ashley revealed the house in all its splendor.

Drop cloths still covered the foyer floor, but the oiled dark wood railing on the staircase gleamed brilliantly under the light of a mock-gaslamp chandelier. The marvelous stained glass window had been dusted and cleaned, its colors shining brightly on the half landing where the stairs split off in opposite directions.

I grabbed Beau's wrist and tugged him into the foyer. "Look! Look at the window! Isn't it gorgeous?"

Beau looked at me, then up at the window. "Sure?"

Only when I was fully in the foyer did I notice the blush wallpaper covering the whole room. "Ash! You picked the wallpaper I sent!"

Ashley leaned against the doorframe. "Since the other spaces have a neutral palette to accommodate different decorations for events, I wanted the foyer to be more iconic."

I rushed to the nearest wall and spread my hands across the thick wallpaper, admiring the dusty pink peonies arranged in a perfect repeating fan pattern. "Ugh, it was so difficult to find a pattern that considered the natural influence in the early Art Deco era and didn't go too geometric. Thank God this worked out."

Beau's boots made the floor creak behind me as he stepped over. "You really like pink, huh?"

I whipped around and pointed to the green glass in the window. "Pink goes well with green!"

He gave me a tight-lipped smile and nodded. "Noted."

"And the pink paper helps pull the red tones from the purple parts of the glass, too," Ashley said. "Ties the whole room together."

"I thought rugs did that," Tyson said as he walked in. He wore a set of overalls that perfectly matched Ashley's, down to the embroidered "Ash & Ty" on the front. They must have just finished filming a segment for their channel.

I couldn't help but notice Beau stiffen as soon as Tyson entered the foyer.

Tyson pulled a notebook out of the embroidered pocket of his overalls and flipped to a page with dozens of numbers. "Just double-checked the measurements in the kitchen. The cabinets should fit just fine."

Ashley's face lit up. "Even in that weird corner where the chimney used to be?"

Tyson nodded and gave her the same smile that secured him a toothpaste sponsorship. "It's all perfect."

Ashley jumped up and kissed Tyson on the cheek. "God, you're such a math genius. I'm going to give you *five* more babies."

Beau swallowed tensely, but only I noticed.

Ashley took her arms off Tyson and turned to me. "Liv, come check out the kitchen with me!" She fluttered her hands at Tyson and Beau. "You two…talk about man stuff."

Beau handed me my green cup before Ashley grabbed my arm and led me into the next room. I tossed Beau a brief pitying look, but left him behind to admire the rest of the house.

"This used to be the parlor," Ashley explained as she led me into a room that was painted an antique ecru. "It'll be tight, but this will be a great space for wedding ceremonies."

Though the walls were neutral, Ashley had left the fireplace lined with small green mosaic tiles perfectly intact. Above the shining wood mantle was the iconic portrait of Miss Kaye herself. Even in black and white she exuded success as she posed, draped in furs and dripping with pearls.

It was her "I survived the Great Depression" photo, and even one of those old-fashioned cameras had captured the triumph shining in her eyes.

The kitchen was less finished than the other rooms. The upper cabinets were missing and the industrial-grade appliances still had the factory labels on them, but the lower cabinets were sporting freshly-installed quartz counters.

Ashley sighed and laid her upper body onto the white stone, spreading her arms across the slightly dusty surface. "Tyson tried to convince me to use butcher block for the countertops, but a certain *somebody's* donation allowed me to splurge a little."

I laughed. "You're certainly welcome. Anything to make this place shine like it should."

Ashley sat on the edge of the counter and her eyes softened. "How are you feeling?"

I shrugged. "I'm surviving. Every day is different, but I feel worse when I remember what I used to be able to do…like working or tying my shoes."

I took a sip from my water and glanced down at my slip-on shoes with rubber grips. I had fallen *one time* and Beau freaked out and bought me ugly nursing home shoes. I never wore anything else.

She gave me a sympathetic smile. "It's all temporary, babe. But that doesn't mean it doesn't suck."

I nodded. "My pregnancy journal is really helping me cope. Beau's mom had been right on that one."

"Speaking of which…" Her green eyes flitted to the doorway. "So…?"

I sighed and leaned on the counter, not caring that I was getting dust on my elbows. "I don't know."

"What do you mean?" Ashley asked before she dropped her voice. "You've lived with him for three months, you're already having kids with him, you just told me you're fucking again, and you *don't know* if you're in a relationship with him or not?"

"Because I don't want to be in a relationship," I answered. "I never have!"

"Why not?" Ashley started counting out her points on her fingers. "He's set for life financially, he's healthy, he's the father of your kids, he makes you come *every time,* he isn't mean to you—"

"Well, no meaner than I am to him."

"Then make it make sense to me."

I ran a hand through my hair. "I just…I don't know if he's being tolerable because of the babies or if…" I stopped and switched gears, refusing to question if he liked me just in case he overheard. "I don't even know who he is."

"What are you talking about? We went to school with him!"

"We knew the stuck-up boy who played football and only talked to the snobs that hung around him because they wanted his money," I answered. "I still don't know who he is as a person. He's quiet, Ash, so I barely know what he even likes other than his dog and sports. He doesn't...gush about things like I do!"

She shrugged. "He's a Capricorn. Capricorns don't *gush.*"

"Regardless," I said, ignoring the twins bumping around inside me. "You told me a man changes after he becomes a father. Why would I make any sort of commitment when Beau could just... unmask and become someone completely horrible?"

Ashley swung her legs a little and smiled. "Well, Tyson became an *even better* man after Kierra was born." She tossed her head back and smiled. "God, you're making me want to get pregnant again."

I rolled my eyes. "You're missing the point."

"Hell, I'll ask him to bend me over this counter and—"

"Ashley!"

She rolled her head to look at me. "You're missing out on being loved and adored and why? Because you're scared?"

I folded my arms on the counter. "Beau is not loving and adoring—he is controlling and nosy!"

She quirked an eyebrow. "I thought you didn't know him? Also, aren't *you* controlling and nosy?"

I smacked my palms against the cold stone and a vein in my neck began to throb. "My mom was *loved and adored* by my dad, and he ruined us."

"Come on, Liv, I have daddy issues too, but—"

"And then Mom was loved and adored by that guy who drank those nasty little bottles of bourbon," I stressed. "Then the guy who had the apartment that smelled like old cheese. Then the guy she met at the county fair."

Ashley shuddered. "Oh yeah, I remember the tilt-a-whirl guy..."

"You think I looked up to Miss Kaye as a kid because of her fashion sense?" I gestured to the old parlor where her portrait was hanging. "She didn't have men cycling in and out of her life to distract her, to steal her ideas, or to weigh her down with domestic duties."

"Well, she was from a different time and could have just been into women."

"She was successful because she didn't rely on anyone," I said, holding back a grimace as my back muscles spiked with pain after standing for too long. "Annie and Brady are an unexpected surprise, but I still intend to live my life as I promised myself I would when I was in third grade—unburdened, uncompromised, and *unmarried.*"

Ashley's face fell. She opened her mouth to say something, but then the voices of the men echoed through the parlor as they approached.

"So, how's your mom enjoying retirement?" Beau asked.

"Ah, former educators can never take it easy," Tyson answered. "She's been a real blessing, though—keeping the kids so Ashley and I can work. We're really fortunate to have her."

Ashley's voice brightened. "Yeah, we're really cutting it close to your due date, but we'll definitely have the house done in time for your baby shower."

The men walked in and Ashley turned toward the doorway and acted surprised to see them. "You guys having fun?"

Beau gave her a smile that I knew was *only* polite. "You've done a great job with the house. Grandpa always spoke fondly of Miss Kaye, said she would give him candy when he visited the department store with his mom. She adored him."

I took a sip of water to keep myself from giggling. Miss Kaye didn't adore Beau's grandfather, she just had good business sense. Keeping Mrs. Fontaine's child happy and distracted while shopping was a great way to get her to spend as much money as possible.

Though I could have word-vomited about Miss Kaye's successful business practices until the sun went down, I needed to give Beau an out. He didn't have to say anything for me to know he was ready to leave.

"I think we need to go," I groaned as I leaned back to stretch my spine. "My body has reached its limit."

As soon as I grabbed my water and stepped away from the counter, my eyes widened as my uterus suddenly tightened like a period cramp. I dropped my hands to my belly—it was hard as a rock.

"I...I think I'm having a contraction," I said.

Beau pulled his phone out of his pocket. "Get in the truck—I'm calling the hospital."

Ashley hopped off the counter and waved her hand at Beau. "Calm down, big guy. It's probably just a Braxton Hicks."

Beau's eyebrows furrowed. "How can you be sure?"

"It doesn't feel...big." I let out a long breath as the pressure in my abdomen released. Annie and Brady kicked me over and over, probably panicking like they had just experienced an earthquake—the poor dears.

"Yep, that was just a practice contraction." Ashley said as she patted my belly. "If you can talk through it, it's not the real deal. We should still pick up the pace with the renovation, though. Just in case."

After we finished assuring Beau that I was just fine, all four of us walked to the front door. Beau gave Tyson an awkward farewell handshake before helping me down the porch stairs and into the truck.

As soon as we pulled away from the curb, Beau scoffed and muttered "Those damn overalls," under his breath.

I turned to him. "Why do you hate Tyson so much?"

A muscle feathered in his cheek as he drove. "I don't hate him."

"You sure act like you do. What did he ever do to you?"

"Nothing, he just…" He fell into silence for a few moments as we drove through the historic neighborhood. "Tyson is…lucky."

I scoffed. *"You're* lucky. You're one of the richest men in the state."

"Yes, but…" He let out a long, slow breath. "You see, my grandpa—"

"The first Beau," I clarified.

He nodded. "The first Beau. He would always tell me, 'Boy, you used up a lifetime's worth of luck just being born with my name.' I never knew what he meant until I met Tyson. You would think the man was born on a bed of four-leaf clovers with how good everything went for him. He had great grades, always had friends who actually liked him, and then at the state championship game…"

Beau shook his head, but kept his eyes locked on the road. "I fucked up, but the college recruiters who came for me only saw *him.* He walked on my back straight toward a full scholarship at a major university."

I shot him a look. "What? You expected him to pass on a great opportunity to spare your pride?"

"No, I—" He ran a hand through his hair. "Look, I know I sound like a bitter asshole bemoaning a high school football game, but that's just one example. The man scored a national championship, he's famous, people want to sponsor him for everything, he has two kids, a wife who is *insane* about him, loving parents who are still around—"

"You're threatened by the man who needs his wife to tell the waitress his steak is underdone?"

"I'm not threatened by him, or *anyone*," he said pointedly. "Tyson Copeland is a measuring stick—the more fortune favors him, the more I'm reminded that I never had *anything* good in my life once I was born. He proves that my Grandpa was right."

Beau could deny it all he wanted, but he was competing against his old teammate. He was the only one keeping score and he was still losing.

"I lost my..." he swallowed, "...the state championship, then my shot at playing pro—the only chance I had to do anything other than work for my family's company—, then I lost my spot as top of the class, then I lost all my friends once they inevitably turned out to be greedy little snakes, then I lost the *love of my life* because she was just as bad as them."

I stiffened as he choked on his words. It always came back to Katie, didn't it?

He took a quick breath and regained his composure. "But I actually get to be a dad now. Maybe this time, fortune will finally favor me."

I folded my arms on top of my belly and glanced out the window as we headed into the country. "Maybe so."

But only if Beau could learn to let things go.

"I have my doubts, though." He let out a shallow laugh. "You know, back when I was in middle school, Grandpa forced me to volunteer at his family center because he was afraid my dad was raising me to be a spoiled brat. I'll never forget him thumping the platinum handle of his cane against one of those cardboard Thanksgiving boxes and saying, 'You're closer to needing one of these than having anything good ever happen to you again.'"

My blood suddenly ran cold. The Thanksgiving boxes. "How... how long did you work at the Fontaine Family Center?"

"Until I graduated high school," Beau answered. "Grandpa had me packing boxes full of food for every holiday drive they did."

My lip trembled. He put the food in the boxes that I ate. He saw my mom's name on that highlighter yellow clipboard. Had he also seen me in the car line, ducking my head from shame?

Regardless if he saw me, he knew. He knew the whole time that I had taken his charity, and not once in the years I had known him had he thrown it in my face, even when we had been at each other's throats.

Hell, I don't think he had never even mentioned it—to *anyone.*

I turned to him, hoping he could catch the look I was giving him even though he was driving. "Th-thank you. Thank you for never teasing me about...coming to the holiday drives."

He turned onto the manor's driveway. "Why would I? I had no control over the circumstances of my birth and neither did you." He flashed me a little smile. "If I was going to tease you, it had to be about something you earned."

I swallowed as we circled around the fountain in the driveway and headed to the garage. I knew Beau was keeping his own secrets, but I never suspected that he was also keeping mine.

I wouldn't know him completely until after the twins were born, but unlike my dad, or the guy with the smelly apartment, or the guy who laughed at me when I vomited on the carnival ride...

...I at least knew Beau was a good person.

17
Beau

The night we got back from the Kaye house renovation, Olivia stopped breathing.

I bolted upright in bed when I heard her gasping across the hallway. I threw off my blankets and sprinted into her room to find her in bed, struggling to get up.

My hands found hers in the darkness and I pulled her into a sitting position. Her hand pressed against her heaving chest as she gulped in air.

"I...I got stuck...on my back," she panted. "Th-the babies just...*crush* my lungs now..."

"Hey, you're all right," I said softly as I rubbed her back. "Just take a breather and get some rest, OK?"

I took her blue water cup off her nightstand and offered it to her. She took a few small sips and I stepped back toward my room.

"Wait," Olivia said, "what if I get stuck again?"

I turned back to her. Even in the barest of moonlight filtering through the lace curtains, I could see Olivia's wide eyes shining with tears.

My mouth suddenly went dry. "Do you...do you want me to stay?"

She gripped her cup with both hands and nodded.

I walked around to the other side of the bed and stared at the mattress like I was looking over the precipice of a cliff. My eyes flicked up to Olivia and she gave me an expectant look back, silently giving me permission to enter new territory.

I held my breath as I slowly got in bed next to her and rested my head on the pillow. The mattress was soft enough to sink into, but the air around us was stiffer than a board.

I cleared my throat. "I'm a pretty light sleeper, but don't be afraid to shake me awake if you need me."

Olivia sank down onto her side of the mattress and cuddled her pregnancy pillow. "Don't tempt me, Beau."

Only after she closed her eyes did I dare to close mine.

I didn't go back to my bed the next night, or the night after that. We made an unspoken agreement that I was her bedroom sentinel. I helped her get out of bed each morning and also in the middle of the night if she needed. I propped her feet up at the end of the day and watched documentaries with her until she passed out. I even brought Titus's bed into Olivia's room so he wouldn't feel left out.

Though we shared a bed, I didn't consider us sleeping together. The mattress was big and Olivia stayed within the confines of her U-shaped pregnancy pillow, so it felt like we were in our own separate twin beds.

Sometimes, when the glow of the TV hit Olivia's sleeping body just right, I caught a glimpse of one, or even both, of my babies moving beneath her pajamas. As much as I cherished the sight, I didn't dare touch. The edge of Olivia's pregnancy pillow made an invisible wall topped with barbed wire between us and I knew better than to venture where I wasn't welcome.

But once, I caught myself stroking the tail of Olivia's braid that had crossed over to my side of the bed. When we binged season two of "Murder in the Heartland," I turned to ask her if the defense lawyer was full of shit only to be disappointed that she had already fallen asleep. When my thoughts were too loud at night, I would glance over at Olivia and wonder how her soft, round face would feel in my hands. Sometimes I'd even catch her worrying her bottom lip during a dream. Other times, I would mentally trace the generous curve of her hip and just…miss her.

I started to doubt that my devotion to Olivia was borne purely from obligation, or out of gratitude for the mother of my children, or even from a paternalistic instinct to protect and control.

What I felt for Olivia was similar to what I had with Katie— the urge to give, and give, and give. But with Katie, I was a young man dizzy with love, with Olivia…

…well, with Olivia, I was too busy thinking about what I felt so I wouldn't actually have to feel it.

At some point, I had stopped putting aside my annoyance with Olivia for the sake of the twins and just…enjoyed being around her. I slept better near her. Her argumentative ass kept me mentally sharp. Even though I wouldn't confess to it under prolonged torture, her little murder shows were damn entertaining.

But any time I started breathing easy around her, a steely voice in the back of my mind reminded me of the cold, hard facts of our situation.

She never wanted to be with me.

She was only in my house because of the babies.

She's leaving me as soon as they are born.

Though I tried to convince myself our situation was only temporary, the logical parts of my brain wouldn't accept it. No matter what could happen, we were Annie and Brady's parents forever. Olivia and I would see each other every holiday. We would sit next to each other at our children's graduations and weddings. The rest of our lifetimes were tied together with twin ribbons, but Olivia acted as if she were about to be dragged by her neck beside me for all eternity.

As I paced the upstairs hallways, mentally sorting the facts and my feelings into orderly little boxes to file away, my phone buzzed with an alert that someone was outside. Before I could check the camera, the doorbell rang.

Puzzled, I headed down the stairs. Titus ran across the foyer and beat me to the front door. I gave him a little scratch behind the ear and ordered him to sit before I opened the door.

A huge delivery truck was parked out front and two men were unloading dozens of large cardboard boxes onto the front steps. Had Olivia been shopping again?

One of the men slid a stack of boxes off a dolly onto the concrete and I read the address label of the top box—they were all addressed to Cheryl Fontaine.

I furrowed my brows and pulled out my phone to call Mom. She picked up after a few rings, but the faded sounds of laughter and Celtic music hit my ears first.

"I'm in the city for the St. Paddy's parade," Mom answered quickly. "Make it zippy before I have to order more green beer."

I gestured toward the growing stacks of boxes. "Mom, what the hell did you buy? The front lawn looks like a warehouse!"

"You sent me the baby registry, so I got it all," she said casually.

"Mom, that registry was supposed to be for everyone coming to the baby shower!"

Mom's lips smacked like she had just pulled them off a glass pint. "And? You need that stuff don't you?"

I wasn't exactly sure what all Olivia had put on the registry, but I couldn't imagine that her prudent ass would want anything unnecessary.

"Thank you, but—" I looked over my shoulder into the foyer to make sure Olivia wasn't listening. "She didn't want all of that here. She's going to set up a nursery back at her apartment once she recovers from delivery."

"Well, that's stupid," Mom said bluntly. "Especially since I've already been setting up the nursery at the manor."

I instantly turned on my heels and headed up the stairs. "You *what?*"

"Damn, son, I don't think I'm drunk enough to be slurring my speech," she replied. "You heard me—I took down the crap from the fake baby and started prepping for the real babies. Olivia left some decor ideas on her registry and I got inspired."

The questions racing through my mind stalled from the panic of Mom getting inspired with house decor again. I quickly walked down the upstairs hallway to the old nursery and opened the door. To my pleasant surprise, all I could find inside was the Fontaine family rocking chair and newly-installed striped wallpaper the color of silver mist.

I hadn't even smelled any wallpaper glue. Mom must have used special low-fume adhesive for Olivia's sake, but how did I not know that she was in the house renovating?

"Wh-when did you do this?" I asked. "How did you get into the manor without anyone knowing?"

"You're always messing around in the gym or on the phone with your finance guy whenever I come in. Your kids are going to get into all sorts of trouble if you don't learn to pay attention!"

I sighed and pinched the bridge of my nose. "Noted. I'll deal with this, you have fun at the parade. Please don't get arrested."

"The law isn't fast enough to catch me, unlike some," she teased. "Love you!"

After she hung up, I went downstairs and gave the delivery guys a fistful of bills so they would take the cardboard clutter up to the nursery and off my front steps.

I rubbed the back of my neck as I went to check on Olivia. I wasn't sure how she was going to take the fact that the twins' nursery was being set up here, or that my mother took it upon herself to buy the whole registry list, or even that she had been in the house.

I grabbed a small box of tissues from my bedroom before crossing the hall. Olivia had so very little that she could control anymore, she would probably burst into tears when I told her the nursery had slipped out of her control too.

Slowly, I entered her room. Olivia was lying on her side in the bed. Though her breathing was slow, it wasn't in her usual sleeping rhythm. The TV wasn't even on.

I cleared my throat to make sure she knew I was there. "Hey… Mom bought everything off the registry and it all got delivered today. I'm sorry, I know you wanted to manage that yourself."

Olivia let out a low hum of acknowledgement and didn't move.

I passed the box of tissues from one hand to the other. "She also, um, started setting up the nursery down the hall. I didn't tell her to, she just…wanted to help, I guess. She put up the silver wallpaper you liked."

"Is that what all that noise was last week?" she asked dully.

I let out a silent sigh—Olivia was having another low day. With the third trimester just around the corner, her movements have gotten slower, she was in bed more often, and she was somehow even quieter. The only time I had seen her spark back to life was when we went to Miss Kaye's. I never knew someone could be so ecstatic over paint and paper on walls in an old house. Had Mom not ruined half the manor with her…*eccentric* style, maybe Olivia would have been just as excited about *this* old house.

Well, Olivia had a history degree. Maybe she spent time with her smutty books and murder shows because she craved a good story.

I carefully put the tissue box on the nightstand next to her mom's ashes and then held out my hands. "Come on, Adams. We're going on an adventure."

She groaned. "I don't want to move."

"It'll be short, I promise." I placed my hand on her shoulder and gave it a little rub. *"And* it involves me info-dumping about historic home design for at least twenty minutes."

Her hands wrapped around her belly and she slowly rolled over to face me. I gently slid her glasses onto her face and helped her out of bed. She wore a little green lounge set meant for nursing, so the underside of her belly peeked out from her blousy top. Even though her hair was a fluffy mess and she wore those clunky, yet practical, anti-slip shoes, she still looked quite cute.

And if I could get her to smile, she'd be damn adorable.

Olivia didn't even bat an eye at the delivery men wheeling the stacks of boxes into the nursery as I led her into the hallway. We stopped on the second story landing in front of a small portrait of a man with a snowy white beard sitting with his bright-eyed wife.

I gestured at the portrait. "This is Jacques and Adelaide Fontaine, my great-*great*-grandparents. As one of Elren's founding families, they were the first to buy up the land around the city and they struck oil. Thanks to that bit of luck, they went from being moderately well-off to unmanageably wealthy almost overnight."

Olivia admired the portrait. "Adelaide had a fantastic sense of fashion. If I had oil money, I'd sparkle like that too."

My eyes wandered from the jeweled hairband that held back my great-great-grandmother's dark pin curls to her draping pearl necklaces and the shining rings on her slender hands. "Not all of it came from oil money."

I pointed to the ring on Adelaide's left hand. "Jacques fell in love with Adelaide when they were children, so he spent ten years saving every penny he earned until he had enough to buy her a proper wedding ring."

Olivia took a closer look at the photo. "He must have saved a lot of pennies. That diamond is huge, especially for the time."

"Love is worth waiting for, I guess." I turned over my shoulder to look at the foyer below. "After the black gold flooded their bank account, Jacques and Adelaide built Fontaine Manor. The manor was a spectacle back then mainly because of its massive size. The idea was to have lots of kids and have everyone live together…but turns out the Fontaines aren't all that fertile."

Olivia cut me a sly look. "Until you."

I bit my tongue to hold down a smirk. "What can I say? I'm the oddball of the family." I turned her attention to another portrait. "Jacques and Adelaide did have an heir to the family fortune, though—my great-grandpa Louis."

She turned to Louis's black-and-white framed portrait. He gave her a cheeky smile beneath his pencil-thin mustache.

"He looks like a trouble-maker," she remarked.

I held down another smile. "We'll get to him in a minute." I pointed to another portrait. "In complete contrast, here's a man you actually know—the first Beau."

Despite being a young man in his portrait, Grandpa was just as buttoned-up as I had remembered as a kid. His cold blue stare even kept the yellow tint of the mid-century photograph from looking too warm. Grandma stood next to him in the portrait with her hair teased a foot high and her pink lips stretched into a smile.

I just hoped I wouldn't have to come up with an excuse for why Dad wasn't on the portrait wall.

Olivia pointed to a smaller framed photo. "And who is this? Do you have a female cousin?"

I swallowed as my eyes found the photo of a squinting baby being devoured by an ivory monster of lace and ribbons. "No...that's me."

She bit her lower lip. "What an outfit."

"That lace gown is a Fontaine male tradition that I intend on breaking." I turned toward the elevator. "I hope Brady heard that."

"He just punched me in the liver to express his earnest relief," she replied dryly.

"Anyway," I said as I pushed the call button on the elevator. "Since great-grandpa Louis was the only child, Jacques and Adelaide tended to spoil him. If he wanted it, he got it."

The elevator doors slid open and Olivia stepped inside. "That doesn't sound like anyone else I know."

I rolled my eyes and entered the elevator. "Louis was...a bit of a partier, to put it lightly. So, instead of allowing their son to get rowdy on the streets of Elren night after night, Jacques and Adelaide made a compromise to try to contain him."

Olivia's eyebrows furrowed as I pressed the third floor button. "They contained him in the attic?"

The elevator rose and I laughed. "Who said the third floor was an attic?"

The golden cage doors parted and Olivia gasped. She wandered onto the polished marble floor and I couldn't contain my smile. Not since the twins' last ultrasound had I seen a more beautiful sight than Olivia admiring the manor's ballroom. She stood in the middle of the dance floor designed to look like a sparkling pool and looked up at the huge stained glass window on the ceiling. The hand-crafted window featured pink water lilies, green lily pads, flying egrets, and lagoon blue marbled glass.

Where I had hoped for a smile, I was instead treated to pure wonder.

I hadn't taken anyone up to the ballroom since Katie and I practiced our first dance for our wedding. Maybe I could replace that bittersweet memory with a better one.

I pulled out my phone as I entered the ballroom and opened my playlists. In an instant, swing music blasted through the nearly invisible speakers around the ballroom.

Olivia jumped as I wrapped my arm around her shoulder.

"Go back in time with me, Adams." I turned her toward the row of tall windows facing the circular driveway. "Picture it—cars from everyone in Elren, and even people from all over the state, lined up out front."

I spun her around to face a clamshell alcove in the far wall. "A big band is set up there. The best musicians from the city would come all the way out here to play for Louis's parties."

I ran off to the opposite wall and stood in front of a large mural of a willow tree. "Elren had a complete prohibition on alcohol until forty years ago." I gave her a wink. "But laws don't apply when you're a Fontaine."

Olivia covered her mouth to hide a giggle as I opened up the panels in the wall that the willow tree hid, revealing a full bar with shining bottles of old booze lining the glass shelves.

"And that wasn't all." I turned back to face her and gestured to the far wall as if I could conjure a party from the past. "He had towers of flowing champagne, trays of delicious food, and…"

I took Olivia by the hands and pulled her in as close as her belly would allow. I looked into her eyes as a soft smile played on her lips.

I won.

I gave her a triumphant smile back. "…everyone at the party would dance until dawn."

She let out a little yelp as I spun her around in time with the music, leading her in the first couple steps of a swing dance. Her little moment of shock brightened into a laugh and I felt nothing less than golden.

Olivia stumbled over my feet. "Beau! You're going too fast!"

I slowed to a stop in the middle of the dance floor and splayed my hand across her back to brace her. "How much dancing experience do you have?"

She gave me a sheepish look. "Does dancing on tables at bars count?"

"No." I pulled out my phone and quickly selected another song on my playlist. A slow piano waltz softly played throughout the ballroom. The first notes of the song sent a pang through my chest that I tried to ignore. "Consider this your exercise for the day—you just have to follow me."

Though I expected a protest, Olivia merely steadied her hold on my hand and slid her other hand up my bicep.

I took my first step back and slowly led her around the dance floor as I taught her how to waltz. Olivia looked around the ballroom instead of up at me, but I didn't mind. I needed to keep an invisible wall up—reminding myself that she wasn't mine and didn't want to be.

Although, at that moment, her belly holding my babies had never pressed against me before. I had never noticed the slight lavender scent of her shampoo, either.

But maybe I had thoughtlessly selected the song Katie and I were fated to waltz to at our wedding for a reason. Beneath the delight of the moment was the undercutting melancholy that every second of closeness was temporary. Happiness was fleeting. Olivia's time in the manor—time with *me*—was running out.

And while I had her in my arms for what might have been the final time, all I wanted was to kiss her. Not ravenously in secret, but slowly as a sigh as the golden sunlight brightened her eyes.

Just once. Just so she knew she could always come back to me.

My feet went still and she paused the dance with me. Slowly, I took my hand off the small of her back. Right as I lifted my hand to tilt up her chin, Olivia sniffed and stepped away. I looked down and caught her eyes glistening with tears.

"I'm sorry, I..." she stammered before covering her mouth with her hands.

She retreated to the bandstand and sat on the step leading into the clamshell as she cried. I followed her, hoping I hadn't pushed her too far.

She pressed the heels of her palms into her eyes as I quietly sat next to her.

I resisted the urge to pull her into a hug. "Are you tired? Are you hurting anywhere?"

"No...it's just..." she wiped away the tears on her cheeks. She put her glasses back onto the bridge of her nose and stared out into the ballroom, deep in thought.

Was I foolish enough to hope that she was having her doubts about leaving? That she realized she would miss me too?

She blew out a shaking breath. "I always hated you because you had what I didn't. When we were in school, you had money, a big group of friends who worshiped the ground you walked on, and everything was just so easy for you. And now..." She swallowed and gestured out to the ballroom. "I hate that you have a history—a good story—because you have a family and I don't."

I rested my elbows on my knees to distract from the heavy disappointment sinking into my stomach. She was only jealous of my family, but she had no idea what the Fontaine family history even was.

I ran my hand through my hair and stared at the blue tile of the dance floor. "Everyone has a history, sugar. You just have to find yours."

Olivia whipped her head toward me. "You think I haven't tried? All I have of my dad is a bad reputation and a name—Johnny Adams. Do you have any idea how many men named John or Johnny Adams there are in this country? Even the best background check programs at my old firm couldn't find him."

She hiccupped. "I want my babies to have my last name because I wanted my mom's last name. I never understood why she wanted to honor that man instead of just using her sense!" She threw out her hands. "The Fontaine name carries a legacy, memories, *meaning*. What does the Adams name carry? Nothing! Because the man I was named for stole everything from my mom and left us with nothing."

My heart started to ache, but then she turned to me with a ferocity in her eyes that I hadn't seen in months. "So every single time you've ever called me 'Adams,' you really just called me *nothing*."

I held my breath, forcing my next words behind an imaginary gate as if it were a race horse rearing in its stall.

Then there's no reason to give Annie and Brady his name.

The argument was sound, and since Olivia was emotional and vulnerable, it was sure to win her over. I would finally conquer the last name debate. I could get her to agree to securing the Fontaine legacy once and for all.

But though the opportunity was laid before me, I couldn't take it. Unlike the Fontaine men that came before me, I was weak. My sense of self-preservation had withered to dust. Just like when she had broken down in the kitchen on Christmas, I wanted to break down too.

I couldn't let the mother of my children believe she was nothing.

Not when comparing herself to the Fontaine legacy. Not when she didn't even know the real truth.

I ran my hands down the front of my jeans. Only because I knew my mother was drunk at a parade and would have no idea what I was about to confess to, I took a deep breath in and gathered every molecule of courage I had left in my body.

"Olivia, don't ever think you're inferior to me because of your father," I said over the soft sniffles of her crying, "especially when I haven't told you about my dad."

Olivia

He had just wanted to talk about his father, but sitting in Beau's bedroom made me feel naughty—like we were sneaking around under our parents' noses.

Beau stood in front of me, his hands gripping the oak dresser behind him, and stared at the floor. Though I merely sat in his bed—on top of the covers, even—, a prickle of unease crawled through me.

My eyes wandered around the room to distract me from the silent intimacy. His room was messier than I expected, with every bookshelf and flat surface filled with clutter from both high school and college. The areas not taken up by old physiology textbooks or football memorabilia were full of dozens of framed photos. Amongst the frames were pictures of his grandfather leaning on his platinum cane, his mom smiling and holding baby Beau at the beach, and even photo strips of him and Katie at a college formal.

Though I quickly averted my eyes from any images of Katie, they always found a man who looked just like Beau in the frames—blonde, always wearing a polo, and flashing perfect white teeth in every snapshot. I recognized his father from the brief glimpses I saw of him at football games and school assemblies. Everyone knew Beau's dad worked a lot to be as rich as he was, so it was like an A-list celebrity had stepped on campus during the rare times he showed up.

Beau blew out a breath and kept his eyes on the floor. His knuckles rippled as he tightened his grip on the edge of the dresser.

"When you have three Beaus in one house," he said, "everybody goes by a different name. Grandpa was, well, Grandpa or Big Daddy, depending on who was addressing him. Dad was Junior or…Dad, obviously. Mom and Grandma called me Beau most of the time since Dad and Grandpa were always out of the house working, but Dad…"

Beau looked up at the frames on his shelves. "Dad called me Buddy."

I tracked his gaze to a photo of a six-year-old Beau holding up a freshly-caught fish, his father beaming behind him.

"He sent me to the best football camps every summer, but he was the first one to teach me how to throw a ball," Beau said. "It became obvious when I was in middle school that he wanted to give me an 'out,' an opportunity to be something other than just a Fontaine heir. Our dream was for me to be quarterback for the Crimson Knights, then go pro, then come back to the company when Dad was ready to retire."

I never knew much about football other than what I could pick up between plays before chomping on my clarinet reed and playing the Elren High fight song. Going to the state championship game senior year had been a big deal, and even though I had hated to admit it, Beau was the main reason the Oilers got that far.

He was big, strong, rich, and talented—even when we were teenagers. There wasn't a single person in school who didn't envy him.

Beau released his grip on the dresser, abandoning his anchor, and paced in front of the footboard. He raked back his hair as his lips twitched, silently practicing his next words.

"Dad said he'd be at the gulf during the semifinals game senior year," he said quickly, as if he had to force it out. "He told me if we won, he'd be at the front row of the championship game. All his recruiter friends from the state colleges would be there too. We'd finally get to have our dream."

I smiled. "I remember the semifinals game. You threw the football sixty yards for that final touchdown." My eyes dropped to my hands on my belly, but I couldn't banish my smile. "I had no idea how you'd done it—throwing a ball so far for someone to catch it *just* in time."

Heat creeped across my cheeks. Was I really bragging on him?

The floorboards stopped creaking under his feet and I looked up. He had stopped pacing and looked back at me with a crooked smile.

"I had to win," he responded.

He held his breath and started to pace again. "The team went out for a late-night dinner to celebrate after the game. When I got back to the house…"

He chewed on his lip. "I just remember hearing a horrible banging noise upstairs as soon as I walked into the kitchen. Then screaming. I sprinted up the stairs and…"

My stomach knotted as Beau clenched his jaw. His hand wrapped around the corner of the footboard and he held on for a few heartbeats.

"I found Mom," he said as he looked at the floor. "She was in their room, whacking at the marital bed with an ax and screaming 'He's gone, he's gone…'"

I glanced at the wall of pictures of Beau's father. Beau wasn't making sense. He said his father was still the CEO of Fontaine Energy. Beau's parents divorcing would have been such a big scandal everyone across the state would have heard about it.

"Gone?" I asked. "What do you mean?"

Beau let go of the footboard and threw out his hands. "You tell me, Olivia. You love a good story. What does it mean when a rich man is gone?"

I bit my lip as my mind ran through every salacious documentary I ever watched, every thriller I ever read, and every juicy rumor about the Fontaines I had ever heard. I combined all the tales of broken families and the rot of wealth into three theories.

"Well," I said quietly. "He could have had an affair…"

Beau's eyebrows raised and a tight smile pulled on his lips. "Come on, you can do better than that."

"He…he committed a horrible crime and fled to another country. Or—"

"Don't be bashful now," he said with a sad gleam across his eyes. "Just tell me what you think."

Slowly, I looked up at the photo of Beau's grandfather—the man who built and funded the Fontaine Family Center, whose name was on multiple buildings in town, and who supplied massive endowments to Lindsay University. The man was a giant, and anyone following him would stumble in the craters of his footsteps.

"Or...he wanted an 'out,' too," I said.

Beau nodded. "That's similar to my theory."

I furrowed my brows. "Wait...you don't know?"

He shook his head. "Mom won't tell me. I've begged and begged but..."

His hand curled into a fist and he lightly tapped the top of the footboard. "When you run a family company, the family has to stay intact. Otherwise, cracks in the foundation send the entire house crumbling down. Regardless of what happened between my parents...they stayed married. Couldn't risk filing for divorce and everyone in town speculating how the company's assets would get split since my dad was the only known heir to the company at the time."

"I thought you had an aunt?"

"Aunt Liz is my mom's sister," Beau said. "Dad does have an older sister, but she took an oath of poverty and runs an elephant sanctuary. She's not part of the business or the family estate."

Another Fontaine who wanted out.

"I still looked for him, though," Beau said. "I looked for him at the championship game. I kept turning my head to his usual seat in the bleachers, waiting to see him there like he promised."

I rubbed my belly, cradling my babies in my arms. *That's* why we lost the game. Back then, I had gleefully thought Beau's luck had finally run out when the game-ending whistle blew. I relished in the sight of his head hanging in shame, finally humbled after all those years of him being the top dog.

Never would I have guessed that he had actually lost something much bigger than a football game.

Beau turned to the shelves. "And as much as I hate to admit it, even ten years later, I still look for him. I used to always turn my head when I saw a tall blonde man in the corner of my vision—even when I was at a club. Sometimes I think he's backpacking across the world like I did after Katie and I broke up, and one day he'll come back like I had to."

I chewed on my lower lip. "Has he ever talked to you?"

"Once," Beau responded. "High school graduation day. Right before the ceremony, he sent me an email from his business address."

Oh God, no wonder he had been such an ass when I walked across the stage. His dad disappeared and then sent a fucking *email* about it?

His throat bobbed as he swallowed. "He said, 'Someday you'll understand, Buddy.' I thought maybe when I got to college I'd get it. Or after Katie and I got married. Even now, holding the company and family legacy on my back and my back alone…I still don't understand why he left me."

My throat went tight as he turned to face me. How many times had I stayed awake at night wondering the same thing? Why did my dad leave? Why wasn't I enough to stay for?

How many times had I forced myself to prove that I was enough to stay for…but still never gave any man the chance to leave?

"And now that Annie and Brady are coming," Beau said, "I never will understand why he left."

I swallowed a lump in my throat that felt heavy as an anchor. Beau might have been rigid, secretive, and a bit of an ass sometimes, but he wasn't going to be like either of our dads.

A tear escaped and I quickly wiped it away with the heel of my palm. "We've got some fucked up families, don't we?"

Beau scoffed and shook his head. "You don't even know half of it. Grandma had a pill problem. Great-grandpa Louis got into so much trouble that his parents had to bribe police departments in multiple states just to keep him out of prison. And Grandpa..."

He threw out his hand to his grandfather's portrait. "If I had followed through with that trial suing the hospital, everyone was going to find out Grandpa had dementia, diagnosed even before my dad left. If that information got out, the managers at headquarters would have questioned every one of his decisions. Dad could have even come back and challenged the changes in the will."

Beau's eyes widened and he cursed under his breath.

I shifted on the bed. "Listen, I used to be a witness for will updates at my old firm. You don't have to explain to me how tragic it is."

Beau let out a shallow laugh. *"Tragic."*

He shook his head, his jaw ticking like he was making a decision. Before I could say anything, he crossed to his window and pulled the curtains open.

He pointed out to the pasture bathed in the blue haze of twilight. "Who do you think owns all that land?"

Where was he going with this? "Um...the company? A family trust?"

Beau turned from the window. "Who owns the company itself? What about this house? And the stocks? And all the other investments? And buildings? And mineral rights?"

My only other guess would have been Beau's father, but then why would Beau worry about his dad contesting the will? Then my eyes slowly widened as the realization dawned on me.

"Your dad is just the CEO of Fontaine Energy," I said softly. "But *you* own it all."

He stepped around the footboard to stand on the side of the bed closest to me. "Imagine not only dealing with the death of your grandfather on your 20th birthday, but also finding out that he left you everything. I went from drunkenly puking on the dirty bathroom floor of the frat house to being worth $860 million with a single fucking phone call."

My internal calculator whirred. I had thought my $98 million Herringbone verdict was an incomprehensibly large amount of money...but Beau's fortune was worth more than *eight* of them.

I had always considered Beau rich, but with his *family's* money, not his own. Knowing that he was in complete control of nearly a billion dollars before he could legally drink...and his estate was certainly worth *even more* now...

I wanted to throw up.

Beau placed his hands on the mattress and leaned in, his eyes tightening. "Everyone I let close to me only wanted a bite out of that fortune. I couldn't take it anymore. Dad ran the company, so I just...ran. I traveled the world. I had five fake names. I crawled through every club and bar I found to escape the deep, cold loneliness."

My lip trembled. "You weren't the only one. I used to toss back shots on a Tuesday night and crawl into bed with *anyone* just so I could forget that I was working myself to death."

Even Ashley had never heard me admit that. Had my old firm not fired me, my heart probably would have given out and I would have died at my desk. My ambition was both a drive and a disease, but I didn't know how to stop.

When you grow up with nothing, nothing is ever enough.

He canted his head. "But did you get arrested? When I was twenty-five, I beat up a guy because I saw him spiking a girl's drink. When the cops showed up, they found some party drugs in my pocket and put me in cuffs. I spent three days in county jail before Mom bailed me out and then covered the whole thing up."

Was he trying to scare me? Didn't he realize I was a lawyer and had seen people do more than just a pocketful of party drugs in an evening?

I leveled his stare. "Do you think I'm going to judge you?"

Beau laughed. "I tell you all my biggest secrets and you think I'm worried about you judging me?"

He leaned in closer, the weight of his palms making the mattress sink deeper. That familiar heat bloomed across my cheeks as his face was mere inches away from mine.

"I don't care if you judge me, Olivia Adams," he said softly. "I want to know if you'll destroy me."

I was better than to kick a man when he's down, but the Olivia I had been in the past might have done it. I would have weaponized his secrets and humbled him, sent him crashing down until we were finally at eye-level. I wanted him to be nothing, just like me.

But now that I was a mother, and now that I might have even been Beau's friend, I could never dream of hurting him.

"If you're so afraid of me," I asked in a measured tone, "why tell me everything?"

Beau took in a quiet breath. "Up in the ballroom, you said that at least the Fontaine name means something." He pushed off the mattress and stood tall, gesturing to the shelves of photos behind him. "Now you know what the Fontaine name really means. We run. We hide. We guard our money and our truth like dragons in a cave, and we behave just as gruesomely. My name is nothing to be proud of."

I turned to the shelf of photos, but a flash of blue on the bottom shelf caught my eye. There, next to a yearbook open to a photo of Beau and I standing with the rest of the debate team, was the sticky note I had left on his birthday coffee months ago. Next to it, almost like it was a companion to the first one, was my crumpled pink note that read: *Work until your name is on the building!*

I had written that note and pasted it to the bottom of my computer monitor in my old office, dreaming of the day when the firm's sign read "Parker, Hill, and Adams." After a lifetime of a name with a bad meaning, I wanted to give it a new story and a better reputation.

My dad might have been a crook, but I wanted to prove to the world that I was worthy enough to have my name on a building, just like Beau.

The twins rolled around inside me. I was about to tell Beau exactly why I wanted to build a new story of my name by giving it to my babies…but that idea suddenly seemed so shallow. Neither Annie nor Brady would be just an Adams or a Fontaine, they would be themselves. They would make their own stories and have their own mistakes and triumphs.

Maybe we both cared too much about winning a battle over a name and not enough about who our babies were going to be. For better or for worse, they were going to have parts of the both of us.

If we were going to truly love our babies, we needed to love ourselves first.

Beau's eyes locked with mine. "You thought your name made you nothing, but how valuable is the Fontaine name now?" His mouth turned up in a bitter smirk. "What am I *really* worth?"

The air around us tightened, winding around my lungs like rope, as Beau waited for me to respond. His elbows remained locked as he propped himself up on the mattress, his biceps flexing beneath his sleeves. He was bracing himself for a scathing appraisal from his old rival.

Instead, I reached up and hugged him.

Beau's chest froze as I wrapped my arms around his shoulders, my fingertips running against the soft, waffled fabric of his shirt. His elbows buckled as I pulled him closer to me. My cheek rested against his neck as his scent filled my nose—like a warm winter, evergreen.

The mattress shifted as he sat beside me, freeing his arms to wrap around me with a deep exhale. We held one another in the haunting silence, but I wouldn't let the ghosts of Beau's past hurt him again.

"You are worth staying for," I whispered. "You always were."

He let out another deep exhale against my hair and tightened his arms around me. His quiet voice rumbled in his chest as he responded, "And so are you."

We were the kids without fathers, but just for a few minutes, we had each other.

My eyes started to get misty, but I was so damn tired of crying. How long had I spent fighting the numbness of loss that I completely neglected to leave room for joy?

The twins were coming, after all.

Slowly, I released Beau and leaned back. He unlocked his arms but rested his hands on either side of me, making the mattress dip.

I looked into those pretty blue eyes and tried to swallow away the tightness in my throat. "This pregnancy has been hard, so hard on the both of us, but…"

I choked down a sob, but that didn't stop a tear from falling. Slowly, he reached forward. He wiped away the tear on my cheek with his thumb and tucked a stray hair behind my ear.

"I'm sick of soaking in my own misery," I whispered, choosing not to add that I was sure Beau was tired of my misery too. "I want to…I want to do something fun. I think we've spent so much time surviving that we forgot how to live."

His hand lingered by my ear, his fingertips lightly smoothing my hair back. A soft smile played on his lips and I had to calm the fluttering in my stomach.

"You're right," he said softly. "I've worried about you for months, but maybe hiding in the house wasn't good for either of us."

I chewed on my lip and bashfully looked away. "I…I liked being in the house, that's not it." I glanced down at my belly peeking out of my nursing top. "It might sound silly, but…I want to get dressed up again. Living in lounge wear hasn't been great for my morale."

Beau lowered his hand and let out a hum of consideration. I glanced up to find him chewing on his tongue, his eyes fixed on a nondescript point on the floor.

Whatever decision he was making, it wasn't an easy one.

After a heartbeat, he looked up and gave me a half smile. "All right, it's a date. You'd better brush up on your dancing skills, sugar."

Olivia

All I wanted was one day to dress up and feel like a person again.

Beau, of course, took that to mean a night at the ritziest gala in the city.

My old firm had purchased a table at a gala a year ago and I was over the moon when they asked me to attend. Though I expected a night of glamour, I instead got to saw through an unseasoned chicken breast as the partners got drunk and schmoozed with wealthy potential clients. I wasn't even sure what charity we were even supporting.

So, when Beau handed me the embossed invitation for the April Showers gala, I was a little skeptical that he would deliver on the fun time he had promised.

But then my dress came in.

I was always a "buy a gown off the rack at the mall" kind of woman, so I doubted that anyone could secure a dress for a body that was thirty-one weeks pregnant with twins.

I should have known better than to doubt Beau Fontaine.

My dress shipped to Fontaine Manor in a large white box that I gleefully opened like it was Christmas morning. I had only told Beau that I wanted my dress to be comfortable, but I squealed when I unwrapped the tissue paper to find pink tulle.

The night of the gala, I slipped the dress over my head and allowed myself a few minutes to admire myself in the bathroom mirror. The dress had gauzy flutter sleeves, a bodice embroidered with large pink and tiny phthalo green flowers, and a tulle skirt that flowed over my belly. Lines of varying lengths of rose gold sequins sparkled throughout the skirt and bodice, catching my eye each time I moved.

I ran my hands over my bump to smooth the tulle and cradled my belly. I rocked my babies side-to-side as I smiled at my reflection in the mirror. I might have been enormous, but *damn* I was pretty.

Beau knocked on my bedroom door as I was putting on my last coat of candy pink lip gloss. I smelled his cologne before I caught a glimpse of him in my bathroom mirror.

He wore a simple black tuxedo with a pink carnation pinned to his lapel. His hair was perfectly combed and gelled, but his neat composure broke when his pretty blue eyes widened. A muscle in his jaw ticked, but otherwise he kept silent.

I looked to the floor as my cheeks heated. Despite the beauty of my dress, the rest of me wasn't up to "gala" standards. My hair was in a simple half updo and I hadn't put on makeup other than blush and mascara since I couldn't stand long enough to do a full face. I didn't know who would be at the gala, but I hoped my plain appearance wouldn't embarrass Beau.

He cleared his throat. I looked up and noticed he was carrying a stack of boxes in his hands—two flat boxes covered in blue velvet and a matte black shoe box.

Beau placed the stack of boxes on the counter.

"Turn around," he ordered.

I brushed my hair over my shoulder and turned my exposed back to him. Though rationally I knew he was just helping me with the zipper I couldn't reach, I still held my breath as his hands found the small of my back.

I stared at the iridescent tile floor, my hands holding my breasts in place as Beau carefully zipped my dress all the way up. His hand lingered at the top of the zipper's track, right where my tattoo was, before releasing me.

The dress was a perfect fit, but Beau was still speechless.

Eager to break the tense silence, I glanced over my shoulder at the boxes on the counter. "What did you bring?"

He lifted the lid of the first blue velvet box, revealing an antique hair comb topped with two butterflies with marbled green glass wings. He quickly opened the second, which held an emerald pendant on a gold chain.

"Pink goes well with green!" I said with a smile. "You remembered!"

He held up the shoe box. "Those are on loan from great-great-grandma Adelaide, but these are all yours."

Beau opened the shoe box to reveal a pair of nude mesh flats dotted with rose gold gems. My hands couldn't yank them out of the box fast enough. The gems glittered and the lacquered red paint on the soles shone brilliantly under the bathroom lights.

I lifted an eyebrow. "What's the point in buying red-bottom shoes if no one is going to see the bottoms?"

Beau gave me a quizzical look. "Because…you like them?"

I turned the sole of the shoe toward him. "I'm surprised you didn't glue non-slip rubber pads onto these. Are you sure you trust me waddling around without my precious safety shoes?"

He gave me a half smile. "Just hang onto me all night and you'll be fine."

I bit my lip and turned around to face the bathroom mirror. With my guidance, Beau securely worked the butterfly comb into my half updo. Then he brushed aside my hair to put on the necklace. I sucked in a breath as he placed the cold emerald pendant on my flushed chest. The hair stood on the back of my neck as Beau's gentle hands fastened the antique clasp.

Once the jewelry was secured, he guided me to one of the bedroom chairs. He knelt in front of me and slipped on my new shoes, one by one.

I could barely breathe at the sight of him on his knees in a damn tuxedo. Slowly, he rose to his feet and gave me an appraising look before extending a hand. "Ready, spring queen?"

I bit my tongue to temper my growing flush and took his hand. He escorted me through the house and helped me into the truck. I cuddled with a pillow and a fluffy throw blanket he had put in the front seat and took a nap while he listened to the Bored Bros on the drive to the city.

When I woke up, the sun was setting and Beau was handing the truck keys over to a valet. Another male valet opened the passenger door to help me out, but Beau quickly stepped in.

"She's delicate," he said to the valet as he offered me his arm. "I've got her."

Beau helped me out of the truck and we walked on a strip of red carpet into a hotel lobby. The light smell of jasmine tickled my nose. A huge chandelier surrounded by dazzling rectangular crystals hung overhead as Beau escorted me across the polished marble floor to the row of elevators.

"So, I'm *delicate* now?" I asked with a raised eyebrow as he called an elevator.

The golden elevator doors opened and we stepped inside.

"It's better than what I wanted to say," he replied. "Which was, 'She's carrying my babies. Touch her and I'll break your arm.'"

I rolled my eyes as the elevator ascended. "Since when did you get so protective? Doctors and nurses touch me all the time."

"*Female* doctors and nurses."

The elevator doors slid open and a crowd of people in pastel gowns and black tie finery waited outside. I clung a little tighter to Beau's arm since I didn't see a single face I recognized in the crowd, but luckily Beau didn't talk to anyone as we waited to sign in.

A cheerful woman at the registration table sat beneath a banner for the Harmony foundation...oh! That was the charity that bought my clarinet when I was in middle school! My inner band kid almost jumped out of my throat and cheered.

"Mr. Fontaine! What a surprise to see you!" The registration woman beamed as she scrambled for a clipboard. "Just a moment and I'll get you set up for the silent auction."

Beau pulled out a folded-up check from his jacket pocket and handed it to her. "Don't bother."

Beau quickly turned away and led me into the gala, but I glanced back just in time to see the woman's face turn stark white when she read whatever number was on the check.

As obnoxious as Beau was with his money, at least he would give kids just like me new instruments that weren't held together with duct tape and band directors' tears.

We parted a shimmering blue tinsel curtain to enter the dark ballroom. Blue and gray uplights along the walls created the illusion of being caught in a rainstorm. White umbrellas full of blue balloons hung upside-down from the ceiling, each decorated with strands of silver beads ending in teardrop-shaped jewels that glittered in the low light. A four-piece band played soft jazz music from center stage.

"You almost gave that woman a heart attack," I said as we weaved through the tables. "I appreciate the sentiment since I used to be a little kid with a song in her heart but moths in her pockets, but do you have to literally throw your money around?"

"Galas are *fundraisers,* Olivia," he replied, "I don't get invites for my dazzling charm and cutting wit. I'd rather just give them the money outright than go through the humiliating circus of an auction."

He led me to the table closest to the stage and pulled out a chair so I could sit before he left to get food. Feeling lost without one of my steel tumblers at my side, I reached for the water goblet in front of me and took a drink. Though I didn't expect anyone else to join us at our table, all eight place settings had a full goblet of ice water in front of them. Beau could get a drink at the bar—those waters were mine.

I clinked my nails against my goblet when I caught sight of the little table sign. I picked up the sign that read "The Fontaine Family."

We weren't having a night out on Fontaine Energy's dime? Businesses usually purchased tables at galas, not private individuals.

Beau would have danced in the town square wearing a clown costume if it gave him a tax write-off, so why wouldn't he try to buy the table as a business expense?

My thumb brushed over the words on the folded cardstock sign. Apparently, business was the last thing on Beau's mind tonight.

Footsteps approached and I quickly shoved the sign into my clutch. Beau placed a plate full of pasta, salad, and rolls that glistened with butter in front of me.

I glanced up at him. "You look like a waiter."

Beau shot me a sly smile as he took his place at the table next to me. "Well, if the feds seize all my assets, I know what my next career move is. Although your child support payments are going to suffer."

"I'm still a lawyer, you know." I laughed as I stabbed my fork into my salad. "If your *dazzling charm* and *cutting wit* doesn't score thousands in tips every night, I'll pay *you* child support."

He picked up his fork and winked. "Good to know you'll always take care of me."

After we ate, he headed to the bar to get us drinks and I took the opportunity to visit the bathroom. After I banished four goblets of water from my body, I stood at the sinks and touched up my lip gloss. A beautiful woman wearing a bright green dress stood at the mirror next to me, wiping away mascara fallout from beneath her eyes.

The bathroom door burst open and another woman in a yellow gown rushed toward the woman in green.

"Tiffany, oh my God," the woman in yellow said. "You'll never believe it—*Beau Fontaine* is here!"

My hand froze, the lip gloss wand pressing into my lower lip. Slowly, I kept applying my gloss so it wasn't obvious that I was eavesdropping.

Tiffany rolled her eyes and opened her clutch. "You're right, I don't believe it." She pulled out a tube of champagne lip gloss and swiped it across her plump lips. "No one has seen him in the city in years."

The woman in yellow folded her arms and leaned against the wall. "Oh yeah? Do you know anyone else who is tall, blonde, and orders Old Fashioneds like they're prescribed to him?"

Tiffany's eyes widened as she dropped her tube of lip gloss into her clutch. "We have to tell her—this is her chance."

Her? Who was this *her?*

The two women left the bathroom as I twisted the lip gloss tube closed tighter than it was designed to go. I eyed "The Fontaine Family" sign at the bottom of my clutch, but I tossed my lip gloss in and snapped it shut.

Just because Beau lived with me didn't mean I had any claim to him. So what if those women were excited to see him? They were the kinds of women he was going to end up marrying, anyway. Hell, the future stepmother to my children could have been outside enjoying the gala and I couldn't do anything to stop it.

I shoved open the bathroom door and made a beeline for the table. I sat down just in time to spot Beau heading toward me with an Old Fashioned in one hand and something fizzy and red in the other.

He sat down and handed me the red drink. "They call it the Cherry Blossom. No alcohol, of course."

I gave him a tight smile as a thanks and took a sip from the straw. Cherry syrup flooded onto my tongue like a sugary punch to the mouth. I stirred my straw to mix the syrup with the soda when I spotted what looked like a tiny stick amongst the ice. Carefully, I plucked out the stick only to find that it was a stem—a cherry stem.

I laughed. "Would you look at that." I pointed to the two cherries hanging from the short stem. "They're twins!"

He rested his cheek on his fist. "Fitting, and adorable."

I held out the cherries and a naughty gleam crossed his eyes. Instead of just taking the cherries from me, he leaned forward and bit the fruit right off the stem.

A giggle burst out of me. "Damn it, Beau, I wasn't trying to feed you!"

He shrugged as he swallowed the cherries. "My mistake. After that child support comment, I thought you were waiting on *me* hand-and-foot for once."

I rolled my eyes and took another sip of my drink as I looked around the room for the women in the yellow and green dresses. Maybe they were off in a corner with their mysterious friend, plotting a way to approach Beau and secure a proposal before the night's end.

If they were willing to put up with his sassy ass for all eternity, they could have him.

As I scanned the room, my eyes caught a familiar face at one of the back tables—one of the partners at my old firm. In fact, the whole table was full of people from my old firm.

I stared at them until I locked eyes with the gray-haired asshole who fired me. Emboldened by my pregnancy super power of not giving a fuck, I raised my drink in acknowledgement. Flustered and embarrassed, he looked away.

Cowards, all of them. Good luck ever getting a $98 million verdict again.

I turned back when I spotted Tiffany and her friend sitting at a table. They whispered to a woman with golden hair twisted in an elegant chignon and all three women glanced at our table.

The blonde woman's eyes widened as she looked past me to find Beau and—*oh*.

Oh my God, it was Katie.

I stared down at the black tablecloth and sucked down my drink, wishing more than ever that I could have actual alcohol.

Of course Katie would be at the gala. Of course she was still interested in Beau. Of course she was wearing a slinky periwinkle dress that showed off just how slim and perky she still was.

If I wasn't sure Beau and I weren't going to end up together before, I was absolutely certain now. The man still kept photos of Katie in his room, for God's sake. He could lament over her breaking his heart and having no integrity, but he'd been secretly wanting her to come back all along.

I swallowed my last sip. There was no way he hadn't seen her by now. I had left him to drink his whiskey and let his eyes wander. The strange relationship purgatory that Beau and I had lived in for the past few months would end tonight. In five minutes, he would make an excuse to get up and go find her.

No, I couldn't wait five more minutes. If I saw him looking at her the way he used to, I'd know where his heart was.

I took in a deep breath and held it, refusing to let myself breathe again until I took the plunge and confirmed my suspicions. As my lungs tightened, I forced my eyes to flick to the side and I caught him.

Beau had his hand wrapped loosely around his drink. His eyes were soft and his jaw was relaxed—like he was gazing at the moon.

It was the exact look he had given Katie in their engagement photos, only he wasn't looking at Katie.

He was looking at me.

My cheeks flushed as my eyes met his, but I turned my head to the stage as the music changed from soft jazz to a gentle, romantic beat.

Beau got up and held out his hand. "Time for your exercise for the day."

I held my breath as he helped me out of my chair and led me to the dance floor to begin a slow waltz. I followed his lead, just like when we had practiced back at home, but I couldn't focus on dancing.

Why had he been looking at me? Were his paternal instincts just that strong? Everything Beau had done for me was to keep me happy and healthy for the good of the twins, but Annie and Brady gave him no reason to look at me like…like *that*.

Beau slowly spun me and I forced myself to come back to earth as he pulled me into his chest, the front of my belly resting against him.

I looked up at him. "You paid the band for this, didn't you?"

He smirked. "Of course I did."

"Do you even know this song?"

"No. Do you?"

I shook my head. He glanced back at the band before looking down at me. "We'll just call this one 'ours,' then."

Other couples joined us on the dance floor as I retreated into myself.

What did *ours* even mean?

Ashley and I had anthems we would belt in the car, songs that I would definitely call ours. The time we both went viral in college was ours. We had jokes that were ours, memories that were ours, and sacred gossip sessions that were undoubtedly ours.

Beau and I had spent so much time together that we would inevitably have things that were ours, too. I supposed a slow waltz was just the first one either of us would name.

Beau was my friend, just like Ashley was.

But Ashley had never looked at me like Beau just did.

And as Beau gently led me around the dance floor with my pregnant belly pressed against him, I didn't think anyone watching us would say we were just friends.

My back started to ache, giving me the perfect escape that I needed.

I swallowed and my eyes flicked up to meet his. "I think I've given this all I can handle."

He spun me once as the song ended. "As long as you got what you wanted out of tonight, we can end it early." He held his arm out for me to grab. "Do you want me to get you a dessert plate before we head up to the room?"

I smiled as I wrapped my hands around his bicep. "Is that even a question?"

Beau had booked a king bed suite on the top floor of the hotel. I sat on my usual side of the bed in my baby blue nightgown, the eucalyptus smell from the hotel shower gel still lingering on my body. My e-reader rested on top of my bump as I read a very spicy dark romance and listened to the gentle rainfall sound from the bathroom as Beau took his shower.

Just as the dark-hearted hero was about to chase the heroine through the woods, my e-reader wobbled. Annie and Brady were awake.

The heat drained from my cheeks—suddenly my book seemed much too vulgar now that I had company.

I lifted my e-reader and looked down at my bump. "There was a content warning at the beginning of the book, you know. Nothing in this story is appropriate for babies, so settle down!"

The bathroom door opened, sending wisps of steam toward the bed, and Beau strolled out as he towel-dried his hair. He hadn't bothered to put on his usual sleep shirt and the pajama bottoms I had gotten him for Christmas rested low on his hips.

He tossed me a look. "Do your dark and twisty little books have you talking to yourself now?"

I scoffed and set my e-reader on my nightstand. "No, the children are just being rambunctious."

"And who do you have to blame for that?" Beau said with a smirk as he put the towel back in the bathroom.

"I don't know," I said as I took off my glasses and placed them on top of the e-reader. "Probably the parent who spent time in *jail*."

Beau sank into the bed beside me and rested his cheek on his fist. "Fine, deny any responsibility. I'll just update my will in case you go off the wall and make me the subject of 'Murder in the Heartland' season three."

I rolled onto my side to face him, but then my breath caught in my throat when I realized we hadn't brought my pregnancy pillow. Our bodies were no closer than a usual night, but now we didn't have a barrier separating us.

A little tingle crawled up the back of my neck as I looked at him, but then Annie and Brady kicked each other so violently that I gasped.

Beau let out a sympathetic hum. "They really are giving you a hard time, huh?"

"Every day," I sighed as my belly rocked.

I clocked his gaze, fixed on my bump and the precious children inside. The tingle on my neck returned and the air around us thickened like honey.

I gnawed on my lip, silently debating my next move, but I gave in. "Do you want to feel them?"

His eyes widened a little as he looked up at me, but he nodded. Slowly, I took his hands and rested them on my belly.

"And...there," I said as I adjusted his hand to my left side. "That's Brady, and on the right is little Annie."

The twins rolled and kicked, each one of their tiny movements popping off like miniature fireworks across my belly. Beau splayed his long fingers across the satin fabric of my nightgown, certainly determined to catch every flutter and bump.

"They're magnificent," he whispered after a few minutes. "You've done a wonderful job, sugar."

My heart swelled. My cheeks ached with my smile as I watched Beau finally feel the twins. His thumbs stroked my belly as he talked to them, telling them how excited he was to meet them and how happy he was to be their dad.

Soothed by his words, the twins settled into stillness.

"You put them to sleep," I whispered.

He let out a little hum and patted my belly. "Goodnight, babies."

He paused, just for a moment, before placing a gentle kiss on the left side of my bump, then my right.

I held my breath. Beau gazed at our babies for a moment more and said, "I love you."

The inside of my chest seized. He said it to the twins, not me— *not me*—, but I still heard him, still savored the words like the first sip of warm tea on a cold night.

This was why I hadn't let him feel the twins sooner. We were close, much too close, and I needed to ground myself back into reality.

I pursed my lips and swallowed. "So, you saw Katie at the gala."

His eyes flicked up to meet mine and his brows furrowed. "She was there?"

He didn't have to lie to spare my feelings. "How could you not see her? She was only a few tables away from us. She certainly saw *you.*"

I instantly hated how bitter I sounded. Beau looked down at the mattress, a muscle feathered in his cheek, and a line formed between his knitted brows as he looked like he was rifling through a dust bin.

After a few moments, his eyes met mine again.

"I don't remember seeing her," he said, "I...I didn't notice any woman there but you."

My lips parted, but I couldn't breathe. All the air in the room suddenly became too tight, too heavy, because he was giving me that look again.

Even though I was stretched and swollen, carried bags beneath my eyes and hunched with the weight of motherhood on my shoulders, Beau still looked at me like I was the only woman in the world.

Though I knew I shouldn't, I couldn't back away. Couldn't stop myself from reaching up and holding each side of Beau's jaw as I drowned in his eyes. Couldn't fight the gravitational pull that drew me closer, or the weight of my lashes as they fluttered closed, or how my lips gently pressed against his.

I had to have him.

Beau slid his fingers through my hair to cradle my head as he kissed me back. I played with the soft hair at the nape of his neck and breathed in the spearing scent of the hotel soap. The sheets rustled beneath us as he pulled me against him as closely as he could. His lips softly trembled against mine with every kiss, as if at any moment either of us could activate a landmine.

But kissing him wasn't enough, just like sharing a bed with him wasn't enough, and dancing with him wasn't enough, and spending nearly every waking moment with him wasn't enough.

"Beau," I whined between kisses. "Please."

"Please, what, Olivia?" he whispered into my mouth.

My hand trailed down the muscles on the side of his body until the very tips of my fingers disappeared beneath the waistband of his flannel pajama pants. My body had ached so much that we hadn't had sex in weeks, but I needed him so badly that I didn't care if it hurt.

"Please," I begged against his lips.

"Just one more," he promised, then he pulled my mouth to his again. The kiss was long and lingering, his thumbs stroking my hair as he gently breathed me in. My toes curled against the sheets—I could have melted like chocolate right onto his tongue.

He slowly broke the kiss and then whispered, "Get comfortable and I'll come to you."

I rolled over, facing away from him so I could rest on my left side. Beau slipped off my underwear and lifted the hem of my nightgown over my hips. He settled in directly behind me, his warm chest against my back and erection pressed into the soft curve of my ass.

He slipped his hand between my legs and traced circles around my clit as he kissed my shoulder and the back of my neck. I moaned and shuddered as he worked. My skin prickled with goosebumps. Pleasure flowed through my body.

When I couldn't take the emptiness any longer, I reached back and wrapped my hand around him, guiding him into me. He groaned as he entered me and I gritted my teeth, fighting against the tightness in my hips to open up to him again.

"Liv," he huffed against my shoulder, "are you sure?"

I reached back and grabbed his thigh, pulling him closer and driving him deeper. I gasped at the sharp stretch inside, but I craved more of him.

"Please," I repeated.

So gently, patiently, he eased his way in until my body finally accepted him. I rolled my head back against my pillow and moaned from deep within my chest as he took me nice and slow, teasing my clit all the way.

His breath huffed against my shoulder blades as he kept pace, placing possessive kisses on my tattoo, my arm, and the top of my breast—everywhere his mouth could reach. He slipped ragged whispers in French across my earlobe that I couldn't understand.

I didn't know how to respond, and even if I did, I didn't want to. So, I arched my back, dug my fingers into his thigh muscle, and let my body talk.

Too long had my different identities been at war with one another—a caring mother holding out against a ruthless lawyer, an independent adult imprisoning the inner child who yearned to be held. Each role placed a new burden on my back, forcing me to question who I was going to be.

But when Beau touched me, all I had to be was a woman.

The tension between my legs mounted until I spilled over. The climax was a long, languid unraveling of my entire nervous system that kept going long after I had surrendered. Just as I thought I couldn't take anymore, my limbs trembled and then went slack.

A sweet exhale left my lips as my eyes felt heavy. I had only barely felt the warmth of Beau finishing inside me before I let out the sigh that sent me to sleep.

The nightstand clock read 3:14 a.m. when I woke up. Beau was still behind me, his chest rising and falling with his easy breath and his arm wrapped around my belly. I quietly peeled myself away from him and got up.

After I left the bathroom, I found myself staring out the window at the lights of the city. A quiet chill settled over me as I spotted the tower where my old firm was, then I found my apartment building—still waiting for me after all this time.

I looked back at Beau, still fast asleep, and then returned my gaze to the window.

Maybe I didn't want to live in the city anymore. An apartment wouldn't be ideal for young children, anyway. I could buy a house in the suburbs so Beau could be closer to the twins.

None of the big firms would work for me anymore, either. I could find a law firm that would let me work from home, or just live off Beau's generous child support and do contract work for other lawyers.

But the idea of continuing to survive from Beau's charity sent off alarm bells in my head—the weaker parts of my psyche were winning. My nervous system woke up again, every instinct in my body blaring so loudly that I had to release the noise.

I rifled through my suitcase until I found my pregnancy journal. I crawled onto the cushioned seat beneath the window and opened my journal to a blank page.

I clicked my pen, and under the glow of the glittering lights of the city, I wrote:

"I can't marry. I just can't. The world is messy, cruel, and unstable, and I learned early on that the only person I could rely on was myself. Everyone in my life either left me or died, so why would Beau Fontaine be any different?

He's not the same Beau from high school, and I don't even think the hateful, snobbish person I remembered had ever even existed. But is enjoying my new companionship with Beau like falling asleep in a poppy field right before a deadly frost rolls in? What if his personality changes? What if he gets sick like Mom did? What if he eventually thinks I'm not worth staying for like my dad did?"

I bit my lip so hard it nearly bled as tears filled my vision, but I let the confession spill out.

"I love him. I love him, I love him, I love him...but I can't keep him. Even though Beau and I are broken in identical places, he deserves someone who will love him loudly and boldly. Someone who will cheer for the Crimson Knights next to him. Someone who already knows how to waltz. Someone who isn't awkward, or defiant, or who fights with him. Someone who will allow herself to be delicate. Someone who isn't afraid to stay.

And if I can't be what he deserves...I have to let him go."

20

Beau

Eyes were windows into the soul, I had once read, so did that mean a window was an eye into the soul?

No, I couldn't open with that. She would think I was high.

I stood at the foot of the stairs in the Kaye house, staring up at that purple and green stained glass window that Olivia loved. My internal poet scribbled down and then struck out line after line as the din of conversation from the twin's baby shower rumbled on.

When I was too afraid of what to say, I said it in French. During intimacy after the April Showers gala, my chest had ached with so much sticky and messy emotion that I only let it escape in a language I knew Olivia couldn't understand.

I had told her that she looked beautiful in her pink dress—that she was the star of the gala, my rose in the rain, and everything I had ever wanted.

I told her I loved her, over and over, and I begged her to stay with me.

But I wasn't brave enough to say it in English.

I kept staring at that window above the landing as I failed to form a solid plan for my next move. The landing where the stairs split off in opposite directions was large enough for two people to stand, making for picture-perfect framing.

Of course, there would be no pictures. I wouldn't take Olivia up to the landing until the baby shower was over and everyone left the house. I'd hold her soft hand as I led her up the stairs and then ask her why she loved that window so much. Then, I'd listen to her talk for as long as she wanted about the history of the house, of the craftsmanship of Art Deco design, or whatever research rabbit hole she had fallen down that led her to adore that window in particular.

Once she was done, I'd just have one other question to ask her.

I held my breath as I reached into the internal pocket of my blazer, ensuring the small leather box was still there.

I'd tell her that she was worth ten years of waiting.

A familiar groan from behind made me turn around. Olivia stood in front of a bronze plaque on the opposite wall with both hands splayed across her belly.

I yanked my hand out of my jacket pocket and ran over to her. "Are you all right?"

She let out a breath. "Just another Braxton Hicks contraction…I think I'm getting them more lately."

"Maybe you should get off your feet, then," I said. "Shouldn't you be seated on your throne or whatever Ashley made for you?"

Olivia rolled her eyes. She wore a beautiful flowing white dress and had aptly-themed sprigs of baby's breath worked into her hair. She was thirty-four weeks pregnant and glowing, looking effortlessly bridal.

The small box in my pocket felt heavier and heavier with each passing second.

"Let me read the rest of the names and *then* I'll sit," she bargained.

Ashley and Tyson had solicited donations for the Kaye house renovation from people all over the world, but they had given a special spotlight to donors that honored female-owned businesses in Elren in the form of a tasteful plaque.

The bronze plaque read: *"To all the Elren businesswomen who made it."*

Nicole Liu's name was on the plaque, and so was Marisol Martinez and her mother, Lupita, who had been cutting my hair since I was a toddler. John Whitecloud donated on behalf of his mother, Charity, who owned the coffee shop downtown.

It was a lovely detail of the house. If Mom had been a businesswoman, I would have put her name on the list too.

But if Olivia had truly read the list of names of all the Elren women who followed in Miss Kaye's footsteps, she didn't pay much attention to them. Instead, her fingertip traced the raised bronze letters of the woman she donated on behalf of—her mother, Annie Brady.

"She'd be so proud of you, you know," I said softly.

Olivia finished tracing the "y" at the end of her mother's name and slowly pulled her hand away from the plaque. "Damnit, Beau, I already almost lost it when I put her ashes on the mantle in the other room. Don't you make me cry in front of all these people."

I reached down and held her hand. "Come on, maybe opening some presents will help."

We walked into the big white room that was filled floor-to-ceiling with pink and blue balloons and twisting crepe streamers. Even though the twins' nursery was going to be purple and green— or *lavender and sage*, as Olivia put it—, Ashley chose classic boy-girl colors for the baby shower. Olivia and I even parked the pink Bel-Air and the blue Mustang on the front lawn to go along with the color scheme.

Olivia pressed into my body as we weaved through the tight crowd toward Olivia's chair. Though the baby shower was technically for the twins, it was also an open invitation for the community to debut the house renovation. I hated the idea of that many people squeezing into our family moment, but Olivia wanted it and who was I to tell her no?

Although I wondered if even *she* expected half the town to show up.

I sat Olivia down in the large wicker chair that Ashley had decorated with vines of fake blue and pink flowers. Olivia started opening her gifts while I stood to the side and hoped no one would notice me.

Unfortunately, our audience was less interested in the purple and green baby outfits that Tyson's older sister had made and was more focused on darting their eyes toward me and whispering to the person next to them.

I bit my tongue to keep my face from going sour. I would have thought the shock of a Fontaine pregnancy out of wedlock would have worn off by now, but everyone in Elren had to ruminate on their gossip like cows chewing cud until something new came along. They were probably calculating the twins' conception date back to the class reunion. Or wondering why my parents weren't at the shower. Or taking bets on which twin would get sacrificed to the magical catfish in our cow pond that allegedly maintained my family's wealth.

Nothing I wouldn't expect from Elren's mouth-breathing finest.

Still, all the eyes on me made my skin crawl.

"Oh, this is so cute!" Olivia gasped as she pulled a green blanket out of a large silver bag. "Beau, look at how cute this is! Destinee's wife knitted this!"

"So cute," I parrotted back. I swallowed a lump in my throat. "Let me get you a snack so you can keep your energy up."

Olivia gave me a thumbs-up and I held back a relieved sigh at the dismissal. I crossed through the foyer and walked past the tables full of food in the dining room to hide in the kitchen.

I leaned against the quartz countertop by the sink and took a deep breath. I might have been alone, but the ring lights and cameras scattered around the kitchen made me feel so exposed. Ashley and Tyson had filmed all their precious content before the shower started, but couldn't they have found anywhere else to stash their fucking equipment?

I raked my hair back as cold sweat began to form on my temples. I needed to calm down.

Quietly, I pawed around the plastic catering containers scattered all over the counters until I found an open bottle of champagne from the pre-shower mimosas Ashley had made.

I held the neck of the bottle like a damn freshman and took a sip. The champagne had gone flat, but I needed something to cure the tight dryness in my throat.

I gripped the champagne bottle in one hand and pulled out the leather ring box with the other. The box weighed in my palm, grounding me to the earth. No matter what anyone at the shower said about me, or my family, or my babies…none of it mattered because I was about to finally win Olivia.

She might have never said she loved me, or even that she wanted to make whatever we were permanent, but Olivia changed after the April Showers gala. First, she started grabbing my hands and pressing them against her belly any time one of the twins moved. Then, I caught her reaching over the pregnancy pillow and gripping my bicep in her sleep.

When she held my hand during her last ultrasound, I knew I had her.

I sucked down a deep breath and put the ring back into my blazer pocket. No more running, no more hiding. I had to go back out there.

As stealthily as I could manage, I slipped out of the kitchen. Relief flooded through me when I noticed fewer voices echoing through the house. The stragglers remaining were probably only people Olivia liked.

I grabbed a plate at the end of the food table and started gathering a snack for my future wife. I piled chicken nuggets onto her plate—not the most dignified food, but she couldn't have the deli meats on the charcuterie board and she was craving protein lately. She probably needed a little sugar boost at the end of a long party, so I reached for a brownie—no, those were topped with walnuts and Olivia didn't care for nuts and chocolate mixed together. I spotted a vanilla cupcake with a swirl of pink icing on top, so I grabbed it and set it on the plate next to the nuggets.

"Are you feeding a five-year-old?"

I turned. Mom stood in the entryway between the dining room and the foyer. She wore thick black sunglasses and her fingers twitched at her side, as if she were about to quick-draw a cigarette. Aunt Liz stood next to Mom, holding a large pink-and-blue gift bag in her hands.

"I-I'm surprised to see you here," I said.

"We've actually been here for over an hour," Aunt Liz said. "We sat in Cheryl's car and waited for the crowd to thin before—"

"So, how bad was the riff raff?" Mom interrupted. "Did anyone ask Olivia if we've inducted her into our cult yet? Or audibly debated if the twins were actually human?"

I raised an eyebrow. "You think I wouldn't have laid someone out if they spoke that way to my..."

I stopped myself right before saying wife.

Aunt Liz cut Mom a sly look. Mom lowered her glasses to look me in the eyes.

"Your what, Beau?" Mom said with a smirk.

I kept my eyes on the floor as I nudged past them. "My *very hungry* co-parent. There's stale champagne in the kitchen if you want some."

Mom scoffed. "You act as if I have no standards."

As I left Mom and Aunt Liz behind, I breathed a little easier once I went back into the big white room. Just as I had hoped, only Ashley and Tyson's family were left. Ashley had her phone on some kind of stabilizer rig, running around the room like a mad woman filming more of the party. Tyson was tossing a blue balloon in the air as his kids ran underneath it, their hands splayed up as they tried to keep the balloon from touching the floor. Dr. and

Mrs. Copeland sipped on their punch from straight-backed acrylic chairs as they watched their grandkids play.

I turned and found my lovely Olivia on her flowery throne, talking to Tyson's sister and her wife. Olivia's brown eyes lit up as I approached.

"What took you so long?" She spread her hands over her belly. "The babies need a snack."

I smiled and handed her the plate. "Ran into my mom. Hope you forgive me."

Olivia smiled back at me. The apples of her cheeks were rosy and her skin looked so soft. The gentle daylight from the windows lit up the curves of her face and made her hair shine.

She was so damn beautiful I could hardly stand it.

And because she was carrying our babies, and she was my best friend, and I was about to ask her to be my wife, I bent down and gave her a soft kiss on the cheek.

Her skin flushed beneath my lips before I pulled away. She froze, but looked up at me with doe eyes, her lips parted slightly.

"Aww!" Destinee's wife cooed, her hand flush against her chest. "You two are so cute together!"

Olivia's head snapped toward the pair, her mouth clamping shut and her chin jerking up. "We aren't together."

As the final word left her lips, time stopped.

During my first game as quarterback, another player hit me so hard that I ended up on my back with no air in my lungs, staring up at the moths flying around the stadium lights amongst the black void of the night sky.

That feeling of shock and emptiness stayed with me. I hadn't been hit that hard again until I got that email from my dad at graduation, and then when Katie came clean about her fake pregnancy.

Even though I had convinced myself that I grew stronger after every blow, Olivia's cold, decisive, and public rejection was worse than being hit by a freight train.

But even as Destinee and her wife glanced at me with wide eyes, the four of us steeping in the leaden aftermath of Olivia's declaration of nothingness between us, I stayed on my feet. The Fontaine facade slid into place, even as my heart crumbled.

"Excuse me," I said quietly to the ladies, "I need to get Olivia some punch."

I left the room decorated in celebration of our impending parenthood and breezed past Mom and Aunt Liz whispering in the foyer. My hands stayed in my pockets so no one could see them shake.

I found myself in front of the pink and blue glass containers of punch but couldn't bring myself to get a drink.

How could I have miscalculated so badly? Olivia and I never put a label on our relationship, but how could she say we weren't together? We were always together. We were going to be parents together. Our whole lives were going to be together.

No matter what I did for her, or gave her, I still wasn't enough for her.

I nearly retreated to the kitchen again when I caught Tyson approaching out of the corner of my eye.

God fucking damnit. Of course.

I fixed the furrow in my brows, but my hands gripped the refreshment table as I turned to face him. "Hey, great shower. Your wife did a good job with everything."

Tyson gave me a half smile. "You don't have to pretend with me, Beau. I know how you're feeling."

I was in a fucking free fall, hiding behind twenty-eight years of practiced indifference. Tyson "born with a horseshoe up his ass" Copeland had no God damn clue what I was feeling.

I bit back the urge to tell him to fuck off and instead merely shook my head.

He gave me a knowing look. "You can't hide that 'oh-shit' look on your face. I felt the same way at our first baby shower for Kierra—that's when the reality of being a dad really sank in."

Beads of sweat formed at the back of my neck. I swore the leather ring box threatened to burn a hole through my pocket and fall to the floor. Pain bubbled up inside my chest like I was a freshly-shaken soda can, ready to explode.

I had to escape—make an excuse that I was going to clean the kitchen.

"Y-yeah," I answered. "You caught me."

Before I could run, Tyson put a hand on my shoulder and smiled. "Being a dad is one of the hardest jobs out there—not everyone is cut out for it."

I forced my face to keep still as I swallowed a lump down my shaking throat. My eyes darted around the room, finding Ashley scooping up a giggling Tarik and setting him on her hip, then Dr. Copeland mixing blue and pink cups of punch to create a pretty purple drink for Kierra.

"You've got a good family, Beau," Tyson continued. "Don't be afraid to rely on them."

My eyes settled on the light streaming in from the window on the front door. My heart pounded as I waited for it to open, waited for that tall man with blonde hair to walk in at last.

But just like Olivia had rejected me, my dad had rejected me too…and neither of them were ever coming back to me.

"Just lean on your girl like I did," Tyson said, "and you'll be just fine."

I shrugged out of Tyson's grip and bit my tongue before I said something I would regret. I only caught the briefest glimpse of Tyson's brows furrowing in confusion as I left the dining room. My hand wrapped around the brass handle and I flung the front door open. The air was sticky, but I ran face-first into it as I made my great escape.

"Beau," my mom called behind me. "Where are you going?"

I ignored her, running down the steps two at a time before heading to the Bel-Air parked on the lawn. I opened the door just as Mom ran up to me.

"What the hell are you doing?" Mom hissed. She glanced over her shoulder at the house. "Everyone is watching you!"

I was halfway into the car when I looked back at the house. Aunt Liz stood on the porch, her hand over her mouth. Ashley clung to the purple front door as Tyson stood behind her, watching me fall apart.

But my heart skipped a beat when I saw the white dress hiding within the shadows of the foyer, the ghostly silhouette of the woman I still loved—the one who, despite everything, would never love me back.

I tore my eyes away from Olivia and sank into the driver's seat. Mom tried to stop me, but I jerked my arm away from her.

"Everyone is always watching," I bit out. "Doesn't mean we're any less alone."

I jerked the Bel-Air door shut and turned the key as the ignition roared to life. I slammed on the gas, tearing through the lawn and bumping down onto the curb as I sped away.

My heart pounded as I gripped the steering wheel. I gritted my teeth so hard I swore they were going to crack. The tension in my chest bubbled over as I maxed out the speedometer toward the manor, each painful thought morphing into a white-hot tear on my cheek.

I was a fool, a damn fool, but it was all over now.

I would never open Fontaine Manor to anyone ever again.

21
Olivia

Despite Ashley's protests, I got in the car.

"Fine, chase after him in your condition," Ashley said through the Mustang's window. "But Tyson and I are going to be right behind you."

I nodded. Ashley lightly patted the roof of the car before jogging across the lawn of Miss Kaye's house and telling her kids to get into Tyson's truck.

My heart thudded as I adjusted the seat back to get my belly off the steering wheel and fumbled with the keys. Beau was probably at the manor by now. His mom and aunt had likely beaten me there since they wasted no time getting into Cheryl's white BMW and speeding off.

I blew out a breath as I gently rolled across the lawn and dropped onto the curb below, holding my rocking belly with a wince. Tyson said he had no idea what had gotten into Beau when he stormed out of the baby shower, but I knew. I knew as soon as Beau looked back at me as he got into the pink Bel-Air.

He had trusted me not to hurt him and I had just blown through him like a cannonball.

Tears trickled out of the corners of my eyes as I drove, but I wiped them away and sucked up the ones that threatened to fall. I didn't regret announcing that Beau and I weren't together because it was true. I was never anything more to him than his friend and the mother of our twins, but that look he gave me before he drove away nearly tore me apart. I didn't want to disappoint him by staying with him and I hadn't wanted to hurt him when I eventually left, but Beau had made that impossible. I couldn't fucking win!

My belly twitched as Brady thumped in my belly, then Annie followed.

I gave the babies a reassuring pat. "Don't worry, kids. We're just going to find Daddy and…have a hard conversation."

I turned onto the country road that led to the manor and cursed every bump I hit. No matter how slowly I drove, Annie and Brady knocked into each other at the slightest dip in the pavement.

The sun was beginning to set when the Mustang crawled up the driveway to Fontaine Manor. I parked in front behind Cheryl's BMW and slowly heaved my body out of the car. I smashed the pad of my thumb against the front door's sensor. As soon as the lock clicked open, I flung open the door.

"Beau?" I called as I waddled into the dark foyer.

No answer.

I hissed out a breath and headed to the elevator to see if Beau was hiding in his room when I caught a blur of white fluff in the corner of my vision.

I turned my head toward the back doors and found Titus jumping up and pawing at the glass. I met him outside and he let out a booming bark just before a crack like a gunshot echoed through the dusk.

My heart leapt into my throat. My head whipped around to the source of the noise—a copse of pecan trees down the hill. What the hell was Beau doing?

Titus pressed his wet nose into the palm of my hand and then ran off the patio toward the trees.

I furrowed my brows just as a series of cracks broke the silence, the sounds not uniform enough to have come from a gun. Cursing under my breath, I picked up the hem of my white skirt and followed Titus down the gentle slope into the trees.

Cows mooed from the distant pasture. My hands cradled my heaving belly as I struggled to keep pace with Titus. Didn't Beau consider that I was too fucking pregnant for his nonsense?

I was damn near out of breath when I finally found him. His face and bare chest glistened with sweat as he picked up a nearby log and set it on a stump. He swung the ax in his hands and split the log in two with the same loud crack I had heard earlier.

Titus sat beside me, on guard. I leaned my shoulders against the trunk of a pecan tree as I caught up with my breath. An unorganized pile of newly-split wood rested only a few feet away. Amongst the grass and leaves were long scraps of fabric, like Beau had torn his shirt clean in half before deciding to play lumberjack.

Once I had enough air in my lungs, I called out, "What the *fuck* are you doing?"

Beau looked up right before he raised his ax again and his eyes turned steely. "What does it look like I'm doing? I'm preparing for a bonfire."

He swung the ax on another log. *Crack.*

I swallowed. "And…what do you intend on burning?"

Beau hissed out a tense breath and picked up the splintered half of the log. "*Wood,* Olivia. If you want to make up a story for your little friends about how I incinerated your clothes or the twins' teddy bears in a fit of rage, be my fucking guest."

I folded my arms. "How dare you think that I'd ever lie like that. I'm only concerned about you."

"Why?" he huffed as he tossed the log into the grass. With a big swing of his arms, he stuck the ax into the stump and turned to me with his hands resting on his hips. "We aren't together, remember?"

I closed my eyes and let out a long breath. "Beau, I told you months ago that I never wanted anything serious."

"A bit late for that, isn't it?" He scoffed. "Having babies together is pretty serious. So is living together, and sleeping together every night, and taking you to every doctor's appointment."

My eyes popped open. "Don't you twist our circumstances—as if any of it was my idea! You inserted yourself into every aspect of my life because you said it was for the good of the twins, not because you wanted a relationship with me!"

Pecan shells crunched under his feet as he took a few slow steps toward me and leveled my glare. "And you didn't have to keep fucking me, but you did. You can't stand here and say *that* was for the good of the twins."

An imaginary fist wrapped around my heart and squeezed. My lower lip twitched once, the only hint of emotion I dared to let show. "That was a mistake."

"You don't have to remind me." He turned away and walked toward the stump. "I'm the biggest mistake of your life—that's what you said at Christmas. The pregnancy was like prison and your only crime was me."

He yanked the ax out of the stump and flashed me a cruel smirk. "Well, good news, sugar. Your sentence is almost up."

He picked up one of the split halves and set it atop the stump.

I rested my head against the bark of the pecan tree as another *crack* shot through the air. "Beau...you aren't a mistake. I don't want a relationship, but it has nothing to do with you."

He ignored me, tossing the split pieces of wood into his pile and picking up another half of the log.

I chewed on my lower lip. How could I possibly get him to understand? I didn't want to hurt him—not by leaving him and not by being with him either.

"I j-just..." I stammered, my eyes falling to Titus as if he could help me. "I promised myself I would never commit to anyone after my dad left."

Crack.

"For fuck's sake, Olivia," Beau huffed as he tossed the ax aside and stomped through the grass toward me. "Really? You're going to blame your dad?"

I furrowed my brows. "It's the truth!"

"It's pathetic." He folded his arms across his chest and stared down at me. "You're going to deny yourself a potential lifetime of happiness with another person because of what some asshole did more than twenty years ago?"

"It's a lot more complicated than that!"

"It's a bullshit excuse and you know it. What if I blamed my dad for all my fucked up choices?"

"You *do.*"

He flung out his arms. "And look where that got me! I'm practically a hermit. I have no friends and no real accomplishments. The only bright spot in my life was you, but that crashed and burned too."

Beau pinched the bridge of his nose and let out a long sigh. "At Christmas, we had that conversation about trying." His hand fell from his face and he looked at me with softer eyes. "I tried, Olivia. Everything you needed, I provided. Everything you wanted, I gave you. And…I'll keep trying. Every day. If it's for you, nothing is too much."

I took quick breaths as I squeezed my arms into my chest, forcing myself not to cry. I couldn't crumble now, not when I was drawing the line in the sand that I should have made long ago.

But I was a weak, foolish woman, and I had to know.

"Why?" I asked breathlessly. "We wouldn't have picked each other if circumstances were different, so why do you keep trying for *me?*"

"If circumstances were—?" His brows furrowed for a moment before he let out a short, exasperated sigh. "Damnit, Olivia, you're so focused on how we got here that you can't even see where we are."

"And where are we?"

His brows stayed pinched as his eyes bored into me. "How can you not see—?"

Beau held his breath and his strong frame shook like he struggled under an invisible weight. Though in that moment he was Atlas with his whole world on his shoulders, his brows softened and his fists loosened at his sides. A gentle breeze brushed the strands of sweat-soaked hair off his forehead. His throat bobbed with a slow swallow, like he was preparing to announce a verdict.

I suffocated at the sight of him, realizing with paralyzing horror exactly what he was about to say.

My head shook as I whispered, "Beau, don't."

"Too late," he replied softly, a wan smile on his face. "I'm in love with you, Olivia."

I clenched my teeth to stop the tears that threatened to fall. My poor Beau Fontaine, what had I done to you? How could I have let you spiral this far?

I had to stop this, for his own good.

My lip trembled, but I lifted myself off the bark and straightened my spine. "Beau, I...I tried too. You gave me everything I could have ever wanted, but I can't go where you want to lead me."

His face fell as I turned away and my heart nearly split in two.

I clutched my arms as I forced out my next words. "I'm...I'm going to stay with Ashley until the twins are born."

The air crumpled around us as I walked away from him, each of my steps heavier than the last. I was nearly back to the manor before I heard grass crunching beneath boots.

"So that's how you really are, huh?" Beau called. "You get what you want out of me and then you just leave!"

I whipped around. "Don't you dare, Beau Fontaine. I am not Katie!"

"I never said that!" he shouted. "God, is the imaginary version of me in your head really that horrible? Is that why you don't want to be with me?"

"No, *this*," I gestured to the empty space between our bodies, "is why. We're fighting worse than we did as kids! We would never make each other happy!"

He shook his head, his brows tightly knitted but his eyes soft. "You can't really believe that."

I didn't believe it. Beau did make me happy. He made me feel safe, and content, and...stable. I loosened the fists that had formed at my sides and shifted my weight to the balls of my feet, ready to run forward and wrap my arms around him.

But wasn't that exactly how Mom had felt after a fight with my dad? Or after being humiliated and degraded by her other worthless boyfriends? The submission to romantic feelings is what perpetuated the cycle that turned into my mom's downward spiral.

And as much as I loved Beau, I loved my babies more. The idea of drowning in a man when I only had myself to lose was frightening, but dragging my twins down with me was unthinkable.

I adored and respected my mother, but I had to make different choices—even if it meant leaving Annie and Brady's father behind.

I took Mom's words to heart and silently recited, *I can do hard things.*

Though it hurt like hell, I forced myself to turn away from him. "I'll let you know about the twins, but please don't come after me. I'm...I'm fine on my own."

He sucked in a breath and held the tense silence for a pounding heartbeat. "I'll look forward to my weekends with them, then."

I listened to the fading crunch of his footsteps as he walked away. Titus, however, remained by my side. I hooked my fingers around his collar and fought through the aches in my back and the weight of my belly as we headed to the manor together.

My chest was hollow as I opened the manor door to let Ashley and Tyson in. I slumped in a chair in the foyer, absently scratching behind Titus's ears as I watched my friends haul my suitcases and newborn supplies out to the truck.

Tyson had just carried out the double bassinet when a spike of guilt shot through me. I knew I had to leave the manor, but I couldn't leave Beau torn and frayed.

Nothing was more important to Beau Fontaine than the truth, so I could at least tell him that I loved him back.

I heaved myself out of my chair and Titus followed me into Beau's study. My hands rested on the handles of the top drawer of the desk when I paused, taking in the six ultrasound photos Beau had framed and set on the mahogany desktop. Each photo marked the beginning of every milestone in the pregnancy—from the very first snapshot of our wiggly twins, the anatomy scan where we saw their sweet profiles for the first time, and the most recent ultrasound that captured the curves of their cheeks and their pouty little lips.

He had taken their care, and mine, so seriously. I had been annoyed at first, but as I stared at the beautiful yet blurry photos of my twins' faces, I couldn't help but see the benefit of the rainbow cups of water, the daily pancakes, and all the rest I got to have.

I wouldn't have had any of it without him.

I bit my lip as I yanked open the desk drawer and pulled out the blue pack of sticky notes that rested near dozens of identical pens. I held a black marker right above my note before the glossy corner of a photo in the drawer caught my eye.

I pinched the corner of the photo and slowly pulled it out from behind the box of pens. It was the picture we had snapped as we were walking out of the April Showers gala. My hands cradled my bump and Beau held a bright yellow prop umbrella over my head. We both gave the camera tired, but genuine, smiles—a portrait of what "The Fontaine Family" would have looked like.

I couldn't lie to myself and believe Beau was just storing the photo until the right frame came in. I thought of the shelves of photos hidden away in his room—of his grandfather, of Katie, and of his lost father—not memories, but prisoners of the past.

Everything I wanted to lock out, he wanted to lock in. He clung to his own heartbreak as if he had nothing without it. He claimed to be a dragon guarding his secrets, but his real treasure was everything he had lost but couldn't bear to forget.

A neon blue sticky note with my confession would just become another part of the hoard.

My heart grew heavier as the felt tip of the marker hovered over the note. I practiced what I had wanted to write and rejected each message, one by one, refusing to give him the heartbreak he would hold on to for the rest of his days.

"I love you."

"I will never be good enough for you."

"In another life, I would have worn matching Christmas pajamas with you."

In the end, I held back. I saved him from himself. Hopefully, his love for me would wither until it was harmless.

After the ink was dry on the paper, I capped the marker and tossed it into the darkness of the top drawer along with our family portrait.

At least I still told him the truth.

My hand gently brushed back the fur around Titus's ear as I silently read the note:

"Thank you for everything. You're going to be a great dad."

Titus and I quietly left the study behind and met Ashley in the foyer. She reported that she grabbed everything out of my room, but couldn't find my pregnancy journal. My tongue was too leaden to respond, but I didn't have enough in me to even care.

I closed my eyes and took a deep breath, memorizing the way the manor smelled. Orange oil, from the wood polish. French lavender, from the air freshener in the formal living room. Dried grass, from Titus's paws. Slowly, I released the breath as I turned to the front door with Ashley—silently giving a farewell to the place I unexpectedly came to know as home.

Before I crossed the threshold, I bent down as low as I could and gave Titus a kiss on the head.

"Take care of him for me, OK, boy?" I whispered as I scratched the fluff on the sides of his face.

Titus gave me a sad little whine, but lowered his body to the tile floor and rested—ready for Beau whenever he came back.

And though I wanted to lock myself in, to run up to Beau's room and become part of his hoard of precious things, I couldn't just think about what I wanted.

Annie and Brady needed parents who wouldn't break each other's hearts.

With a silent sigh, I resolutely took my first step out of Fontaine Manor for what was likely the final time. I was finally the independent mother I always wanted to be. I had complete control of my life, my career, and my future.

And it hurt.

Beau

The toe of my sock pushed against the floor as I rocked back and forth in the wooden nursery chair and stared at the striped wallpaper. Titus rested on the rug near my feet—he had stuck to me like glue since Olivia left.

The Bored Bros podcast played on my phone as it rested on my lap. We still had three months until football season, but the Bored Bros were running a whole segment on the new recruiting classes for Lindsay University and Plains State. I couldn't even pretend to give a fuck, but the noise filled the haunting silence.

"Lindsay's starting quarterback took some time off at the end of last season after that big injury," Bret Bogeman said. "I have some serious doubts about his recovery going into what the coaches say is going to be a new era of Crimson Knight football."

"I bet $500 Coach replaces him with new blood," said Bobby Ballinger. "I've watched enough football to know that once you're out, you're *out.*"

I took a sip from my whiskey. The ice ball had halfway melted and washed out most of the flavor, but a little hydration wouldn't hurt me at this point.

I had all a man needed—a good dog, a good drink, and some good football.

Footsteps echoed in the hallway and Mom opened the nursery door.

She wrinkled her nose at the sight of me. "Beau, it's been a week. You need to stop moping."

I took another drink. "I'm not moping, I'm relaxing. Leisure time is about to become pretty fucking rare once the twins are born, so forgive me for wanting to soak up as much 'me' time as I can."

Mom put her hands on her hips. "Quit lying to yourself. You look worse now than when I picked you up from jail!"

I wiped a drop of whiskey off the scruff on my chin. Fine, maybe I hadn't shaved in a while, or showered, and I couldn't remember the last time I changed out of pajamas, but who was around for me to impress?

I paused the podcast and set the whiskey glass on the side table. "Fine, Mom, I'll go put on my best tuxedo to stand by the door and wait for my children to be born."

She sighed and leaned against the doorframe, her purse swinging from the crook of her arm. "You really haven't heard from her?"

I shook my head. Aside from the blue sticky note that was currently in the pocket of my pajama pants, I hadn't seen a trace of Olivia since our argument.

Olivia's c-section wasn't scheduled for another three weeks—well, two weeks and six days, to be exact. I wasn't sure if she would let me drive her to the hospital for her next doctor's appointment or if I wouldn't hear from her until the birth.

Hell, she might even drop the babies off on the front steps whenever she determined my first "weekend" would be. I shouldn't expect anything more from a cold-hearted sadist.

"Have you thought of reaching out to her?" Mom asked. "Maybe checking in and seeing how she's doing?"

I furrowed my brows. "You know, for someone who demanded that I stay mum with Olivia, you sure want me to get chatty with her. What made you change your mind?"

She pursed her lips. "Call it a mother's intuition." She paused, considering. "Or…"

My eyes widened as Mom pulled out a black and white striped journal from her purse.

She flashed a feline smile. "You can call it a plan paying off."

I jumped out of the rocking chair and my phone clattered to the floor. "What the fuck, Mom? You stole her pregnancy journal!"

Mom shrugged. "Stealing would imply that I gave it to her, which I technically never did. Her job was to write her truth in the journal and my job was to read it to ensure she wasn't swindling you like the last gold digger." She tapped a fingernail on the back cover of the journal. "Adding a tiny tracker under the endpaper made sure I could always find it. There were no secrets between us girls."

My mouth hung open. Mom had no limits, but I never thought she would go so far as to spy on Olivia!

"I can't believe you!" I said. "That is a disgusting invasion of her privacy! Let me read it."

Mom shoved the journal into her purse just as I reached for it. "No! This scheme was for my snooping purposes, not yours!"

I threw down my hands. "Damnit, Mom! No wonder Olivia didn't want to be part of this family, not when we constantly hide the truth from each other."

I turned and held onto the rail of one of the cribs, part of the little furniture Olivia had let me keep. I stared down at the delicate green leaf pattern of the crib sheet, silently wishing that I could just blink and my baby would be there.

More than that, I wished with every pounding heartbeat that Olivia would just come home. I wished for her glasses on my nightstand, a house full of Christmas lights, and long car rides with snacks on the center console.

But just as I had to learn when I was eighteen, wishing for someone wouldn't make them appear.

"I gave her everything," I muttered, "I *told her* everything, and I still couldn't make her stay."

"You...*what?*" Mom hissed.

I whipped around. "I came clean about Dad, and Grandpa, and Katie, and everyone else. Call it one of my self-destructive urges or my trust issues if you want, but I had to see if she would hurt me. I gave her all the knives she could use to stab me in the back and..."

I closed my eyes and rested my fist against my forehead as my temples throbbed. When Olivia left, she didn't rub the truth of

Dad in my face like I had feared she would. She didn't tell me I was weak, or too broken, or unworthy to be a father to her babies.

No, Olivia only did exactly what she always said she was going to do—leave.

"...she passed the test I gave her," I said, opening my eyes to the empty nursery. "She didn't hurt me, I just hurt myself. I should have never tried to propose."

Before I could stop her, Mom grabbed my chin and forced me to look at her like when I was a little kid. Her eyes strained and the faded smell of menthol washed over my face as she nearly growled, "You tried to *what?*"

I held her stare. "I wanted to marry her, Mom. I was going to propose after the baby shower."

She pursed her lips and held her breath, her hand trembling beneath my jaw.

"I know I'm stupid," I admitted. "I know I put our reputation, and our estate, and the entire family business at risk, but..." My voice cracked and I swallowed to keep tears away. "...she was just worth more."

Mom released my chin and tossed her purse into the crib before plopping onto the rocking chair. Her eyes were fixed on the subtle star pattern on the ceiling as she sucked in a deep breath. Her fingers twitched atop the armrests, like she was fighting a tremendous urge to light up a cigarette.

She let out a tense breath. "I don't know who to be more pissed off at—her or you."

I folded my arms across my chest and cut her a look. "Why would you be pissed off at Olivia? Did you learn nothing about her while snooping through her intimate thoughts? She didn't want to be a Fontaine wife, she wanted to work."

"Who said she wouldn't work?" Mom retorted. "She's a lawyer who took on one of our company's biggest competitors and won. She would be a great asset for the family business!"

I scoffed. "Who are you to say what's an asset for the family business?"

Mom froze and her voice dropped. *"Excuse* me?"

The intimidation act might have worked when I was a kid, but I was tired of dancing around her bullshit. "You heard me. Grandpa was the CEO of Fontaine Energy and now it's Dad. All you ever did was go shopping and tear up a house that you refuse to even live in! You go on trips and attend parties while I'm answering emails and flying across the country any time Dad remembers I exist, so don't you tell me what's good for the family business when you have *never* had to shoulder its burden."

Mom's eyes went glassy. "You have no idea what I did for this family."

"You're right, I don't, because you refuse to tell me!" I stepped away from the crib and stood in front of her. "It's been a decade, Mom, and you still won't tell me what really happened with Dad."

She shook her head. "And I won't. I told you back then, and I'll tell you again now, you aren't ready to hear what happened."

"And maybe I'm not," I conceded, "but how can you ignore that not knowing hurts me." Hot tears beaded in the corners of my eyes. "I still look for him everywhere. I'm still waiting for him to come back and give me the answers because you won't."

Her face stayed still, but silvery tears lined the bottom of her eyes. "Baby, I just need you to trust me a little while longer."

I took a deep breath in, but still forced myself to let the truth out. "And I know that whatever happened, he hurt you too. That's why I never pressure you to be with me for holidays anymore. And I enable your drinking, and say nothing about your smoking, and still try to recognize my mother under that frozen mask you had a doctor sculpt onto your face."

Mom's phone buzzed in her purse—more message notifications. Probably Aunt Liz beckoning her out for drinks.

I gestured to the still-vibrating purse. "But I can't hide like you—not anymore. I might not get to be a husband, but I'm going to be a father and I'm going to be a CEO whenever Dad decides he's done with the company like he decided he was done with us."

Mom's phone buzzed again and I gritted my teeth, biting back the urge to pick up the phone and launch it through the window. "So answer whoever is fucking texting you and go lose yourself in vodka or coke or whatever your chosen coping mechanism is for tonight."

She swallowed. "They aren't texts, they're emails."

I threw up my hands. "Whatever, Mom. Just go and let me *mope* in peace."

Mom slowly rose from the rocking chair and retrieved her purse. She pulled out her phone and read whatever was on her screen. She looked at me, then back at the screen, her frozen face unreadable.

When she turned to me, the air in the room thinned and weighed on my shoulders all at once.

"Baby," Mom said quietly, "I will be on my deathbed before you find out the truth about your dad, maybe even after that, but…"

She pursed her lips and weighed her phone in her hand before blowing out a trembling breath. "As long as I'm alive, you don't have to worry about becoming the CEO of Fontaine Energy."

Her screen lit up as another notification came in. I looked from the screen back up to her face as she fought back tears. All the air instantly left my lungs as my mind took me back to high school graduation when I read that email from the CEO of Fontaine Energy.

"Someday you'll understand, buddy."

My throat trembled as I tried to gather the air to speak. When I got that message, I thought my father was teaching me a lesson about duty, responsibility, or a love greater than I could comprehend.

Instead, I came to understand how far a mother was willing to go for her child.

"Y-you..." I stammered, "...you've run the company this whole time, pretending to be him."

Mom slipped her phone back into her purse. "It's easier than you would think. None of the managers ask questions if their salaries are high enough. I can keep the ruse going for decades."

I put my hands on her shoulders. "Mom, no. I'm an adult now. You don't have to—"

"I *want* to," Mom said firmly. She gently placed her hand on my cheek and smiled. "You have one shot at a family, baby. Focus everything on them...I'll be happy to take care of the rest."

She dropped her gaze and took in a quick breath. "And...you don't have to keep looking for your father any more."

My face fell as her words carved themselves on the insides of my ribs.

Dad...was never coming back.

My knees weakened. My vision swam and I slammed my eyes shut. The finality of my never-ending search for my father, my hero, crushed me like a giant had his fist wrapped around my chest.

But when I opened my eyes, the nursery looked brighter and more crisp. The giant's fist released me and I could breathe more easily than I had in years. I didn't feel the need to run away, or hide beneath the neon lights of a club, or push my body to its physical limits.

I...I didn't know what to make of it.

I swallowed and looked at my mother. "Mom...I'm sorry. I shouldn't have said what I said just now. If I had paid better attention, I would have known that you—"

"Oh, hush," she scolded. "That's just what parents do. You'll find that out soon enough."

Mom lowered her hand from my cheek and shrugged her purse onto her shoulder. She gave me a pointed look. "Now, take a shower! I'd prefer you after two-a-day football practices than whatever—" she gestured to my pajama pants "—*this* is. You're a Fontaine, damn it. Have some pride!"

I gave her a soft smile. "Yes, ma'am."

Mom started to walk out of the nursery, but then she stopped and tossed me a look over her shoulder. "It's not too late with Olivia, you know."

My heart skipped a beat. "How can you be sure?"

She paused in the doorway and gave her purse a pat. "Like I said...Olivia doesn't guard her secrets that closely."

I swallowed, but that fledgling hope that had awoken in my chest didn't go away.

With a cautious first step, I walked to my bedroom. The tips of my fingers tingled in anticipation as I rifled through the drawers of my old desk.

What I was planning was risky, but I had to go for it.

The night after Olivia left, I had dragged my carcass into the kitchen after staring at the flames in the backyard fire pit and found the keys to the Mustang on the island. Seeing the keys nearly crushed me—I would have let her keep the car, or even one of my kidneys if she wanted—but the note next to the keys had given me hope.

The note scrawled on graphing paper wasn't from Olivia, but from Tyson, leaving his address and phone number. Olivia might have run away, but I knew exactly where she was.

I pulled out an old red notebook from high school and started flipping through the pages. I'd jot down a few practice proposals until I got it right, and then I was getting in the car. I didn't care if I had to get on my knees and beg like a worm in front of Tyson Copeland, I couldn't let Olivia slip away.

As I tore through the spiral-bound notebook, my confidence began to wane. What if she was going to reject me again? Mom said I still had a chance, but I wasn't that lucky. Hell, the entire reason I was even with Olivia in the first place was because of how incredibly unlucky I was.

I got her pregnant with an IUD after one night together. Then she lost her job and we both struggled with her loss of purpose. We had hated each other so much in high school and now we were irrevocably bound through parenthood.

The portraits of my grandfather on my shelf bore holes into the back of my head. I'd never have anything good happen in my life again, ever. What made me think Olivia would actually accept my pathetic proposal?

I picked up the notebook and sat on the edge of my bed with a dejected sigh. My eyes slowly traveled down the beginning of an essay from junior-year English class.

"The purpose of this essay," I had written, *"is to analyze the author's choice of certain colors of clothing on the characters as a signal of their intentions. Over the next few paragraphs, I intend to show—"*

Oh, dear Christ.

I might have aced the class, but I had been shit with words back then and I was scarcely any better now. How could I possibly win her over when I still didn't know what she was really thinking?

My hand slipped into my pocket and pulled out the note Olivia had left in the study. Thanking me for taking care of her and assuring me that I would be a great father felt too fake, like writing "Have a great summer!" in a yearbook.

The Olivia I knew would have left a note wishing I would choke on a dick after the fight we had. I tapped the edge of the note on my knee. After all this time, Olivia was still holding back the truth.

Just as I was about to abandon the proposal plan all together, I thought back to Mom's confession in the nursery. Women had lied to me before, but no one had ever lied for me until now. Who could say Olivia hadn't done the same thing?

I absently flipped through the notebook as I chewed on the thought. As I turned a page, Olivia's name caught my eye.

"Why won't Olivia Adams shut the hell up?" I had written. *"If she answers one more question, I'm throwing my desk. I hate her voice. I*

hate her grungy sweatshirts. I hate her glasses that make her look like a bug. I hate…"

The whole page was full of her name. I couldn't tell if I had written it in one red-eyed frenzy or if I had frequently returned to add more vitriol. After reading every line, I turned the page to find even more on the back, the paper embossed from the rage behind a sharp-tipped pencil.

I had only hated a few people in my life, like Anthony Dauphin's cheating ass, but I had never noticed if his shoelaces dragged on the ground like Olivia's had. I had never kept track of an exact grade he had earned on a test, either. I certainly would have never paid attention to if he had printed fanfiction on 16-point font and read it in class.

But with Olivia…I had noticed everything.

"When is Olivia Adams going to realize no one cares about that long-dead department store owner but her?" I had scrawled into my notebook. *"She's going to die a virgin if she never learns to shut her mouth. I hate her so much. I hate, hate, FUCKING HATE HER!!!"*

No, young Beau Fontaine, you don't hate Olivia Adams at all. You never did.

I set the notebook down and turned to look at my shelf full of memories. My eyes roamed from my folded football jersey to my prom photos until I found the open yearbook on the bottom shelf. On the glossy yearbook page was Olivia, her eyes sparkling behind her glasses frames as she smiled for the debate team photo.

I looked at everyone else I had kept within my shelves. First, the cheery, breezy version of my mother that hid her sharp wit behind coral lipstick and teased blonde hair. Then, the photo strip of Katie and I kissing at my fraternity formal. Finally, I found my father, the man who would never come back.

None of them would ever come back. My mother was the CEO of Fontaine Energy now. Katie was invisible to me. And Dad...

...I didn't need him to learn how to be a man and I sure as hell didn't need him to learn how to be a father.

So, with a long exhale, I let all of them go. Everyone except her.

I wouldn't memorialize Olivia when she was still out there, still carrying our babies, and still within arm's reach.

I flicked my eyes up to the picture of Grandpa who sternly looked back at me as he gripped the cold platinum handle of his cane.

"You were wrong, old man," I said with a smirk. "I didn't use up all my luck by being born with your name—Olivia already came back to me once."

I turned from my shelf and flipped through my notebook until I found a blank page. I clicked my pen and began to write.

One shot. One draft. I wouldn't beg or plead, nor would I give her sugary prose. My proposal would be short, truthful, and I wouldn't hold back.

I wasn't afraid of the risk—luck was on my side.

23
Olivia

After I left Beau, I stayed in bed for a week.

I rested on my side, cradling my belly on the foam mattress in Ashley's guest room...which also happened to be her office in the attic. When I wasn't doom-scrolling on my phone, I watched Ashley edit videos for her channel.

Tonight, unfortunately, she decided to work on the video from my baby shower.

My glasses pushed into the side of my face as I watched her edit, but I didn't care enough to adjust them. Ashley kept her big white headphones on as she stared at her dual monitors, sparing me from enduring the repeating audio as she cut and arranged clips from the shower.

My phone buzzed on the mattress and I looked down. With a silent sigh, I deleted the text from Dr. Ornelas's office requesting that I reschedule my missed appointment. I knew I should have gone, and Ashley would have gladly driven me to the city, but I just…couldn't.

I gently tapped the card that read "The Fontaine Family" against the top of my belly. When staring at my phone screen hurt my eyes, I switched to fidgeting with the satisfyingly thick cardstock of my souvenir from the April Showers gala.

The skin of my belly twitched—Annie had the hiccups. I placed the card in its usual place on the tiny nightstand next to Mom's ashes and patted my abdomen where Annie's bottom was. Brady, clearly jealous, pushed against his sister and Annie responded with a swift kick across my ribs. I grimaced, but patted them both to try to soothe them.

They fought worse than Beau and I had.

As soon as I calmed them, a Braxton Hicks contraction stole the breath from my throat. I shifted on the mattress as I tried to breathe. The twin bed that pushed against the sloped attic wall was too damn small, but I was in no position to complain. Ashley and Tyson had already sent their kids to Dr. and Mrs. Copeland's house so they could take care of me before my c-section.

They were making huge sacrifices for me, but I couldn't stop comparing them to Beau. Crinkled plastic water bottles lined the floor by my bed, but they couldn't replace the unique four flavors of water that Beau would make. Ashley checked on my symptoms and told me what was normal, but she didn't scour medical journals for me like Beau had. Pete, their big ginger cat, snuggled by my belly every day, but he was no Titus.

Ashley had said that lying in bed and wanting to do nothing was perfectly fine for the thirty-fifth week of pregnancy, but I didn't *feel* perfectly fine.

Every night, I'd wake up with my arm stretched out across the crowded attic-turned-nursery. I'd panic in my sleepy haze, thinking Beau had disappeared into thin air, and then I'd have to hold back tears when I woke up enough to realize I was the reason he was gone.

So, this is what being an independent woman looked like—lying like a slug in your best friend's attic because you couldn't bring yourself to trust the father of your children.

I sure was a winner.

I glanced up at Ashley's monitor and watched a clip of a tracking shot of the green-tiled fireplace at Miss Kaye's house. Ashley's camera captured the shiny glaze of the tile, then the clip jumped to the wooden mantle that held Mom's ashes.

The clip changed to a wide shot of the white room at Miss Kaye's, right as Beau handed me my snack plate. He kissed me on the cheek and my stomach twisted as I watched my face harden and my lips form the words, "We aren't together."

Beau's shattered spirit flashed across his face before he slipped the mask back on and walked away. I shut my eyes, refusing to see any more.

Another contraction rolled through my abdomen—a more painful one, that time—and I couldn't help but think I deserved it.

I let out a miserable groan and Ashley took off her headphones. She swiveled around in her blue chair and rested her elbow on the corner of the double bassinet that was crammed between her desk and my nightstand.

"That one hurt, huh?" she asked.

"Still just Braxton Hicks," I muttered. As much of a pain as they were, they didn't come at a measurable pattern. It was all just senseless misery.

Ashley glanced to the floor but then looked back up at me. "Liv, I'm tired of seeing you like this. Just talk to him."

I shook my head against the pillow. Despite the temptation that gnawed at my fingertips every time I reached for my phone, I had refused to reach out to Beau.

"No, he needs some space to get over me," I said dully. "He needs to hate me, maybe find someone else out of revenge, and hopefully move on."

Even if the idea of him with someone else made me want to fall to my knees and cry, Beau deserved to finally have happiness in his life.

Ashley's mouth thinned at my response. I knew that look.

I furrowed my brows. "What? He'll find someone better than me. I know you think I'm great, but you should have seen those gorgeous women at the gala who looked at Beau like he was a god descended from the heavens—"

"Remember when I sold Valentine's Day candy grams for student council freshman year?" Ashley interrupted.

I blinked. What did high school have to do with this? "Um, sure?"

Ashley pulled her legs into her chair. "I was in the hallway, shilling those lollipops tied to balloons to anyone who passed, when Beau walked up and demanded to know if anyone had bought one for you. He was a complete asshole about it."

I ran a hand down my belly and smiled as I remembered. "Oh yeah, you bought me five of those candy grams just to spite him!"

Ashley nodded. "As soon as Zach Wilson walked into Geometry class and handed you all those balloons, Beau got *pissed*. He started furiously scribbling in one of his notebooks like he was writing a manifesto or something."

She tucked a loose strand of hair behind her ear. "I thought it was just a one-off, but Beau kept harassing me about you—if you had tricked a poor soul into being your boyfriend, if you managed to find a date for prom, or if you were actually going to college or were just going to slum it around Elren for the rest of your life."

I rolled my eyes. "God, I forgot how much of a dick he used to be. I wanted to strangle Mr. Garza for making Beau sit behind me in English class junior year."

"But that's the thing," Ashley said as she leaned forward. "Mr. Garza never had assigned seating."

I blinked. That's right. Beau had whined in the car months ago that I had annoyed him in class, but he chose to never move.

"And it wasn't just junior English either," Ashley said, "Beau always sat near you if he could. You never noticed because you always sat at the front, but I did because he was so damn tall that I would have to lean on the edge of my chair just to see the whiteboard!"

Maybe Beau had a fascination with me, but didn't that come hand-in-hand with the nature of the competition between us?

"We were academic rivals, Ash," I said. "He probably just wanted to keep tabs on me—*know thy enemy*, and all that."

Ashley folded her arms. "You only think that because you don't know what he asked me before the reunion."

"Wh-what? What did he ask?"

"He asked if you were married."

I blew out the breath I had been holding in. "Well, of course. He was planning to hate-fuck me."

She shook her head. "If that was really what he wanted, he would have asked if you were single. Or he would have just messaged me the question."

"Wait, he left the manor and found you?"

She nodded. "He just walked in while Tyson and I were in the middle of the department store renovation. The question was buried in enough small talk that I didn't think anything of it, but looking back, it was obvious that it was very important to him to know if you were married."

Ashley's eyes fell to the floor and she bit her lip. "I always thought he was just an asshole, but I started re-thinking everything during the middle of your pregnancy. Between the insistence of his questioning before the reunion and how he acted back in high school…"

My heart stopped. "Do you think he was in love with me then?"

She scoffed. "I think he didn't have the balls to admit to himself that he had feelings for you, but something was there—something strong enough where he couldn't move on from you even if he tried. It's like he always wanted to…" Her green eyes rolled around the room, as if she were searching for the right answer.

"He wanted to *what?*" I insisted.

Her eyes landed on my face. "He wanted to keep you."

I took a quick glance at "The Fontaine Family" card on the nightstand as my hands splayed across either side of my belly. Though a very sudden and very warm feeling of being wanted filled my body, I couldn't accept it.

"Well, I don't want to be *kept.*" I scoffed. "How many times do I have to say it? I want my independence, to keep winning million-dollar verdicts, and to never rely on a man, ever."

Ashley's brows peaked and her eyes strained. "And what's the point of achieving all that if you still aren't happy?"

The warmth in my body disappeared in an instant, leaving behind a hollow cavern beneath my ribs. I was about to argue that happiness didn't pay bills when the familiar rumble of a diesel engine echoed outside.

"That's him!" I gasped as I shifted my legs off the mattress.

"Wait," Ashley protested, "shouldn't you—"

"I can't believe he has the gall to show up here," I grumbled as I leaned forward, trying to stand up from the mattress. "I have to tell him to get lost."

Ashley sighed, but hopped off her chair and pulled me to my feet before leading me to the stairs. Before I could descend the first step, pain flared down the side of my belly and I gripped Ashley's hand.

"Are you sure you want to go downstairs?" Ashley asked. "You're obviously in a lot of pain and—"

The doorbell rang and my heart raced.

"I'm in pain all the damn time." I gripped the wooden handrail and took my first shaking step down. "If I don't go down there and tell him to leave, he'll wait on the porch forever!"

Reluctantly, Ashley helped me down the two flights of creaking stairs until we reached her living room. I was nearly out of breath, but I released Ashley's hand and hurried to the front door.

The antique hinges creaked as I opened the door. "Beau, you can't be here—"

But he wasn't there. My heart sank as I scanned the empty porch, finding nothing but Ashley's hanging ferns and a deserted driveway while the faint chirping of crickets filled the night.

A sharp spike like a tearing sensation flared up on the right side of my belly and I grimaced. I looked down and splayed my hand across the aching spot when my eyes caught a flash of white on the welcome mat.

I took a step back so my belly wouldn't block my view and found a folded paper note covering a small dark box like a tent. I widened my stance to bend over and retrieve it, but Ashley snuck around from behind me and picked up the note.

With a soft smile, Ashley handed me the note. It was written on college-ruled notebook paper and had a short message written in ballpoint pen on the front.

"You win," Beau had written.

I swallowed the lump in my throat and unfolded the crinkling paper. I held my breath as my eyes traveled down the paragraphs written in blue ink.

"Olivia,

According to my research, you had a 1 in 100 chance of getting pregnant with an IUD. We had a 30 in 100 chance of making a baby after one try and our pregnancy had a 3 in 100 chance of resulting in twins.

For years, I believed my grandfather that I would never reap the benefits of good fortune for the rest of my life, but putting the odds together gave us a .009% chance of having our twins, and ultimately, of you coming back into my life.

And that makes me the luckiest man alive.

As lucky as I am, you have ruined me. You unspooled me little by little and wrapped me around your finger, but I have no intention of ever untangling myself from you.

You won, Olivia. You will forever have all of me.

Consider this as my complete and unconditional surrender. Accept me, reject me, do whatever you wish, but if you want me to be part of your forever, just come home. I'll be waiting on bended knee for the rest of my days."

My heartbeat pounded against my brain as I read the last line over and over.

How could he? I made it damn clear to him that I couldn't be with him, but he was still trying to win me over! What would I have to do to make him give up? How much more did Beau want me to hurt him?

Pain flared through my abdomen again, but I beared down, staring at Beau's letter like I could have burned a hole through it with the intensity of my gaze. Beau Fontaine was an incomprehensible ass, impossible to reason with, and the most stubborn man to walk the planet, but he *would not* get me to break.

A footstep on the creaking floorboard behind me forced me to tear my eyes away from Beau's letter. Tyson stood in the curved archway between the kitchen and the living room, a cold bottle of blue Tigerade in his hand.

"Thought I heard a truck in the driveway," Tyson said. "Did someone come by?"

My trembling hands made the notebook paper crinkle, but Ashley's lilting voice remained calm. "Beau Fontaine left presents on the welcome mat."

Presents? Oh, right! Something had been under the note. I turned from Tyson back to Ashley, and my breath caught in my throat when I saw the tiny leather box resting in the palm of Ashley's hand.

He didn't. He fucking didn't.

I shook my head, but Ashley's brows softened and she nodded in response. She slowly held out the box.

"Should I kneel?" Ashley asked.

"N-no…" I stammered, but my shaking hand floated up to take the box anyway. "No…how *dare* he? I'll kill him. I'll…"

But all my words failed when I opened the box. Sitting in a cushion of white velvet was a ring that I instantly clocked as being an original Art Deco piece. The central round diamond sparkled like rainbow fire under the living room lights. Eight emeralds shaped like tiny fans surrounded the center stone amongst the metalwork, creating the illusion of a flower in the abstract. I gently plucked the ring from the velvet, holding the platinum band between my fingers as the ring sparkled.

"Oh!" Ashley cooed. "It's beautiful!"

"He left that on the porch?" Tyson said incredulously.

"Beau might be too much of a coward to propose in person," Ashley said as she peered at the ring, "but *damn* did he drop a dime on that ring."

Beau could have purchased any ring in the world, but he didn't buy this one. A sharp pang flared between my heartbeats when I finally placed where I had recognized the ring—his great-great grandmother Adelaide.

It was the wedding ring earned from ten years of patience.

My head swam. I slowly put the ring back amongst the velvet and lowered the box on a nearby credenza.

I told Beau that we weren't together and he responded with a marriage proposal.

If he truly loved me, he wouldn't torture me like this. I tried to give us a clean break and starve him of me so he could find happiness elsewhere, but just like at every juncture of this damn pregnancy, he had to barrel in and smash all my efforts to bits.

He called his proposal his unconditional surrender, but asking me to marry him required *my* surrender. Did he think I was so weak-willed that I would bend at the glitter of the most beautiful piece of antique jewelry I had ever seen? That I could forget everything I was and become the Fontaine wife he wanted?

No matter how much he wanted to keep me, I was still me. Did he want every day to start with an argument? Did the former star athlete want to resign himself to rotting in bed and watching murder shows with me? Did he want to hate me during football season when our alma maters went head-to-head? Did the man who owned a damn helicopter want to share his life with a woman who still stopped at weekend garage sales?

How could Beau have spent all those months with me and still want me? He had no idea how big of a mistake he made by leaving that ring on the welcome mat.

I hated him for ignoring my boundary and for giving me emotional whiplash, but most of all, I hated him for how badly I wanted to say yes.

"I can't…" I whispered to myself. "I…"

Searing pain tore through my belly like I was being split in half and I gripped the wooden edge of the credenza to keep from falling. I gritted my teeth as my body shook.

Footsteps pattered over the pounding in my ears as Ashley and Tyson both ran to my side.

"What's wrong? What's happening?" Ashley asked.

I opened my mouth to try to answer her, but I couldn't. I had no air left as pain reverberated through my body like a church bell.

Suddenly I was wet, *much* too wet, between my legs. I shoved myself off the credenza and turned. Tyson tried to help me, but I brushed past him as I made a beeline for the bathroom beneath the stairs.

I barely had enough time to flick on the light and slam the door shut behind me before I collapsed onto the toilet. My vision blurred. Cold sweat ran down the side of my temple as pain roiled through my abdomen.

Did my water break? Were the twins coming?

Only when the pain waned for a short reprieve did I dare look down. I stared at my underwear stretched between my knees as all the warmth drained from my face.

"Ashley," I called. "ASHLEY!"

The weathered brass doorknob turned and Ashley entered the bathroom. Her eyes widened as she looked down at my underwear—stained with blood.

Ashley's eyes then locked with mine and her face hardened. "Don't move. I'm calling Beau."

24

Olivia

I stared at the larks on the wallpaper in the bathroom as Tyson guided my breathing. Ashley had run upstairs to get me a change of clothes and provided some maxi pads to catch the blood slowly trickling out of me, but I still sat on a folded towel just in case. My head felt lighter as the seconds ticked on. The wallpaper blurred just before I could blink, so I listened to Tyson's deep voice as he tried to help me through whatever was happening to my body.

In, out, in, out—those were Tyson's instructions, but I couldn't focus on my breathing when Ashley was on the phone with Beau just outside the open bathroom door.

"No! Are you insane?" Ashley shouted into her phone. "She needs to go to the emergency room *now.*"

Beau's voice, stressed and hurried, echoed through Ashley's speaker, but I couldn't make out what he was saying. Still, a wave of calm washed over me the instant I had heard him.

Beau would know what to do, he always did.

"No—no! I am not taking her to the manor!" Ashley argued. "I'm driving her to Parkland hospital whether you like it or—"

"I WILL NOT LOSE HER TOO!" Beau shouted, loud and clear.

Something cracked within me at the panic in his voice. I had watched Beau take brutal hits on the football field and still spring up, unshaken and eager for the next play. He had stoically dissected a frog, took a kickball to the face without flinching, and didn't even blink when going against the nastiest opponents during debate competitions, but the idea of me suffering the same fate as his grandfather made his voice break.

And I refused to let him break.

Tyson looked over his shoulder at Ashley and she glanced back at him. Then, Tyson's brown eyes and Ashley's green ones simultaneously found me.

"Take me to the manor," I said calmly.

Tyson placed a firm yet gentle hand on my shoulder. "Liv, you need to go to the hospital. Beau is a nice guy and all, but he might not be in his right mind."

Ashley hit the mute button on her phone. *"Might* not be? He threw a tantrum at your baby shower and just proposed with a 'check yes if you like me' note. You shouldn't let a man who is acting like a *third grader* make emergency medical decisions!"

My hands stretched around my belly, feeling the tiniest movements from both Annie and Brady. My babies were OK, but they needed to stay that way.

I had to get them to their dad.

"If Beau wants me at the manor, he has a good reason," I said softly. "I trust him to take care of us."

Ashley's mouth tightened as she looked down at me.

"Ashley? ASHLEY!" Beau shouted through the phone. "Answer me in the next three seconds, or I'm getting back in the truck and taking her myself!"

Ashley unmuted her phone with a scowl. "Keep your overpriced pants on! We're coming!"

Tyson helped me off the floor and I leaned on his strong arm as I shuffled through their house.

"My mom," I gasped through a contraction as I walked out the front door. "I can't…leave Mom behind."

"I got her!" Ashley called from the living room. "She's in your purse!"

Tyson gently guided me off the porch and to the driveway while I counted the seconds between breaths so I wouldn't fixate on how much pain I was in. The wheels of my suitcase thumped on the porch steps before Ashley threw it into her SUV.

"Hospital bag is loaded," Ashley said, her keys jingling from her hand as she jogged to the driver's side of the car. "And Mama Brady is coming in."

Ashley gently set my purse on the floorboard at the passenger's side of the SUV. Shakily, I lifted myself into the passenger seat and sat on a folded towel. Tyson buckled me in as Ashley started the engine.

"Be careful," Tyson warned. "It's dark and those country roads are dangerous."

"Please," Ashley said with a smile, "I used to top out at 100 miles per hour well after midnight when I would race the Murphy boys. I never wrecked once."

Tyson's eyes went wide and he gripped the handle of the passenger door. "You *what?*"

She hummed. "Forgot you didn't race with me back in high school. That's what you get for having parents who cared."

Reluctantly, Tyson closed the passenger door and took a step back.

"For Olivia's sake," he said, his voice muffled through the glass window, "don't make it a bumpy ride!"

"Kay." Ashley blew her husband a kiss. "Love you, babe!"

I gripped my belly with a wince as Ashley peeled out of her driveway and sped down the street. Even though I kept my eyes closed, focusing on my babies' every movement, I was pretty sure Ashley was running a few red lights and blowing through stop signs.

The ride smoothed as Ashley turned onto the familiar country road. She mumbled to herself about Beau asking her to drive out to the back pasture instead of the house and wondering if he had lost his mind.

My arms tightened around my bump when the pavement turned into grass and dirt.

"He can't be serious," Ashley said as the car slowed to a stop. "He's high, or crazy, or both."

I didn't bother to open my eyes to see what she meant, nor did I even take a breath to ask. When the passenger door opened and two strong arms wrapped around me, I simply leaned toward the warm body that lifted me out of the car. I buried my face into his neck, breathing in the scent of his evergreen soap that made him smell like Christmas, and felt his heartbeat against the side of my ribs.

For one quiet moment, everything was all right.

Beau carried me a few steps before I heard Ashley's car door slam.

"The fuck do you think you're doing?" Ashley called as she stomped through the grass after us.

Beau's voice reverberated in his chest. "I'm taking her to the hospital in the city—Dr. Ornelas was on call this weekend and she's going to be waiting for us."

"In *that?*" Ashley shouted.

I lifted my face off Beau's shoulder and opened my eyes. Blinking red and white lights instantly flooded my vision, but I was able to make out the dark outline of a helicopter in the pasture.

I tensed and gripped his shoulders. "Beau! Are you crazy?"

"This is the fastest and *safest* way we can get there," Beau said calmly as he approached the helicopter's open door. "I promise, it won't feel any different than the truck once we're in the air."

Ashley huffed out a breath as she struggled to keep up with Beau. "OK, asshole, enough with the fucking theatrics. Turn your ass around and put my best friend back in my car so I can take her to Parkland—"

A contraction ripped through me and I screamed. The growing pain clawed my cry back into my throat as I lost all air.

"Get me to the city," I gasped once the pain relented. "I don't care if you have to strap me to a rocket, just get me to Dr. Ornelas!"

Beau quickly ascended the step into the helicopter and took me through the open door. A second pair of hands reached out and took mine, guiding me to lie on the leather bench seat inside.

I blinked in the bright light from the helicopter's interior and an eerily familiar face came into focus. Though he had red hair and blue eyes, and it would have been impossible because he would have been too young, the man who secured me to the seat and propped a small pillow under my head looked exactly like...

"Dad?" I asked wearily.

"Nope," the man said with a smile and a quick shake of his head. "The name is Johnny Charles Fitzpatrick, but everyone just calls me—"

"Chuck?" A small smile tugged on the corners of my mouth. "You're Chuck!"

Another pair of footsteps entered the helicopter and Chuck looked over his shoulder.

"You told your girl about me?" Chuck said as he moved toward the open door. "I'm flattered!"

Beau rolled my suitcase into the helicopter before kneeling in front of me.

"Don't let your head get so big that you can't squeeze into the cockpit," Beau said to the wide open doorway. "We need to get in the air."

My body tensed with another contraction before I could think to be afraid. After the pain crested, I opened my eyes to find Ashley setting my purse near my feet.

Her face was pale, but she gave me a reassuring look and patted my calf. "You can do this. Remember what your mom always said."

"I can do hard things," I mentally recited.

Both babies moved inside me and I closed my eyes and wrapped my arms around my belly. The twins were all right. Beau was going to take care of us. We were going to be fine.

The helicopter door slid shut with a loud click and my eyes popped open. Beau had ignored the wide, comfortable-looking seats behind him and stayed kneeling in front of me.

My hand spread across my belly as I looked at him. "It's today, isn't it?"

His mouth formed a tight line. "Dr. Ornelas told me she's just going to check you out, but statistically half of all twins are born before thirty-six weeks. Odds are in favor of you being right."

Statistics. Odds. The proposal note.

My blood ran cold and my lip trembled. "Beau, the ring—"

"Don't." He took my hand. "Don't worry about that right now."

My chest shook as my breathing became more and more labored. "Damnit, Beau, you can't expect me to look at you and not address—"

He brought the back of my hand to his lips and kissed my knuckles. "Olivia, I waited ten years for you to come back into my life. I can wait a little longer for you to marry me."

A hollow laugh, light as a luna moth, escaped from my lips.

"You are so presumptuous," I whispered with a smile, "and egotistical...and..."

I blinked and Beau's face disappeared. I stared at the upper edge of the wide window on the helicopter door, watching the tiny lights of city buildings approach us in the night.

Wait...lights of city buildings?

A tiny gasp shot through my throat and I looked down, finding Beau still kneeling at my side.

"How did...how did we get in the air?" I asked breathlessly. "What happened?"

His brows furrowed. "We've been flying for a while. You were just saying that you wondered if the twins were going to be born under a scorpion moon or something. Do you not remember?"

"Scorpio moon," I corrected. "But...no. I don't remember any of that."

What was going on? I hadn't lost consciousness because I had been talking, but what about the blood?

"Beau," I asked timidly, pointedly darting my eyes toward my hips, "am I...?"

Beau took the hint and glanced down. His eyes widened.

"What's wrong?" I said as my heart started to race. "How bad is it? Oh God, this is white leather..."

"Forget about the leather," he said quickly, his eyes straining at the corners. "Hey, remember how you used to annoy everyone with your little fun facts?"

I frowned. "My facts weren't annoying."

He grabbed my hand and held it between both of his. "Start talking. Tell me all your little facts about the Art Deco era. Or serial killers. Or lawyer stuff. Anything—just don't stop."

I took in a breath, but another big contraction stole the air from me. I gritted my teeth as I toughed out the pain, trying to search my brain for any information to play along with his little game. I could have lectured for hours on the progression of Art Nouveau into Art Deco, or rattled off my favorite stories from cases I had worked, or even done a deep dive on some of the most depraved murders from my books and true crime documentaries, but I didn't have the energy to talk like I wanted.

So, I stuck with simple animal facts that I had learned when I was a kid.

I took in a short breath once the contraction waned. "Did…did you know the opossum is the only marsupial in North America?"

"I did know that, actually." Beau squeezed my hand. "Tell me more."

"Did you know elephants are pregnant for eighteen months?"

"See? It could be worse."

"Beau."

"Sorry. You're doing great, sugar. Keep going."

I moaned low in my throat as another contraction ramped up. Fuck me sideways with a rake, were the contractions ever going to stop? Beau's thumb ran over my knuckles as I rode through the next few minutes of torture.

"Sh-sharks don't have bones!" I nearly shouted as I fought through the lingering pain in my abdomen. "Female praying mantises bite the male's heads off while mating!"

"Fascinating," Beau said. "You nearly bit my head off while mating too."

Sweat beaded on my temples. "Di-did you know an echidna's penis has five heads?"

"Shit, really?" Chuck said from the cockpit.

Beau looked past the back of my seat into the cockpit. "How much longer until we land at the hospital?"

"Ten minutes, max," Chuck answered.

Beau's throat dipped and his eyes glanced to my hips again. His mental calculator whirred behind his glassy eyes, betraying his calm face. His grip on my hands tightened—whatever math he had done using my bleeding and the time we had left until I could get medical care did *not* yield an assuring result.

The man who wanted nothing more than to keep me might actually lose me.

Dying in childbirth was not something I ever considered, but I couldn't ignore the gravity of the situation. If the worst were to happen, I couldn't be a selfish coward again.

If he couldn't have me, he could at least have my truth.

"Beau, I'm sorry," I rasped. "You-you're a much better man than I ever thought you could be. I'm sorry I can't be the woman you need. I'm weak, and terrified of commitment, and I love the shoes your mother hates—"

"The fuck are you doing?" Beau demanded. "We have less than ten minutes. Don't you start acting like you're—"

"*Listen,* I'm trying to—"

"Fun facts," he ordered. "Don't you dare exhaust yourself when we're almost at the finish line. You broke up with me, I get it. Or we never broke up because we were never together, whatever. None of that matters now. I just need you to stay awake."

"But—"

"God *damn* it, Olivia!" he said through gritted teeth. "The next words out of your mouth better be 'Did you know?' or I swear I will never speak to you again!"

I clamped my teeth down and glared at him. Another contraction was coming, but I wasn't going to just let him win. I let out a quiet, shaking breath and looked into his pretty blue eyes.

"Did you know that I love you?" I whispered.

His face softened. His lips parted to say something, but then the helicopter door slid open.

"Come on, mama!" Chuck called from outside the door. "Let's see those babies!"

Beau's arms quickly slid under me and picked me up.

I huffed out a breath as he pushed me into his chest. "We landed already?"

"I told you it would be a smooth flight," Beau said as he stepped out of the helicopter.

I blinked in the bright lights—we had landed on top of the hospital. Four nurses and a gurney waited for us just outside the helipad. Beau gently set me down on top of the rolling bed and then all I could see was a blur of bodies and hands.

The bed rolled into the brightly-lit hospital. I confirmed my date of birth with a nurse before she stuck a hospital bracelet around my wrist. A little plastic clamp on my fingertip measured my oxygen. Fuzzy pink and blue bands encircled my belly and tracked two heartbeats.

"How far along are you?" a nurse asked.

"Um…thirty-five weeks and a day," I responded, rolling my head against my pillow as I looked around the triage room. "Or… two days. Is it after midnight? Beau, what time is it? Beau?"

I looked down, trying to find him, and got a glimpse of my body. All I could see were wires and monitors and tubes. My fist gripped the black leather straps of my purse that was wedged between my hip and the side of the bed. I hadn't even remembered grabbing it.

Beau's blonde head popped up amongst the crowd of nurses. "I'm here, sugar. It's a little after 2 a.m." His head turned toward the screen of one of the monitors. "The twins have good heart rates, and it looks like you're about to have another contraction—"

I closed my eyes and gritted my teeth, trying my damn best to breathe through the contraction like Tyson had told me. When

I opened my eyes, I found Dr. Ornelas at the foot of my bed, examining me. She said something inaudible to a nurse before she quickly left the room.

Two nurses held my arms as they stuck IV ports in the back of my left hand and the crook of my right elbow.

"What's happening?" I shakily whispered.

"We're going to the OR," a nurse replied without taking her eyes off my arm. "Ready to meet your babies?"

My heart seized. I had a feeling this would happen, but I wasn't ready. Not at all.

The bed rolled out of the room. I gripped the bedrail and tried to swivel my head around. "Wait, Beau has to come with me. He's the father!"

"No time," the nurse at my right responded. "You have to go under general anesthesia. He'll be waiting for you when you wake up."

"No!" I cried. My hands started to shake. The bed was rolling much too fast. "He's been with me this whole time, I can't finish this without him. I need him to—"

"Olivia, I'm here," Beau said.

I turned to my left. My star quarterback had caught up with us and was keeping pace at my bedside.

I strained to lift my purse a couple of inches. If Beau couldn't go into the operating room with me, they wouldn't let Mom in either.

"Here—take Mom," I said.

Without question, Beau took the purse from me and held it with both hands.

"Anything else?" he asked.

Tears lined my eyes that I couldn't blink away. My chest shook with every breath. "T-tell me I can do hard things."

"You can do hard things," Beau said with a smile. "You're a badass. You've toughed it out through worse. All you have to do now is take a little rest and then we get to snuggle our babies, OK?"

It sounded simple enough, but I couldn't do it. I shook my head over and over.

Beau grabbed my hand. "You beat Herringbone and you can beat this surgery." His eyes shone like glass marbles and he swallowed. "You win—that's just what you do. I love you, Olivia Adams."

The end of the bed pushed open the doors to the operating room and my hand slipped out of Beau's hold. I rolled my head back onto my pillow, tracking his face as long as I could before the white doors swung shut.

I looked up and found a massive lamp of blue and yellow hexagonal lights like a honeycomb directly above me. My heart threatened to pound right out of my chest. A woman in a surgical mask appeared at the edge of my vision.

She put a clear mask over my nose and mouth. "OK, take a breath and count backward from one hundred."

"No," I shakily responded, my breath fogging up the mask. "I want Beau here."

A masked smile reached the woman's brown eyes. "You're a stubborn one, aren't you?"

"That's what Beau says…" I said breathlessly.

Then my eyes fluttered closed and darkness swallowed me.

Beau

Tick. Tick. Tick.

I gritted my teeth to stop myself from ripping the damned ticking clock off the wall of the hospital waiting room. My back ached as I slumped in the hard plastic chair, clutching the straps of Olivia's purse with Ms. Brady's ashes inside. As odd as it was to hold her mother in a bag, I was glad for the company as I waited for Olivia's c-section to finish.

I was happy that the medical team was completely focused on Olivia and the twins, but I would have solemnly sworn to never watch football again if I could have had just one update. Worry tore through each of my muscles and I threatened to crack the tile with how hard the heel of my boot rattled against it.

Despite how hard I tried to stay positive, I couldn't shake the image of all that blood coming out of Olivia. My grandfather's words haunted me. All my luck ran out at birth. Fortune would never favor me or mine ever again. I was going to lose Olivia. Or my babies. Or both.

I squeezed my eyes shut and rested my forehead against my tight knuckles.

God, *please* God, don't let me lose them.

A soft pair of footsteps approached and I lifted my head. A nurse had appeared and I held my breath as she gave me the details of the surgery. My hands loosened around the purse straps when she told me that Olivia was being wheeled into a recovery room, but I only exhaled when she gave me the news of my babies.

My sweet Annie Cherie was born at 2:33 a.m., weighing 5 pounds and 8 ounces. Big boy Brady Louis came just three minutes later, weighing 6 pounds even. Their APGAR scores were perfect and their lungs were fully developed. Even though they came early, they didn't need to go to the special care unit. Instead, they were in the nursery, ready to meet their parents.

Though I could hardly wait to finally lay eyes on my babies, I refused to see them without their mother.

Olivia

Beep…beep…beep.

God, that sound was annoying.

I slowly opened my eyes and blinked through my blurry vision. I scanned the wood-paneled room, trying to find the source of that awful beeping sound, when I discovered a man at the side of my bed.

I hadn't remembered getting in bed or being with a man, but the stranger held my right hand and rested his blonde head on top of it.

"Whoooo are you?" I asked, my tongue feeling like rubber in my mouth.

The man lifted his head and looked at me—wow, he was gorgeous.

"Oh, you're *handsome.*" I giggled. "What are you doing in my bed?"

The man smirked. "Waiting for your anesthesia to wear off."

Ana-what? Whatever, more important matters were at hand.

I tilted my head to the side. "Are you my boyfriend?"

He laughed—God, why was he so hot when he laughed?

"You told me you didn't want a boyfriend," he said. "In fact, you told me over and over that you wanted nothing to do with me."

My chest shook and tears welled up in my eyes. "Why would I say that when you're the most handsome man I've ever seen?"

Beep…beep…beep.

I turned my head. "And what is that noise?" I looked down, finding wires in my hands and arms. "And what are these? Oh God, am I a robot? Is that why I can't love?"

I sobbed as hot tears rolled down my cheeks. The handsome man laughed at me.

"Hush, Olivia," he said, an amused smile brightening his voice as he dried my tears with the edge of his sleeve. "You're not a robot."

He lifted my hand to show me the wire that now looked more like a tube embedded into my skin. "This is just to help the nurses give you medicine." He glanced up to a screen behind me that I just noticed. "That monitors your heart rate—that's the noise you're hearing."

I leaned forward, studying his strong jaw and the devastating cut of his cheekbones. "And why are you here?"

He looked at me with eyes that were blue enough to quench any thirst. "Because I care about you."

He smelled so good, like opening presents under the tree at Grandma's. His face was mere inches from mine, but I wanted him closer.

"Really?" I said, my eyelashes feeling heavy as I moved toward him. "I'm so lucky…"

BEEP. BEEP. BEEP.

His eyes flicked up to the monitor and his breath ghosted against my lips. "If you're this excited now, I can't wait to see what happens when you meet the babies."

I froze, then my brows furrowed as I limply fell back. My pillow caught me and held me upright as I chewed on the handsome man's words.

I took a deep breath—wait, I could breathe again. Why couldn't I breathe before? My hand groped around my ribs, then my abdomen. My belly felt smaller and squishier than it should, like it was empty.

"Babies?" I whispered. "Babies…babies! Oh God, where are my babies?"

I turned as my chest started to shake. "Beau, where are the twins?"

Beau held my shoulders, keeping me steady. "There you are, sugar. The twins are in the nursery, snuggly and warm. They were just waiting for Mommy to wake up."

The tears started again. "What—what happened?"

Beau held my hands as he explained everything. I sat, frozen in shock, as he told me that Annie had a partial placental abruption at Ashley and Tyson's house that caused me to hemorrhage. I had lost nearly two liters of blood by the time I was wheeled in for the emergency c-section.

"Dr. Ornelas said you were very lucky to not need a transfusion after all that blood loss," he said. "You were so tough, I told you that you were a badass."

My lip trembled. "You…you saved my life. If we had gone to Parkland hospital or…or even driven to the city instead of taking your helicopter, I might not have made it."

He shrugged. "Like I said before—if it's for you, nothing is too much. I'd do it again any day of the week."

He said it so casually, like he had merely picked up a coffee for me before work. Beau always had the financial resources to move mountains, but the sincerity of his devotion shook me to my bedrock.

Hearing that he loved me was nothing more than words, bits of breath lost to the wind. Every touch and every kiss I had dismissed as pure physical voracity. Even him caring for me during the pregnancy was a means to an end, and that end was currently waiting in a nursery somewhere else in the hospital.

And Beau was…here. I had awoken to him clutching my hand almost as if he were in prayer and he had stayed with me, patiently, like he always had.

A calm warmth, like a blanket fresh out of the dryer, wrapped around me. I had always thought that all-encompassing warmth, the kind that made my muscles feel woolen and each breath light as down feathers, was an unaffordable luxury, but the feeling was not completely unfamiliar.

I had felt it, pieces of it, at doctor's appointments while staring at a flickering ultrasound monitor, in the cab of a truck while ordering at a drive-thru that was just about to close, and in the artificial twilight of the bedroom TV just before falling asleep next to my greatest friend.

Beau's love was something I never thought I wanted, then nothing I ever thought I deserved, but regardless of how I felt about it, I had it—all of it.

And I never wanted to give it back.

A quick knock rapped on the door before it opened. I held my breath as the nurses wheeled in two bassinets, one with a pink placard and the other with blue, filled with precious swaddled bundles inside.

The nurses' voices lifted with their smiles, but their words were a happy blur as they handed me first Annie, then Brady.

My head turned back and forth as I scanned each of their faces. I couldn't match the squishy bundles in my hands to the blurry ultrasound photos that I had studied.

A horrible hollowness grew in the center of my chest. Between the slender cheeks and pointed chins, I couldn't recognize any part of myself in them. There must have been a mistake.

I shook my head. "These...these aren't my babies."

The nurses tried to reassure me, but I ignored them as I instinctively looked up at Beau for help. He held a loose fist against his lips as he looked at the babies, his eyes glistening.

A faint itch of recognition tickled the back of my mind. I had seen the face of my twins before—not in an ultrasound, but on the wall of the second story landing back at Fontaine Manor.

My cheeks rose with a smile as I looked down at the twins, then back up at Beau. "These aren't my babies, they're *your* babies. They look exactly like—"

"I know," Beau rasped, nodding his head slightly. "I...I see."

He was stone still, as if he could freeze his incoming tears in place to keep them from falling.

I wiggled my toes, just to make sure I could move from the waist down, and then scooted over in the bed to make room.

"Well, come on," I said with a pointed glance to the empty spot on the mattress. "Get in here and meet your children."

Beau carefully sat in the bed, easing beside me so he wouldn't startle the sleeping babies. His shoulder brushed against mine and his ribs mashed against my side. He was far too big for the hospital bed, but I still invited him to take up every remaining inch of space.

His face softened as he looked at the twins. He gently stroked Annie's cheek and she gave him a tiny smile. Brady grunted in his sleep and his arm burst out of his swaddle, but Beau caught his little fist and held it.

"Our perfect babies," he whispered as his thumb lightly traced Brady's fist.

With a silent sigh, I rested my head on Beau's shoulder. I had all of Beau's love before, but that soothing warmth grew before my eyes, encompassing not just two, but four hearts.

And it felt wonderful.

The nurses helped us unwrap the babies from their swaddles and I breathed a sigh of relief when both twins latched for their first tandem feed. We braved through their first diaper changes. I discovered a small cleft on Brady's chin that my mother also had. Annie's slender fingers, just like her father's, wrapped around my thumb and I nearly burst into tears.

All the while, Beau snapped picture after picture, his phone constantly vibrating as his mother responded to every image of the twins he sent her.

Sunlight bled through the hospital window and faded into a cool night, but time had become an abstract concept as we cared for the twins. When one baby settled down, the other would instantly start crying. We fed and burped and bounced the babies until we could scarcely keep our eyes open.

On top of meeting the twins' every need, I was occasionally reminded that I was also recovering from major surgery. Nurses came in and out of the room at all hours. I was poked and pressed and given more pills than I could keep track of, but Beau stayed with me through it all—never complaining once.

On the second day of our hospital stay, a nurse came in with a stack of paperwork and a pen—the official government forms for the twins' legal names.

I sat in the bed with the papers in my lap, my eyes scanning the blank forms, but then I looked up at Beau. He sat in the gray leather chair beside me with his eyes closed, holding the twins as they rested on his bare chest. Even though Beau was surviving on his third cup of drip coffee from the nurse's station, his breathing wasn't in his usual sleeping pattern. The twins, Annie under her lavender blanket and Brady under his sage one, had their cheeks smushed against their father's chest as they slept peacefully in his arms.

A faint smile lifted my cheeks and I turned to my bedside table, where my mother's ashes sat beside my breast pump and my hospital water jug.

Mom always told me I could do hard things, and she was right. I had braved through a tough pregnancy, swallowed my pride and accepted help, and survived a life-threatening delivery. Though victory after victory, one achievement was always out of reach—happiness.

I had always thought happiness was a temporary sunbeam that flashed in the gilt of triumph. I created my own happiness with an expensive pair of shoes, a strand of glittering Christmas lights, or the defeat of a bitter rival. Joy was earned, it wasn't a state of being.

But when Beau came back into my life, I stopped trying to achieve happiness. At first, I was focused on mere survival— counting down the days until I could be back on my feet and continue conquering the world—, but then I found pockets of joy in mere existence. What began as quiet contentment with Beau had turned into deep comfort that led to occasional glitters of exhilaration—and he hadn't made me earn any of it.

I had sworn off commitment because I had seen men take and take from my mother, but Beau was different. He gave. Not just money, cars, or jewels, but he gave himself, even when I wouldn't reciprocate. Being with him had been so easy that I had thought I was falling into a trap, but what if I deserved an easy life? What if I deserved happiness?

Accepting that I deserved comfort and happiness from another person might have been the hardest thing for me to do, but like my mother said, I could do hard things.

I put the pen down on top of the forms. "Beau?"

He opened one eye. "Hmm?"

I wrung my hands in my lap. "You said you love me, but do you trust me?"

He blinked both eyes open and then stared off into a corner for a moment. Just when I thought the sleepless night had caught up with him, he turned back and looked at me.

"You've always been true to yourself and true to your word," he responded. "Everything you said you would do, you've done. So, yes, I trust you."

I pursed my lips and dropped my eyes to the stack of forms. I glanced back up at him. "What do you want from me, Beau?"

Beau looked at the sleeping babies on his chest and then turned his attention back to me, his eyes soft. "You know exactly what I want, Olivia."

I nodded, my decision locking in place. I picked up the pen and started filling out the first form.

Beau leaned forward a little. "What are you doing?"

"Giving the twins their full legal names," I responded as I wrote.

He swallowed. "And…what name are you giving them?"

"I'm doing exactly as I said I would do," I said as I filled out the second form. "Our children are going to have *my* last name."

A tense silence enveloped us for a moment, but then Beau gave a short nod in acceptance, leaving me to complete the forms in peace.

When I finished, I straightened the sets of documents and set them neatly in my lap.

"I'll take the babies so you can sign," I offered.

His mouth formed a fine line and he slowly rose from that stiff hospital chair. Gently, he handed me Brady, then Annie. The babies cooed and grunted as they settled against me, their bodies warming my chest. I held them close as I watched Beau take the stack of forms and settle back into his chair.

Beau's eyes lazily roved over the beginning of the form for a second, but then he paused, his brows furrowing. He blinked and read the form again. The paper crinkled in his hands as he pulled out the second form from behind the first and held them side-by-side, his eyes bouncing between the two.

He looked up at me over the papers. "Wh-what does this mean?"

"I told you," I said plainly, "the babies will get my name."

Beau looked down in disbelief, staring at the forms where I had written "Annie Cherie Fontaine" and "Brady Louis Fontaine."

"So...?" Beau asked.

Maybe the sleepless night *had* gotten to him.

A flush crept across my cheeks and I smiled. "Yes, Beau. I will marry you."

The forms fell from his hands as he rose to his feet. He stared at me, wordless, as the sunlight from the window cast him in a golden glow. Then he smiled, softly at first, but then that smile grew until he was laughing.

A giggle formed in my throat, but he stole it with a kiss before it could leave my lips. He cradled my head, kissing my temples and the tip of my nose before giving each twin a kiss on the head.

When Beau moved back next to me, the sunlight caught the fine hairs on Annie's head and made me pause.

"Look," I said as I brushed Annie's hair back with my palm. "Do you see—?"

"I do," Beau responded.

We both looked at our daughter, snuggled in her blanket, as I smoothed down her very *red* hair.

I blinked. "Beau, you like statistics. What are the odds that Chuck and I are related?"

He hummed. "Mathmatecally speaking, it would be a long shot. But with my good luck, I'd bet the ranch on it."

Beau gave me another kiss and wrapped his arm around my shoulder. We rested our heads together as we watched our babies sleep in the warm afternoon sun, making a perfect picture of the Fontaine family.

And then, with a quiet exhale, I made Beau Fontaine III a silent promise.

I was going to stay with him, forever.

EPILOGUE

Beau

Splash.

"Damnit, Titus!" I jerked my arm into the air to protect my beer. Thankfully, the tidal wave after Titus leaped into the pool stopped just short of me. My beer might have been free since it was part of Tyson's new sponsorship, but I wasn't about to waste a good drink.

"That was a close one," Tyson said. He sat beside me on the pool's edge, wiping a few droplets of water off his own beer can.

I groaned at my big silly dog. "Boy, have some self control!"

Titus ignored me, happily paddling around the sparkling pool while Kierra and Tarik laughed from their floaties in the shallow end. A square of blue fabric floated toward me and I plucked it out of the water.

"And you ruined your outfit too." I dropped the sopping bandana beside me. "Olivia isn't going to be happy."

I knew as soon as I tied that blue bandana around Titus's neck that it wasn't going to last. I had told Olivia that maintaining matching outfits for the twins' first birthday party was too ambitious, but did she listen to me? Of course not.

The sun started to dip toward the horizon, casting a warm glow over Titus's fur and making the water glitter as he swam.

Aw, I couldn't stay mad at the big guy. He had been very patient throughout the day, after all.

Other than some adorable messiness during Annie and Brady's cake smash, the party had gone off without a hitch. Olivia had chosen a retro theme for the party, so she covered the manor in pastel balloons and ribbons. Annie wore a fluffy powder blue dress and Brady had a very dapper bowtie-and-suspenders combo for the first half of the party. The family had sent the twins an egregiously large pile of presents, my mother being the main culprit.

Olivia's favorite gifts were the stuffed elephants from Aunt Daphne. I was partial to the tiny motorized cars the twins were too little to drive. I couldn't wait to watch them race across the pasture the instant they could reach the pedals.

I sipped my very orange beer as I listened to the easy jazz playing over the patio's speakers and tossed a glance to my wife. Olivia stood on the other side of the deck with Annie on her hip as she talked with Ashley, who floated in the pool below.

Damn, Olivia could work a blue polka dot bikini. The tight knots securing the bottoms created a dip in the curves of her hips. Her stretch marks glistened in the sun across her soft tummy. She tested the strength of the top's fabric each time she bounced as she talked, and I sure wouldn't have minded if one of the straps broke from the weight of her breasts.

I tried to limit my shameless ogling since the whole family was still around, but I was a mere man. Besides, Olivia just looked so cute holding Annie, who wore a matching blue polka dot swimsuit with a ruffled skirt.

Did that mean that I was wearing a ridiculous pair of blue polka dot swim trunks to complete the family set? Yep. Happy wife, happy life, after all. Good thing I spent most of the birthday party taking pictures instead of being in them.

I couldn't hold back a smile as I looked at my girls. Annie still had pink frosting from her cake smash smeared on her round cheek, but she was still cute as a button. Her auburn hair was pulled into pigtails with white bows and she wore a pair of tiny white sunglasses that had pointed corners, like something my grandma would have worn as a teenager. She had certainly inherited her mother's love of accessories, but I had started to suspect that wasn't the sole trait she had received from Olivia.

"So I was getting ready for court and who did I get a call from at the eleventh hour?" Olivia said to Ashley. "Herringbone's attorney! He started acting like it was the first time he had seen my settlement offer when I had been trying to get a response for months!"

"Wow, what an asshole," Ashley said sleepily. She rested her cheek on top of her folded arms on the edge of the pool as she looked up at Olivia. "Did you settle?"

"Only after I added another million to the offer." Olivia held up a finger, her nail painted a pretty delicate blue. "You want to waste my time? You pay for it."

"Ya!" Annie cried, holding up a finger to mimic her mother.

"Ouch," Tyson said with a smile. "Olivia is killing 'em out there."

I shrugged. "She's the ballsiest in-house attorney Fontaine Energy has. When your name is on the building, you can do anything you want."

Chuck came around the deck and handed Annie a juice box. She looked up at Chuck with furrowed brows and let out a string of very demanding babbles.

"More cake it is," Chuck said with a smile.

"You're going to spoil her rotten, aren't you?" Olivia called as Chuck headed toward the snack table.

Chuck turned around. "That's part of my uncle privileges. Just wait until I teach the twins curse words."

I caught Olivia rolling her eyes just as I received a tap on my shoulder. I turned to find Kierra standing next to me.

"Mr. Beau," she asked, "do you have any ponies?"

I laughed. "God, no. Horses are giant babies that eat hundred-dollar bills and are only useful to make glue. I have cows—they're tax write offs that taste delicious."

Too late did I notice the sparkling rainbow pony on the front of Kierra's swimsuit. Just as I thought she might cry from my insult to all pony-kind, she instead looked me dead in the eyes and gently placed a small hand on my shoulder.

"I'll put your name in my prayer journal," she whispered. She gave my shoulder a simple pat and then left to join her little brother in the pool.

Tyson could barely contain his laughter as his daughter passed by. "Oh no, she's spent way too much time around my mom."

I shrugged. "Hey, the kids have to go somewhere while you're filming the new show."

Tyson sighed and shifted his beer from one hand to the other. "Thanks, by the way, for being part of it."

Letting a camera crew into Fontaine Manor to film the first episode of Ashley and Tyson's new renovation show had been a test of my resolve, but I did it for Olivia.

"No problem, man," I responded. "The primary suite needed some major work, so the timing was perfect. I can hardly wait to move out of my grandparents' old room."

Tyson gave me a half smile. "I don't really tell people this, but I've never liked the cameras."

I paused just before taking a sip of my beer. "Really?"

"Yeah. They make me nervous, I just put up with them to provide for my family." He shrugged and looked up at me. "But being with a friend makes it a lot easier."

I smiled back at him. "Just like the good old days."

We clinked our beer cans together in a silent toast.

"Ugh," Ashley groaned at us as she waded toward the pool's steps with Tarik in her arms. "Can you two stop having so much fun over there? You're making me want a beer."

Tyson gave a sweet apology to his wife as she slowly climbed out of the pool, her very pregnant belly visibly dropping as she left the water.

"I still can't believe it," Tyson said with a shake of his head as he watched his miserable wife waddle to the snack table, "identical twin boys. How lucky can a man get?"

"Well," I said with a soft smile as I turned my eyes to my own wife, "you could get lucky enough to reunite with the love of your life after ten years. Or finally get your mother to come to holidays again. Or find out that your most trusted employee is actually your half-brother-in-law."

Olivia caught me looking at her and smiled back.

"You might have never expected twins," I said, "but they're just the beginning of everything good that's coming to your life."

Olivia bounced Annie on her hip and pointed at me. Annie looked at me and waved, shouting "Dada!" from across the pool.

Speaking of twins, where was Brady?

I turned my head just as my mother squealed with delight. She stood by the manor's back doors with Aunt Liz, holding an ugly lacy bundle in her arms.

Wait, that wasn't a mere pile of ivory frills—it was my son!

I jumped up from the edge of the pool and rushed over. "Mom, what are you doing?"

"The Fontaine gown still fits!" Mom said triumphantly as she held Brady out. "It was still in storage from when you were born!"

I had spared Brady from the God-awful tradition of being stuffed in that frilly abomination for a year, but my damn mother took advantage of me being distracted with the party. Though Brady had more strawberry in his blonde hair than I did, he looked horrifyingly like me in that abomination of a gown.

I took him from my mother's arms, but Brady still looked at me as if to say, *"Father, why have you forsaken me?"*

"I'm going to change him," I said as I brushed past my mother and aunt.

"Go ahead," Mom responded with a cackle. "I already took pictures!"

I opened the French door into the manor and crossed into the foyer. Brady rested his head against my shoulder and let out a miserable whine.

"I know, I know," I soothed as I patted his back. "I'll liberate you from that gown as soon as—"

The portrait on the wall caught my eye and I stopped. It was my favorite photo from our wedding—Olivia and I stood in front of the stained glass window at Miss Kaye's house as we each held a twin.

I lightly bounced Brady as I remembered just how small the twins used to be—they had looked like perfect little peanuts in our arms. Annie had on a sparkling white dress with a flower headband and Brady had somehow managed to keep his white tuxedo clean for most of the wedding. Brady had completely outdressed me, but Olivia looked like a queen as she held our princess. Olivia's big pink—or as she had called it, *blush*—dress flowed down the first steps of the wooden staircase and Adelaide's emerald brooches glittered in her hair.

When the photographer's camera clicked on our wedding day, I felt like I had finally won that last football game or crossed the graduation stage with a gold medal. It was the portrait of a perfect ending, I had thought, but the conversation with Tyson scratched at the back of my mind.

Maybe the portrait hadn't been an ending after all.

I ruminated on the thought as the party wrapped up and the manor slowly quieted. After we kissed the twins goodnight, Olivia sat on the edge of our bed and stared at her slippered feet for far too long.

I sat down next to her just as I heard her first sniffle.

"They're getting too big, aren't they?" I said.

She looked up with me with glassy eyes. "Did you know they aren't infants anymore? We have *toddlers* now."

I folded my arms and chewed on the inside of my cheek for a moment. "Feels like we're at an ending, doesn't it?"

Olivia took in a ragged breath and nodded.

I looked out the open door into the hallway. Our new bedroom suite was mere steps away. The only lock on the door was a flimsy promise to the TV producer that Olivia wouldn't see the room until they could film the "big reveal."

But what they didn't know wouldn't hurt them.

I stood up and took Olivia's hands. "What do you say we break in a new bed?"

That got her to smile. She followed my lead as I guided her into the hallway.

"But Beau," she said in a conspiratorial whisper, "we promised—"

I flashed her a wicked smile as I grabbed the doorknob. "My manor, my rules."

Olivia peeked around me as I pushed open the bedroom door. She gasped and gently brushed past me to explore the room. I leaned on the doorframe, admiring her as she ran her fingertips down the mahogany bedpost of the custom bed. She moved on to fluff a decorative pillow made with the exact fabric she had put in her "inspiration" file and then smiled when she glanced at the floor beneath the bed.

"The damage from the ax is gone!" she remarked.

When Ashley had asked me on camera what made the deep gashes in the wood, I made sure to stare directly into the lens and let my pointed silence choke the air. Let Elren come up with stories behind a new mystery at Fontaine Manor. They needed something new to gossip about, anyway.

Olivia's eyes glittered as she surveyed the room. The floral wallpaper had been her choice. The carved wooden dresser? Another find from her inspiration file. Everything in the room had been carefully crafted to be entirely "hers."

Well, except for my one small contribution.

Olivia turned around and her hand flew to her mouth. "Beau, is that…?"

I slowly walked into the room as we both admired the antique couch.

"It's newly refurbished," I explained. "A rescue from the dusty attic of an old department store."

Olivia tentatively approached the couch. "I'm almost too afraid to, but I can't resist."

She slowly sank down onto the center cushion, waited a moment, and then bounced.

She could bounce on that couch all she wanted—it wouldn't break again. Tyson Copeland really could fix anything.

Olivia sweetly looked up at me. "Thank you. This is a wonderful surprise."

"Who said I was done?" I walked over to the armoire and retrieved a black shoebox. "It's the one-year anniversary of you braving that surgery and becoming a mother. Did you really think I wouldn't get you a present too?"

I handed my wife the box and she eagerly opened it. She unwrapped two high-heeled shoes with red paint shining on the soles. The leather was a princessy pink and they had silk ribbons instead of straps or buckles.

"I figured you might enjoy those when you go to court against your old firm next week," I said.

Olivia's brows knitted as she admired the shoes. "These aren't from the Spring collection."

"I know," I said with a smile. "They're custom made."

She squealed in gratitude as I knelt in front of her. She kicked off her slippers and I slid the new shoes onto her feet. I wrapped the ribbons around her left ankle and tied it off in a bow, but when I moved to her right ankle, I couldn't help but let my eyes wander up her bare legs. She wore that lacy little nightgown that barely covered her thighs—the one that never stayed on her body for very long.

I held her right heel in the palm of my hand after I tied off the silk bow and gently placed a kiss on her ankle. Then my mouth worked its way up the inside of her calf, kissing her smooth skin, before she kicked out of my grip.

Olivia pressed her foot into my shoulder and pushed me away, the point of her stiletto digging into the muscle of my chest, right over my pounding heart.

God, she was so pretty when she looked like she was about to kick my ass.

She looked down at me. "I caught you making eyes at me from across the pool, Mr. Fontaine. Are you making a move for more children?"

I smirked. "The prospect did cross my mind."

Her face was still all iron. "Did you know that once a woman has twins, her odds of having another set of twins shoot up by thirty percent? Do you really want to do all of that again?"

"Again?" I repeated. The word bounced around in my head and crashed into my jumble of thoughts from earlier, clicking into place amongst the chaos like the final puzzle piece.

"You know, when you think of life in terms of achievement, every milestone feels like an ending," I said. "You rush to the finish, celebrate the end of some sort of struggle, but then what? You move on to a new struggle and the process repeats into eternity."

Olivia canted her head. "So, you're agreeing with me?"

"Not at all, let me finish." I ran my thumb across her ankle, right beneath the ribbon. "But you don't triumph every time, do you? Sometimes the struggle wins. Sometimes you're up against an unbeatable opponent like time, or fortune, or death. And when you're so focused on those endings, you end up mourning what you've lost."

I looked up at her. "Like just now—you were mourning that our infants have disappeared and babbling toddlers have taken their place. You're also probably mourning that the birthday party you spent months planning is over. Margot is going to clean everything up tomorrow and put all your pretty decorations in the trash."

Olivia folded her arms. "Wow, Beau. You're really killing the mood."

"Only if you're focused on the ending," I said. "For way too long, I was focused on endings. I wasted years mourning what I lost and clinging to the pieces left behind. Hell, I thought I lost you, and yet I get to wake up to you every morning."

Her hard facade broke with a smile. The pressure of her foot against my shoulder softened and I dared to lean closer. Her leg yielded to me as I rose onto my knees and rested my hands on the couch cushions on either side of her body, bracketing her with my arms.

We were eye to eye, a mere breath apart.

"Why mourn the end of a first birthday party when you get to do it all again for their second birthday? Then their third? And their fourth?" I said. "Why miss our tiny babies when we still get to wake up as Annie and Brady's parents again and again? Why grieve the end of our wedding day when I marry you again every time I come back to bed after an argument?"

She leaned in closer, her eyes half lidded. "Get to the point, Mr. Fontaine."

"There are no endings, Mrs. Fontaine," I whispered against her lips, "only beginnings—because everything good in my life I get to have again and again."

I kissed her, long and slow, savoring the taste of her mint toothpaste. She slowly wrapped her arms around my neck and pulled me in closer, but I broke the kiss, just for a breath. Her eyes fluttered open as she looked back at me. A warm flush was spread across her cheeks. She was perfect, completely perfect, and somehow completely mine.

How lucky can a man get, indeed.

I glanced at the old couch beneath us. "You ask me if I want to do this all again, but I'm not sure if we ever stopped."

"We'd lose nothing, but could gain so many new beginnings," Olivia said wistfully. "More first steps, more first Christmases, more new adventures."

"I knew you'd catch on." I reached up and gently held her chin as she looked me in the eyes. "You always were the smartest person in the room."

A beautiful smile played on my wife's lips before she leaned in and kissed me, again and again.

I really was the luckiest man alive.

Acknowledgements

To Taylor, my editor: Thank you for turning Olivia and Beau's mess into a lovable mess. Sometimes you can fix what is broken.

To Erin and Georgie: Thanks for giving "the rich love interest" a name and thanks for growing up with me. They wouldn't last an hour in the asylum that raised us.

To Becca and Rachel, my beta readers: Thanks for polishing this little beauty and helping me make it slightly less unhinged.

To Rachel, cover artist extraordinaire: Thanks for keeping your DMs open through multiple drafts. O and B look fantastic!

To El Reno, Oklahoma: Don't let that fancy new Starbucks change you. You're still small, you're still weird, and I still love you. Go Big Blue!

To my husband Ryan: Thanks for helping me concieve this book idea. Driving around New Orleans with you to make the Fontaines real will always be one of my treasured memories.

To my daughter, T.J.: You are the best big sister of all time.

To my twins, R.L. and R.J.: Bringing you into this world was tough, having you in my world is easy. You complete me.

More from Perci Jay

**In the mood for a Romantasy that hurts a little?
Ok...hurts a lot?**

**"When you are brought up to be only a bride, you are nothing
until you are married. Then someone else decides what you are."**

Serafina Ravenwood is a liar. Caught between bloodthirsty giants
destroying her homeland and a cruel Duke who shatters her family,
Serafina only has one option to survive—marry the heir to the
Dukedom of Lycaster

Serafina spends seven years charming and deceiving him into securing
her place as his wife. As her promised marriage was within her grasp,
a notorious half giant known only as "the Beast" crushes her plans.

But the half giant is only the beginning. She learns the glittering life
of Lycaster's court is nothing more than a world of beautiful lies. To
survive in the endless labyrinth of deciet, Serafina must become more
than just a bride. She will shed her white dress and transform into a
plotter, a lover, a manipulator, a rival, and an assassin—or else her fate
is sealed.

**Check out the Lycaster series, a heart-wrenching romantic
fantasy full of magic, twisted fairytales, and dark family secrets.**

About the Author

Best known for her best-selling Lycaster series, Perci Jay is often found embarassing herself on BookTok and other corners of the internet. When not writing yet another kissing book, she is with her husband and three children causing a ruckus all over Central Texas.

Want to be part of Perci's next viral moment? Follow along with her red-lipped journey to infamy on her socials:

www.percijayauthor.com

@percijay_fantasyauthor

www.ingramcontent.com/pod-product-compliance
Lightning Source LLC
Chambersburg PA
CBHW031332020726

47499CB00005B/1229